WHAT'S IN A NAME?

"Do you know, Cassie, how much prettier you look with your hair loose like that?"

She took a step back. " 'Tis the wind. I assure you, it was neat a little while ago."

"I like it." He reached out to touch her cheek. *Pull back,* she warned herself, but she couldn't. There was something magnetic in his gaze, something that compelled her, and the touch of his calloused fingertips on her skin was somehow exciting and soothing at the same time. "Soft, so soft," he murmured. "You don't freckle, Red."

"No, I'm lucky that way. My lord—"

"I liked it better when you used my name." His lips hovered a mere breath from hers. "Say it."

"I can't."

"Say it, Cassie."

"Nicholas," she said, helpless to resist, and his head lowered. . . .

A Memorable Collection of Regency Romances

BY ANTHEA MALCOLM AND VALERIE KING

THE COUNTERFEIT HEART   (3425, $3.95/$4.95)
by Anthea Malcolm
Nicola Crawford was hardly surprised when her cousin's betrothed
disappeared on some mysterious quest. Anyone engaged to such an
unromantic, but handsome man was bound to run off sooner or later.
Nicola could never entrust her heart to such a conventional, but so
deucedly handsome man. . . .

THE COURTING OF PHILIPPA   (2714, $3.95/$4.95)
by Anthea Malcolm
Miss Philippa was a very successful author of romantic novels. Thus
she was chagrined to be snubbed by the handsome writer Henry
Ashton whose own books she admired. And when she learned he considered love stories completely beneath his notice, she vowed to teach
him a thing or two about the subject of love. . . .

THE WIDOW'S GAMBIT   (2357, $3.50/$4.50)
by Anthea Malcolm
The eldest of the orphaned Neville sisters needed a chaperone for a
London season. So the ever-resourceful Livia added several years to
her age, invented a deceased husband, and became the respectable
Widow Royce. She was certain she'd never regret abandoning her girl-
hood until she met dashing Nicholas Warwick. . . .

A DARING WAGER   (2558, $3.95/$4.95)
by Valerie King
Ellie Dearborne's penchant for gaming had finally led her to ruin. It
seemed like such a lark, wagering her devious cousin George that she
would obtain the snuffboxes of three of society's most dashing peers
in one month's time. She could easily succeed, too, were it not for
that exasperating Lord Ravenworth. . . .

THE WILLFUL WIDOW   (3323, $3.95/$4.95)
by Valerie King
The lovely young widow, Mrs. Henrietta Harte, was not all inclined to
pursue the sort of romantic folly the persistent King Brandish had in
mind. She had to concentrate on marrying off her penniless sisters
and managing her spendthrift mama. Surely Mr. Brandish could fit in
with her plans somehow . . .

Scandal's Lady

Mary Kingsley

ZEBRA BOOKS
KENSINGTON PUBLISHING CORP.

ZEBRA Books are published by

Kensington Publishing Corp.
475 Park Avenue South
New York, NY 10016

First Printing: February, 1994

Printed in the United States of America

DEDICATION

To Patty "Shmoe" Harrington, Kelly "Cookie" Harrington, and Amy Kruger.
"Mis angeles."

Chapter 1

Sussex England
Spring, 1814

The news spread quickly through the neighborhood. The new Earl of Lynton was at last coming to take up residence at his estate. For over a year the big house had stood empty, since the death of the last, unlamented, earl. The accession of the new earl had caused a great deal of excitement. He was said to be a young man, and a hero of several naval engagements in the late wars with France; he had, rumor said, distinguished himself at Trafalgar. Most importantly, he was unmarried, and it was that which caused most of the excitement. There were several unattached females in the neighborhood, and all had hopes.

Cassandra Aldrich folded away a much-darned shift in her narrow attic room, smiling to herself at the excited chatter of the girls behind her. The earl's arrival had been the only topic of conversation in the Lamb house in the last week, and even Catherine and Mary, the youngest girls and Cassandra's charges, weren't immune to it. After all, there were five daughters in the Lamb family, the eldest two of marriageable age. The earl could do worse in his choice of wife.

" 'It is a truth universally acknowledged, that a single man in possession of a good fortune, must be in want of a wife,' " Cassandra murmured, closing the dresser drawer firmly and turning, clapping her hands. "Catherine, Mary." The two young girls, sitting on the narrow bed, looked up at her. They would be beauties one day, Cassandra thought fondly, with their shining gold curls and bright blue eyes. The fact that they were twins would add a measure of interest to their appearance. "It is high time you got ready for tea."

"Do we have to?" Catherine protested. To outsiders, the twins were nearly impossible to tell apart, but Cassandra had soon learned the difference. Catherine, the oldest, and the bravest, of the two, tried to get away with whatever she could.

"You know you do," she replied in her strictest voice, but her eyes behind her steel-rimmed spectacles twinkled. "Go on and get cleaned up, now, or your mother will wonder what kind of governess I am!" Turning a deaf ear to all protests, she shooed the girls out of the room, her refuge and the favorite place in the house for most of the Lamb girls. Teatime with their mother was not something they enjoyed.

"Brats," a voice commented behind her, and Cassandra turned to see Miss Beatrice Lamb, sitting on the bed with her arms around her knees. Just a few years younger than Cassandra, she was the best friend Cassandra had in this house, and, though not the family beauty, by far the sweetest of the Lambs.

"Just high-spirited." Cassandra closed the door. "You should be getting ready, too, Bea," she said, dropping any pretense of formality now that they were alone.

"Oh, pooh! You're not my governess."

Cassandra sank down on the bed. "Thank heavens."

"Well, I'm glad you're not." Beatrice flopped onto her back, staring up at the sloping ceiling. "We couldn't be friends, else."

"If your mother sees you lying like that, we won't be."

"Oh, pooh! What do you think he's like?"

"Who?" Cassandra's voice was distracted as she reached for another shift to fold, this one trimmed with tattered bits of lace at the neckline.

"The earl, of course, silly! Who else?"

"Who else, indeed?"

"Now you are hoaxing me," Beatrice said, smiling. "But you must admit, Cassandra, this is quite the most exciting thing to happen in simply ages!"

"Quite. There, that's done." Cassandra put the remaining shifts away and turned from the dresser, sitting in the room's only chair, narrow and straight-backed. "I rather wish the dratted man would arrive and get it over with."

"Cassandra!" Beatrice leaned up on her elbows. "Don't you want to meet him?"

"Me? Meet an earl?" Cassandra's eyes crinkled. "I'm only a governess, Miss Beatrice. How would the likes of me meet an earl? And besides"—her voice returned to its usual cultured tones—"with you and your sisters, why would he look at me twice?"

"Your background's as good as ours, and if you would just take off those spectacles and that mobcap—"

"Yes, yes, and this dreadful gray gown. I know." Cassandra's eyes twinkled again, and then softened. "Those days are past. I'm quite content as I am."

"Being governess to two brats? What of when they

grow up and don't need you any longer? You may have to go to a family that's not as nice as ours."

"Horrors," Cassandra said, lightly, though the prospect truly horrified her. A family worse than the Lambs? It couldn't be possible.

There was a knock on the door, and Amanda, the third oldest girl, tumbled in, her hair falling untidily about her shoulders. "He's coming here!" she announced, and the others stared at her.

"Who's coming here? Really, Mandy, your hair's such a mess," Beatrice said.

"Is it? But it's so exciting! He's actually coming here."

Cassandra rose. "Sit down, Miss Amanda, and I'll fix your hair for you," she said.

"You're a treasure, Cassandra. Why aren't you excited?"

Beatrice threw a pillow at her sister, making Cassandra duck. "Because we don't know what you're talking about."

"But I told you—"

"Amanda," Beatrice said with admirable patience, "who is coming here?"

"Why, the earl, of course," a cool voice said from the doorway, and everyone in the room straightened. There stood Miss Penelope Lamb, the oldest daughter and an unquestioned beauty. Even Cassandra's eyes left her task for a moment to look at her, pristine and elegant in pale blue muslin, and then lowered again. "Though heaven knows why he'd want to when you look like that! Beatrice, Mother would swoon if she saw you on the bed like that. And Amanda, your hair is a disgrace. Really, Aldrich, have you no control over my sisters?"

Beatrice scrambled from the bed. "The earl is coming here? But I didn't even know he'd arrived."

10

"This morning. Papa paid a call on him—"

"Papa's met the earl and didn't tell us?"

"—and he invited him to tea. Today."

That provoked the exclamations of surprise Penelope evidently desired, for she smiled, coolly. Everything Penelope did was cool, Cassandra thought, retying the blue satin ribbon around Amanda's fine, straight hair. Beatrice had told her, in strictest confidence, that Penelope had earned the name Ice Princess during her season. Cassandra could well believe it. A cold heart, Penelope had. Cassandra knew that well.

"Tea, today?" Beatrice was saying.

"Yes. Where are the twins, Aldrich?"

"Washing their faces, I believe," Cassandra said, calmly, setting the hairbrush down. "Are they to come down to tea?"

"Yes. You're to dress them in their best gowns immediately, and bring them down when you are summoned. And make sure Catherine's dress doesn't have any smudges on it."

"No, miss."

"You're also not to stay when you do bring the twins down. The earl isn't interested in servants."

"But Cassandra's like family!" Amanda protested, as Cassandra gave Penelope a long, unsmiling look.

"She is paid for what she does, is she not? This may be our only chance to be accepted by the *ton*, and I don't want it to be ruined by a servant."

"Penelope!"

Penelope lifted her chin, accentuating her long, arrogant nose. "Come. I wish to look my best for the earl, even if you do not." With that, she swept out of the room.

"What's wrong with my looks?" Amanda said, and

Cassandra saw with comic despair that her hair was coming loose already.

"She's hateful," Beatrice said. "If only I could say so—"

"Pay her no mind," Cassandra said. "Here, let me retie your sash for you, Amanda—there, you look fine."

"I hope so. Not that it will matter." Amanda made a face. "Why would the earl look at me, with Penelope there?"

"Penelope may be beautiful, but you're much nicer."

"As if he'll have a chance to find that out! Thank you, Cassandra." Amanda gave her a quick hug. "Maybe Penelope will marry the earl, and we'll be free of her."

"Maybe." And then Cassandra would be free of Penelope, too, she thought, turning toward the tiny, cracked mirror on her dresser after both girls had flown from the room. Of all the hardships she had endured in the past few years, surely dealing with Penelope was one of the worst. At twenty-one Penelope, in spite of a London season, had yet to catch a husband. She couldn't guess why, though Cassandra, from her own painful experience, could have enlightened her. It wasn't easy to be accepted by the *ton*, even with Penelope's ice blond hair, ice blue eyes, and a slender figure set off to perfection by clinging muslin gowns. Underneath she was shallow, and could be vicious. Cassandra suspected that polite society had been quick enough to see her as she was and shun her, pretty face and substantial dowry or not. Perhaps the earl, having been at sea all these years, would be less discerning and would, indeed, be caught by Penelope. Cassandra devoutly hoped so.

Quickly she pulled off her spectacles and cap and splashed water on her face. Her hair, thick and glossy, was a deep auburn, and her eyes, now revealed to be large and soft brown, with long, thick lashes, stared back at her from the mirror. She couldn't compete with any of the Lamb sisters in looks, not with this red hair and her small, well-rounded figure. Ah, well, beauty wasn't everything, as she'd learned during her own season six years ago, cut so unexpectedly and cruelly short. Nor, looking back, was she impressed with most of her suitors. Still, even a less than spectacular marriage would have been better than what she had had to endure since.

"And that's enough self-pity," she told herself, drying her face with a threadbare towel. She had a roof over her head, employment that satisfied her, and enough to eat. What more could she ask? Firmly she bundled her hair back into the mobcap; firmly she set the spectacles on her nose. It was time to bring her charges to meet the famous Earl of Lynton.

Chivvying the girls into their best dresses of white muslin wasn't easy. Catherine, as expected, protested having her curls brushed and her pink satin sash tied; there was, indeed, a smudge on her dress. Mary, thank heavens, was easier, at least on the surface. She stood still as Cassandra finished brushing her hair, her eyes so far away that Cassandra wondered, as she often did, what she was thinking. If Catherine was the leader in mischief, it was often Mary who thought of their pranks. She had her hands full, Cassandra thought cheerfully, taking the girls by their shoulders and ushering them out of the nursery. Thank heavens she liked them.

Voices from the drawing room filtered up the stairs as the nursery party made their way down. Mr. Lamb's genial laugh mingled with Penelope's silvery tones and another voice, an unfamiliar male voice. Something about it made Cassandra stop for a moment. Who—? But the memory flew away before she could catch it. No one

13

she knew. It had to be the new earl, and how would she know him?

Carey, the Lambs' butler, was standing just outside the double doors of the drawing room, looking in. At Cassandra's approach he straightened, his face austere. She smiled at him, not fooled, and tilted her head inquiringly toward the drawing room. Carey's only answer was an expressive shrug, and Cassandra bit back another smile. The old humbug. Much though he pretended indifference to his employers' affairs, as befitted his position, in truth he was as curious as anyone. Well, they might as well go in and meet the earl and get it over with.

At her nod, Carey stepped forward and opened the door. "Miss Catherine Lamb, Miss Mary Lamb," he announced, and the people in the room looked up as the small group came in. The men rose, and Cassandra felt the color draining from her face, the floor shifting under her feet. It was—no, it couldn't be, but it was. The man she'd thought never to see again, the one man against whom all others were measured. The Earl of Lynton was, apparently, Nicholas St. John, the man she had loved with all her heart, so many years ago.

He wished he was back at sea.

Nicholas St. John, late of His Majesty's Navy and the new Earl of Lynton, scowled at his reflection as he tugged at the neckcloth his valet had insisted he wear. Behind him the valet frowned, too, a pained look on his face. He was, Nicholas thought with sudden humor, finding his new master a trial. As well he should. "Look like a demmed man-milliner," he growled, turning away from the mirror.

"Oh no, my lord, not at all! You look just the thing."

The valet busied himself brushing away invisible specks of lint from the shoulders of Nicholas's new coat of blue superfine, so tight it had taken all his strength to struggle into it. Give him the freedom of his pea jacket any day. Better yet, give him bell bottoms and a smock and bare feet. After being at sea for so long, it was strange to be on the beach again, a landlubber, yet here he was, all rigged out like a monkey, about to pay his first call on his neighbors. Blast! He ran his hand through his carefully disarranged hair, making his valet wince. He wished he were at sea again.

A little while later he tooled his curricle into the wide, curving drive that stretched before a pleasant, half-timbered manor house, the home of his nearest neighbor. A good man, Joseph Lamb, Nicholas thought, handing the ribbons to a groom and jumping to the graveled drive with the grace born of years of climbing rigging and walking a moving deck. At least Nicholas had found him so, when Mr. Lamb had visited him this morning. Nicholas knew his manners; he'd been well brought-up, in spite of his recent occupation. Courtesy demanded he return the call. But no more, he vowed, going into the house, his gait rolling as if he still walked a deck. Bad enough he'd had to take up the title. He'd be demmed if he turned into some kind of dandy.

A stout butler, his expression austere but his eyes curious, led Nicholas up a wide, shallow staircase of sturdy oak to the drawing room. Nicholas's collar seemed tighter than ever, and he resisted the urge to run his finger under it. Nothing so threatening about this house, after all, furnished as it was with good old English solidity, oak paneling on the walls and a suit of armor on the flagstoned tiles of the hall. Much like the house in which he'd grown up, in fact. As if he were back in that house, he had a horrible feeling of being shut in, of needing to escape. By Neptune, he wanted to go back to sea!

Mr. Lamb rose as Nicholas was announced, his hand outstretched. Strange to hear himself called by his title, he thought, and so it was with a distinct sense of relief that he saw only friendliness in his host's eyes. He wasn't so certain about the rest of the family. All daughters, by Neptune! Though slender and dainty, they seemed to fill the room. Nicholas never had been comfortable with ladies; they mystified him, and their delicate airs frankly exasperated him. Years at sea hadn't done much to help him gain any social polish. Had he come across these girls in some waterfront tavern, he would have known what to do, but what did one say to ladies?

As he answered Mrs. Lamb's questions about the state of Sutcliffe Hall, his estate, he studied the girls. Remarkably pretty girls, all blond; they all made him profoundly uneasy. Miss Beatrice, true, had a sweet smile, and Miss Amanda seemed absentminded and somewhat untidy, making her more approachable, but as for Miss Penelope Lamb! She was by far the most polished of the group, and the most terrifying, with her graceful carriage and her fashionable clothing. She'd had a London Season, she was telling him now. How was he, so much a man of the sea, to talk to someone who'd mingled in polite society?

"I beg your pardon?" he said as he heard his name, raising his cup to cover the fact that he hadn't been attending.

"Were you really at Trafalgar, my lord?" Mrs. Lamb said.

Nicholas's face tightened. "Yes, ma'am, I was."

"How exciting." Mrs. Lamb went on with the embroidery in the tambour frame set before her. "Imagine, Mr. Lamb, we have a hero in the neighborhood!"

Nicholas shifted uneasily. "I'm hardly that, ma'am."

"But of course you are," Penelope said, her voice cool and well bred. "How frightening it must have been to be in battle! I am certain I would sink with the fear of it!"

"I wouldn't," Amanda declared, pushing her hair back from her face. "Penelope suffers from seasickness, my lord."

"Amanda!"

"It must have been tremendously exciting." Amanda leaned forward, her chin in her hand. "I've always wanted to go to sea."

For just a moment Nicholas was tempted to tell them the truth of a naval engagement, but at the sight of Amanda's eyes, frank and innocent, he refrained. "Mostly long stretches of boredom interrupted by a few hours of excitement. Do you sail, Miss Amanda?"

Amanda glanced quickly at her mother, who was frowning. "No, my lord, but George, my brother, does."

"George is reading history at Oxford," Mrs. Lamb put in. "He'll be coming down from spring term soon. Do you know, Mr. Lamb"—she turned to her husband—"when he does, we should give a reception for the earl. You'll want to meet George, I'm sure, my lord. He's so interested in history, and he studies so hard."

Amanda muttered something under her breath, and Beatrice bit off a giggle, earning both girls a look of reproof from their mother. Nicholas held on to his smile with an effort. By Neptune, did they really expect him to do the pretty? All he'd planned on doing when he'd decided to visit was to set Sutcliffe Hall's affairs to right, and then head back to Portsmouth. He had no desire to be tied to the land. There was nothing here for him. "There's a great deal to be done at the Hall, ma'am," he

17

said, setting down his cup. "I'm afraid I won't have the time to attend parties."

"But everyone wishes to meet you, my lord," Penelope said, and her cool little voice sent frissons of panic up his spine. No, by Neptune, he hadn't resigned his commission just to fall into the clutches of the first husband-hunting female he encountered. He'd refuse any and all invitations, he'd—

The door to the drawing room opened, and the butler stepped in. "Miss Catherine Lamb. Miss Mary Lamb," he intoned, and two little girls came in, followed by their governess, a mousy woman obviously past the first blush of youth. More blondes, God help him. Fortunately, they were too young. As for the governess.

He looked at the woman, and felt a jolt go through him. By Neptune, it looked like—but it couldn't be—Cassie? Great heavens, Cassandra Aldrich. The years melted away as he saw her again as she had been, looking up at him with worship in her huge brown eyes. She'd changed, of course, as had he, but the essential bond that had always been between them was still there, unchangeable, immutable. Cassandra Aldrich. Part of his past, and now, apparently, his present as well.

Nicholas rose, his eyes catching hers and seeing there recognition and surprise to match his own, along with other emotions he couldn't read. She wasn't entirely happy to see him, but that didn't matter. Not now. In her eyes, hidden though they were behind her spectacles, he had found what he had sought for so many years.

"Hello, Red," he said.

Chapter 2

The hated nickname jolted Cassandra out of her shock. Red! No one had called her that for years, and then it had mostly been him. How she'd hated it, and loved it. "Mr. St. John," she exclaimed. She was aware of Mrs. Lamb's thundering frown of disapproval, but she couldn't stop herself. Nicholas. He'd come back, at last. "What a surprise."

He grinned, that easy, relaxed smile she remembered. He'd changed, and yet he wasn't so very different. There were lines around his eyes that hadn't been there before, and his skin was weathered. His hair was the same, though, dark blond on the sides, bleached to near-whiteness on top by the sun. And he'd filled out. The shoulders that had been a little too wide for his lanky frame now looked exactly right, combined as they were with a broad chest and strong, solid arms. The years rolled back. Twelve years ago she had been infatuated with him, and yet he had been only a boy, younger than she was now. Now he was a man, a different proposition altogether.

"You've grown up, Red," he said, as if they had parted just yesterday.

"Yes, well." Cassandra's hand flew to her mobcap, and

for the first time in years she regretted her attire. "It's been a while. But what are you doing here?"

"Aldrich," Mrs. Lamb said firmly and rose. Belatedly Cassandra remembered where she was, and who she was. Oh dear. This was a blunder of major proportions. "One does not speak so to an earl. My lord, I must apologize," she said, turning to face Nicholas. "Aldrich is not usually so pert. Rest assured, she will be punished for this."

Nicholas glanced quickly from Mrs. Lamb to Cassandra. "You are employed here, Cassie?" he asked, not smiling now.

"Yes, my lord." Cassandra lowered her eyes. "I am the governess. Forgive me if I offended you, my lord."

"Return to your room, Aldrich." Mrs. Lamb stepped forward, standing beside Nicholas. "I shall call for you later."

"Hold now, there's no need for that." Nicholas spoke easily, but something had changed in his face. His eyes were now keen and hard, the set of his features determined. He was, Cassandra realized with a little shock, no longer a polite aristocrat, but a sea captain, accustomed to being in command, self-assured and confident. In spite of the tongue-lashing she knew was coming from her employer, Cassandra couldn't stifle a spurt of delight. Mrs. Lamb had met her match. Nicholas was standing up for her again, just as he had all those years ago.

"You know this person, my lord?" Mrs. Lamb said, looking up at him.

"Quite well, ma'am." His smile was affable, and yet Cassandra could sense the steel within him. "Since she was a girl. I understand, though, Cassandra, if you have duties." He turned to her, smiling. "We can catch up another time."

He was giving her a chance to escape. Cassandra

wanted to smile at him, except that she knew such an action would only intensify the scold she would get. "Yes, my lord," she murmured, curtsied, and fled.

Nicholas stood staring after her for a moment, unaware he was frowning. Cassie Aldrich, here, and as someone's servant. Something was very wrong.

"I am sorry, my lord," Mrs. Lamb said, touching his arm, and he looked down at her. "Please be assured that Aldrich will be punished for this."

"There's no need, ma'am," he said easily, and just as easily eluded her grasp. He detested clinging women. "Surely two old shipmates are allowed to greet each other."

"Shipmates?" Beatrice said. "Was Cassandra at sea with you?"

"No, no, figure of speech." He sat down again, more relaxed. Mrs. Lamb looked decidedly vexed, and that pleased him no end. He'd taken the wind out of her sails by refusing to take offense. For the first time, Nicholas began to see the advantages of being an earl. Just as when he had captained a ship, no one was likely to go against his wishes. "We are old friends."

Beatrice leaned forward. "How do you know her?"

"Beatrice," Mrs. Lamb reproved. "I'm sure his lordship really doesn't wish to discuss this."

"My sister's family and hers were neighbors," he said, ignoring her and enjoying himself immensely.

"Family friends, then, that's understandable," Mr. Lamb said, smiling. "Very natural for Miss Aldrich to want to greet the earl, wouldn't you say, Martha?"

Mrs. Lamb looked even more vexed, and Nicholas had to bite back a grin. "Of course, Mr. Lamb," she said, finally. "Forgive me if I've caused you any offense, my lord."

21

He smiled. "You haven't, ma'am. In fact, it will be pleasant knowing someone in the neighborhood."

"Oh, but surely, my lord, you won't wish to associate with such a person," Penelope said, her voice even colder than before. "Not now."

"Aldrich will be much too busy, I'm afraid," Mrs. Lamb put in. "I'm sure, my lord, we can find ways to entertain you. We must have a dinner party for the earl, Mr. Lamb. And, Penelope, you may sing afterward."

"That would be acceptable, Mama." Penelope smiled. "I am accounted to have a good voice, my lord."

Cassie couldn't carry a tune if her life depended on it, he thought suddenly, irrelevantly, and smiled. "I'd enjoy that. I'll need to meet our neighbors. Tell me, sir, is there someone in the neighborhood who does carpentry? Sutcliffe Hall needs repairing," he said to Mr. Lamb, and the conversation went on to other topics. Ignored for the moment was the surprise of his acquaintance with the family's governess. Ignored, but not forgotten, certainly not by Nicholas. Thus it was with great relief that he rose, sometime later, to make his own escape.

Safe in his study at Sutcliffe Hall, Nicholas at last pulled off the blasted neckcloth and allowed himself to relax. The Hall needed work, no doubt about it, but this room, with its broad partner's desk and leather armchairs, was a comfortable refuge. Sipping from a glass of whiskey, he leaned back. One duty done, but not the last. Looked like he'd be expected to stand watch all over the neighborhood. .Rather, attend all the neighborhood events, he corrected himself. He wasn't at sea anymore. Time to stop thinking that he was.

More than a little wistfulness crept into his thoughts at that. He hadn't been sorry to leave the navy, not after nearly twenty years of it, but he was sorry to leave the sea behind. Sorry to leave behind all his plans, and dreams. He'd have his own ship someday, he'd vowed. He would be in the merchant trade, carrying cargo as needed, as free and unfettered as the wind. Grand plans, and not so unrealistic. He'd saved some during his years at sea, and, with his record in service, he was certain he could obtain a loan for the rest of what he'd need. The news of his accession to the title, reaching him in America, where he was convoying ships against the threat of privateers, had not simply taken away one of the best captains in His Majesty's Navy. It had also meant the end to his dreams. He was an earl now, for what that was worth.

"Cap'n." Kirby came into the room without knocking. He was a small, wiry man with the sharp clear eyes of the true seaman, grizzled hair tied in a queue, and skin like leather, an unprepossessing figure who looked even more out of place in this great barn of a house than Nicholas did. Nicholas had tried to dissuade him, but nothing would do but that Kirby, who had served him well as steward, would come along back to England, to make sure his cap'n was taken care of. Nicholas wasn't yet sure whether he should be grateful for that, or not. "Be you wantin' supper?"

"Not yet," he said, without looking up. Kirby, too, was having a hard time leaving the sea behind after so many years at it; he insisted on keeping shipboard hours, and gradually was terrorizing the rest of the staff to do the same. "Did you bully the cook into making it already?"

Kirby snorted. "Landlubbers. Not a one of them good for anything. That cook, now. Rather have salt horse and biscuits than that swill she served us last night."

"The stew wasn't so bad," Nicholas said mildly, and earned himself another snort. "If you keep insulting the servants, Kirby, they'll all give notice."

23

"And good riddance to 'em. Not a one of them could holystone a deck or take in sail or—"

"None of them need to. We're not at sea anymore." His voice was still mild, but it stopped Kirby in middiatribe. For a moment their eyes met in shared sympathy. No, they were not at sea anymore. "I'll ring when I'm ready to eat."

"Aye, Cap'n," Kirby said finally, his voice subdued, and, flipping a quick salute, he went out.

Nicholas let out his breath. Kirby could be truculent and difficult to get along with, but he was loyal and his standards were high. At another time Nicholas might have spoken more sharply to him, but he had the damnable flaw of being able to sympathize with, and understand, what the other man was feeling. He, too, felt cast adrift, floating upon unfamiliar waters. Not quite so bad as he had, though. Something had happened to him this afternoon in the Lambs' parlor, something he still couldn't explain. It had to do with Cassandra Aldrich, though, and that in itself was a puzzle. Since when had he looked to find peace with a woman? Passion, yes, excitement, yes, but never peace. And yet, that was what he had felt when he had recognized her.

Cassandra Aldrich. Red. Smiling, he leaned back, remembering how she had always hated that nickname, how she would fire up when he teased her with it. It was a sore spot with her, her flame-colored hair, making her an exotic scarlet bloom in a garden of English roses. He had seen something in her even then, though she was just a child, a hint of beauty that promised to be more compelling than her sisters' more conventional looks. Something had gone wrong, though. His Cassie had never been meant to be someone's governess, in dull gowns and mobcaps and spectacles. The promise he had seen was more than hidden. It was dulled, as if it had never been fulfilled. What, he wondered, had happened to bring her to such a pass?

Stretching, he rose and crossed to the bellpull. Time to see what kind of unpalatable mess Cook had made up tonight. Kirby was right, he thought. The servants did leave something to be desired. He'd whip them into shape, though, them and this house, and he felt more enthusiasm for the task than he had since hearing of his inheritance. He wasn't sure what had changed within him. He knew only one thing. When he had looked deep into Cassie Aldrich's soft brown eyes, he had felt all the scattered pieces of his life fall into place. He was at peace, at home. He had, at last, found safe harbor.

"Red!" Catherine let out a giggle and bounced on Cassandra's bed. "Whyever did he call you that, Miss Aldrich?"

"Her hair, silly," Mary said, shooting her twin a look. "I don't think Miss Aldrich liked it much."

"Mama didn't, either. Did you see her face? Are you going to marry the earl, Miss Aldrich?"

"Don't be silly," Cassandra said, so sharply that Catherine looked startled. She rarely spoke to the girls in such a way, but then, this had been a trying afternoon.

"It would be ever so nice if you would." Mary's eyes had taken on that dreamy look that Cassandra had learned to distrust. "Then you could be our neighbor forever and ever."

"Mama wouldn't like it above half."

"It isn't going to happen. Now, girls, please go and put on your everyday dresses, else you'll get those dirty. Go on, now." Cassandra hurried the girls out of her room,

25

wishing for peace but knowing she'd get none. She had yet to account for this afternoon's extraordinary events. Nicholas St. John always had been able to disrupt things. Still. Her mouth curved in her rare, sweet smile. She, too, had enjoyed that look of displeasure on Mrs. Lamb's face, if only for a moment.

Penelope swirled into the room without knocking. She looked cool, composed, not a hair out of place, not a wrinkle in her gown. The perfect ice princess, except for the emotion flaring in her eyes. "I had no idea you kept such exalted company, Aldrich."

"Hardly that, miss." Cassandra stood in the middle of the floor, her head bent, her hands clasped before her. Hard as the pose was, she had long ago learned that it was required in her position. Listen to her employers, even agree with them, and never, ever argue. Not when they held her future in their hands.

"No? Then what was that in the drawing room? I declare, I was never so embarrassed in my life. Though I should have expected it. Others think you're such a meek little thing, Aldrich, but I see you for what you are. You're a forward little hussy, and I won't stand for it, do you hear?"

"No, miss," Cassandra murmured, though anger burned inside her at the insult.

"You think you're fooling everyone, hiding behind those spectacles, but I know what you're really like. You flirt with any man—"

"Miss, that's ridiculous—"

"Pray don't interrupt. I've seen you. Well, you may do what you wish with your own kind, but the earl's not for the likes of you."

Good heavens! Could Penelope possibly be jealous of her? "Oh, miss, I'm hardly a threat to you."

For some reason, that seemed only to make Penelope angrier. "Threat? How could you ever be a threat? Red," she said, scornfully. "That shows what he thinks of you."

That hurt. It was, indeed, what Mr. St. John—the earl, she corrected herself—had always thought of her. Old hurts and insecurities came pouring back. He might tease her, smile at her, laugh with her. When it came to courting, though, it was her sister he had chosen, she of the soft white skin and golden curls. Even then, Cassandra had known that was more important. She had no reason to think that anything had changed. "I have no intention of flirting with the earl."

"I should hope not." Penelope sniffed. "A fine sight you'd make, tossing your cap at him. I'll wager he's at Sutcliffe Hall now, laughing at you."

No, that was one thing he'd never do. The thought gave Cassandra strength, and she raised her head, looking at Penelope with calm, steady eyes. "Is that all, miss? I need to see to the twins' lessons."

"Oh my, oh my." Mrs. Lamb bustled into the tiny room, fanning herself vigorously. Her bulk filled the space, making Cassandra long desperately for escape. "What an afternoon. That was a disgraceful scene, Aldrich. Disgraceful."

"I didn't ask the earl to recognize me," Cassandra snapped, goaded beyond endurance.

Mrs. Lamb seemed to puff up, her head rising, her bosom thrusting forward. "I will not countenance such insolence, Aldrich. One more remark like that, and you will be seeking another position. Do I make myself clear?"

Cassandra's eyes widened with alarm. To have to look for another post, most likely without a character from her employers, was a frightening prospect. "No, ma'am. I mean, yes, ma'am. It won't happen again."

27

Mrs. Lamb sniffed. "See that it doesn't," she said, her tone modifying a bit. Cassandra relaxed. The worst was over, for now. "How do you know the earl?"

"As he said, ma'am. His family and mine were neighbors. It was a long time ago."

"Indeed. See that it stays that way. From now on, when the earl visits, you'll stay in your room."

"Yes, ma'am."

Mrs. Lamb glanced at her, as if suspicious of such meekness, but Cassandra's head was bowed, hiding her emotions. "Good. Come, Penelope. We've wasted enough time here. I don't believe Aldrich will give us any more problems."

"She had best not." Penelope's voice was cool again as she turned toward the door. "Oh, and, Aldrich."

Cassandra looked up. "Miss?"

"Please be certain to wear your cap at all times." she gave Cassandra a pitying, condescending smile. "Red," she said, and went out.

Cassandra tore off her cap and threw it across the room. She didn't think she'd ever been so angry in her life. It rather frightened her, she indulged her anger so rarely, but it felt good, too. Red, indeed. No one had the right to call her that, no one! Except perhaps Nicholas.

At the thought of the earl, her anger abruptly faded, making her sink down onto the edge of her bed and pull off her spectacles, pinching at the bridge of her nose. Nicholas. She'd never thought to see him again. He was a memory, nothing more, sweet and distant, something to hold on to when things got difficult. Thus to walk into the drawing room and realize that he was the new earl had been a considerable shock. The new earl, and now her neighbor, which meant she'd see him again. Not that it would do her any good. Tossing her cap at him, indeed.

With a wry smile, Cassandra retrieved her cap from behind her narrow bed where it had fallen, and pulled it down onto her untidy hair. She'd thrown the cap in anger, but for nothing else. Certainly she had no wish to entice Nicholas. The gulf between them was wider than it had ever been.

Looking quickly in her mirror, Cassandra straightened her cap and then set off toward the schoolroom. Before, the difference in their ages had separated them. Now it was the difference in their positions. Romantic novels notwithstanding, a mere servant could never aspire so high. If Cassandra had learned nothing else, she knew her place. It had been taught her in ruthless, painful lessons such as this afternoon's. She wasn't likely to overstep the bounds again.

She opened the schoolroom door where the sight of the twins throwing wads of paper at each other pushed other thoughts out of her mind. She had made her decision. She would avoid the earl, but not because she had been warned to do so. No. She would do so for her own preservation. She'd lost herself once before. She couldn't afford to do so again.

Nicholas set his mouth in a grim line as he tightened his grip on the reins of his mount. Blast, if he really was going to be a landlubber, he'd best learn how to ride. Blasted nag bucked worse than a frigate in a heavy sea, making him feel like a green hand who had yet to get his sea legs. Life ashore was proving to be as difficult as he'd anticipated.

It was a strange world he found himself in, with intricacies of etiquette and behavior that sometimes baffled him. Nicholas had been well raised, but he'd been a seaman most of his life. In the navy he'd learned other standards of behavior, other rules, and readjusting was hard. Especially for a man now considered to be the leading authority in the neighborhood, simply because of his title.

The thought made him grimace, and the horse took the opportunity of Nicholas's distraction to dance beneath him again. Muttering words learned in the forecastle and better never repeated in polite company, Nicholas regained control and rode on, down into the green valley where the village of Fairhaven lay. Above a band of sturdy oaks a church steeple pointed to the sky, dark against the brilliant blue light reflected off the English Channel, not far distant. Fairhaven had once been a thriving port, hence its name, until its harbor had silted up, forcing larger craft to go elsewhere. All that were left now were the dories of the fishermen, who lived in tiny, ramshackle huts near the shore. They kept to themselves, and yet were aware of all that went on around them, as Nicholas had learned one evening when he'd stopped into the local tavern for a pint. His exploits, especially at Trafalgar, had apparently preceded him.

He passed through the band of trees, and there was the village green, verdant in the spring sun. At the head of the green was the church, its Norman architecture solid and four-square and uncompromising. In the center of the green was a duck pond with a stream leading away, toward the sea, and around the green were houses of various age and descriptions. They were cottages of flint or tile, rather than the half-timbered homes of his childhood village, but somehow he was reminded of that long-ago place. Perhaps it was the peace it exuded, its smallness, its sameness. Perhaps it was the fact that here, as there, he felt out of place. He didn't belong here, though he couldn't say just why.

Stopping before the Crown and Anchor, the inn, he swung off his mount, handing the reins to a groom. Here Nicholas planned to meet with a builder recommended by Mr. Lamb to supervise the work needed at Sutcliffe Hall. As he turned toward the door, however, his attention was caught by the people coming out of the linen draper's across the High Street, a woman and two children. He recognized the children first; their golden curls proclaimed them to be the youngest Lamb sisters. His recognition of the woman was deeper, and not based simply on externals. Cassie.

Peace settled over him at the sight of her, chivvying her charges down the street. Lord knew why. He'd known more beautiful women, better-dressed women. Today Cassandra wore another sacklike gown that effectively hid her shape, this one in an indeterminate shade of blue, with a plain shawl about her shoulders and an unadorned bonnet upon her head. And her spectacles, of course. Quite aging, but then she must be—Nicholas's calculations brought him up short. Good God, she must be about twenty-four, six years younger than himself. No longer a young miss, certainly, but hardly past her last prayers. She had been a quiet child, he remembered, at least on the surface, but not so self-effacing. He wondered what had happened to change her.

The builder was forgotten as he crossed the street. The girls saw him first, and their faces brightened. "Oh look, Miss Aldrich!" the taller one said, tugging at her sleeve. " 'Tis the earl!"

Cassandra whirled around, and the parcel she carried fell to the ground. "Oh, bother. Catherine, do be careful," she scolded, bending down.

"Here, let me," Nicholas said at the same moment, his square, brown hand reaching to pluck the parcel from the ground. Cassandra pulled back in surprise, and her spectacles, already loose, slipped off her face. She caught them before they could fall further, but not before Nicholas, looking up, saw her. "By Neptune, Cassie, you have pretty eyes."

One of the girls giggled, and Cassandra straightened, securely fastening the spectacles back on her nose. "There, that is better," she said, ignoring his comment. "Catherine, Mary, make your curtsy to the earl, now."

Nicholas returned the courtesy with a grave bow. Both girls were dressed in white, one with a pink sash, one with blue. It was, however, easier to tell them apart than he had expected. Already he knew it was Catherine whose eyes sparkled up at him so mischievously, while Mary held back. "Ladies," he said, and held out his hand to Cassandra. "Miss Aldrich."

Cassandra hesitated and then reached out her hand. He had the fleeting impression of fingers that were cool and slender, yet strong, before she pulled back. "My lord. How do you, today?"

"Well, thank you. You've been shopping."

"Yes. Girls, we must be returning, or we'll be late for luncheon. A pleasure meeting you, my lord."

Nicholas turned to walk with them, noting a fleeting look of chagrin on Cassandra's face. "You aren't walking, surely?"

"Of course we are. We do so whenever the weather is fine. It isn't above two miles."

"Then let me escort you," he said, impulsively.

"Oh no, my lord, I couldn't ask you to do such a thing. Not when you must have business in the village."

"Blast." He'd forgotten about the builder. "I do. But, blast it, Cassie, you're the first friendly face I've seen in days."

The eyes she turned to him were unexpectedly merry. "As bad as that?"

"Worse." His hands in his pockets, he walked beside them, his gait rolling. "I took tea with the vicar and his wife the other day. Well may you laugh," he said as Cassandra made a smothered sound. "You did not have to sit through a Scripture reading, a poetry recitation, and hymns played at the organ."

"Reverend Carlisle's daughters are quite accomplished," she said, tactfully. "And rather pretty, too."

He cast her a sour look. "Do the families of this neighborhood have naught but daughters?"

Cassandra laughed outright. It was an entrancing sound, throaty and husky and very real, unlike the artificial giggles he'd heard so much this past week. "Oh no, there are some sons. However, there are a great many unmarried girls."

"Blast."

"My lord, your language," she reproved, her eyes twinkling.

"Well, Cassie?" He stopped and smiled at her. She was enjoying his discomfiture a bit too much. It was time to get some of his own back. "Why aren't you setting your cap at me?"

Chapter 3

Shock held Cassandra briefly immobile. "My lord, I'd never do anything so forward," she said, ignoring the girls' giggles. For a moment she had forgotten who she was, who he was. It would not do. Gathering her dignity about her like a cloak, she laid her hand on the girls' shoulders. "Come, 'tis getting late. Your mama will scold if we're not home betimes."

"Running away, Cassie?" Nicholas said, mildly.

"No. I must get the girls home."

"Of course. I didn't think you'd cry craven. Do you still have a temper, Cassie?" he went on, following behind her. "With your hair, you always did."

Cassandra forced herself to take a deep breath before replying. "Redheads do not always have tempers, my lord. Now, if you'll excuse us—"

"My lord, you walk funny," Catherine said, suddenly.

Cassandra rolled her eyes toward heaven in supplication. It needed only this. "Catherine Louise Lamb," she began.

"No, it's all right, Cassie." Nicholas grinned down at the little girl, who was regarding him with frank interest. Somehow he knew he had an ally here. "From being at

34

sea, Miss Catherine. When you're on a moving ship, you learn to walk a different way."

"Mama says you're a hero. Are you?"

Nicholas paused. "I suppose some would say so."

Cassandra looked at him sharply, but stopped herself in time from commenting. There was something behind his words, darkness and pain, but it was not her task to soothe him. No matter how much she might want to. "I apologize for Catherine's forwardness, my lord, but I fear 'tis my fault. I encourage the girls to ask questions."

"No harm done. Truth is, Cassie, I feel all at sea here." The wave of his hand encompassed the neighborhood. "I need someone. Just until I can get my land legs."

Cassandra swallowed, forcing herself to look away from the appeal in his eyes. "I am persuaded there'll be any number of people willing to help you, sir." Placing her hands on the girls' shoulders, she turned them. "Good day," she said, and hurried away.

Nicholas stifled his protest. "Good day, Red," he called, and had the satisfaction of having Cassandra look back at him, startled. Suddenly cheerful, he turned, returning to the inn. Perhaps life ashore wouldn't be so bad, after all.

Freedom. Cassandra pulled off the hated spectacles, shoved them in her pocket, and began to run across the fields, over the stile in the fence that separated Lambton Manor from the earl's property, toward the cliff. There she paused for a moment, catching her breath. It was a glorious day. Far out in the Channel she could see sails, and she wished, not for the first time, that she was on one of those distant vessels. Closer to home, the dun-colored sails of the fishing fleet contrasted sharply with the sparkling deep blue bay, while, in the cove below her, waves lapped at the edge of a sandy beach. Tide was out, she noticed. Not good for swimming, even had it been warm enough. She'd have to content herself with walking the beach today.

Carefully, watching every step, Cassandra picked her way down the narrow, twisty path that led down the cliff face. It wasn't quite so dangerous as it seemed, being firm underfoot and having stiff brambly bushes to the side to break any falls. Still, she had never brought Catherine or Mary here, nor was she likely to. She loved her charges dearly, but there were times she needed to escape them. This was her own, private place, and she shared it with no one. In all the time she'd been coming here she'd never seen anyone else, nor did she expect to. It was hers, alone.

Not today, however. Something, a sound, perhaps, made her look up when she was just a few feet from the beach, and she caught her breath in a curious mixture of dismay and exhilaration. Someone else had discovered her cove. Nicholas.

Had she said his name aloud? Though she was certain she hadn't spoken, he raised his head from contemplating the foam at the edge of the waves and looked directly at her. It lasted only a moment, that fierce, blue gaze, but it pierced her to the heart. Then he glanced away, his eyes shuttered. "Ahoy," he called, and strode across the beach toward her. "Where are your glasses, Red?"

"I—what are you doing here?" In spite of herself Cassandra retreated a few steps, stopping only when he did.

Nicholas leaned a booted foot on a rock and casually rested his arms on his knee. "Happens I own this."

"The earl—oh."

"Exactly. Oh." He smiled, but his eyes were somber,

36

the dark blue-gray of storms. "Not quite what one thinks of as an earl, am I?"

"Oh, it's not that," Cassandra said, quickly. If anything, she thought he'd make a very good earl. He had an air of authority he wore easily and naturally, perhaps because of his years at sea, perhaps because of his nature. "I meant—"

"Feel like a fish out of water," he growled, stuffing his hands into the pockets of his impeccably tailored coat and looking out to sea. His shoulders were so broad they almost looked bulky, and an unruly strand of hair fell over his forehead. "Don't you?"

"What? No." She recoiled from the impact of that blue gaze turned on her again. "No, my lord. I meant simply that you're very little like the old earl."

At that he laughed, a hearty peal of sound that boomed out across the water. "Were you acquainted with my uncle, Cassie?"

"No. Should I have been?"

"By Neptune, I hope not," he said, though he continued to grin. "Seen the inside of Sutcliffe Hall, have you?"

"No, my lord, I haven't."

"Stop 'my lording' me, Cassie."

"I can't, sir. It wouldn't be proper."

"The devil with proper." He strode toward her and again she stepped back, making him stop. "Blast. My apologies, Cassie. Seems I don't know how to go on in the world."

Cassandra kept her distance, as wary of his sudden contrition as of his earlier forcefulness. She didn't know this man as she once had; he had changed. But then, so had she. "You've been at sea, my lord."

"Cassie," he said through clenched teeth, and then

sighed. "Oh, very well. If you must call me something, why not 'Captain'?"

"Because it wouldn't be—"

"Proper. I know. When we're alone, Cassie. No one else need know." He paused, studying her face. "Well?"

It was her turn to pause. The path sloped so steeply here that, even though he was only a few feet away, his head was below hers, giving her the odd experience of being taller than he. From this angle his face, turned up to her almost beseechingly, looked young and vulnerable. And something else. Unconsciously her tongue flicked out to moisten lips gone dry. "Aye, Cap'n," she said, her voice husky, which was absurd. He was just her old friend. "But, mind, only when we're alone."

He grinned up at her. "What a starched-up little governess you've turned into, Red. When did you become so proper?"

"Pray don't call me that, my lord—Captain."

"Why not, Cassie?" He stepped toward her. "You never minded being teased before."

"I've grown up."

His smile was lazy. "So I've noticed," he said, and leaned his head toward her.

Startled, Cassandra wheeled around, fleeing up the path. Surely he hadn't been about to kiss her. Not when he called her "Red." Red! The very thought of the name made her fume.

"Not that anyone can tell your hair's red anymore," he said, so close behind her that she spun around again. Good heavens, he could move quietly when he wished to! She hadn't heard so much as a footfall. This time he was not below her level. This time, he loomed above her, and she had to crane her head back to see his face. His eyes were azure, with little lines radiating out from the corners, and the sun picked out the highlights in his hair, turning them golden. Cassandra's mouth went dry again. "Now you wear caps. Ashamed of your hair, Red?"

"No." She whirled around and stalked away, not caring if he followed her or not.

"At least you've taken the spectacles off." He was following her, the dratted man. "What are you hiding from, Cassie?"

"Nothing."

"Then why are you running away from me?"

That stopped her. Why was she running from him? He was her hero, the man she had adored with all the fervor and heartbreak of first love, so long ago. What had happened since then had nothing to do with him. "My lord, if Mrs. Lamb knows I've seen you like this, she'll ring a peal over me."

"As bad as that, Cassie?"

The gentleness in his voice was nearly her undoing. It brought her back to days that seemed simpler in memory than they actually had been. "Yes. So you see, I cannot stay to talk with you."

"No, we can't talk here. The path's too narrow." Lightly he nudged her shoulder. "Go. We'll talk at the top of the cliff."

"My lord—"

"Go."

There was no gainsaying that simple command. Cassandra went, trying not to hurry, but to walk her usual, measured pace, though she was aware of him behind her. Uncomfortably aware that, because of the steepness of the path, he was level with a certain area of her anatomy and was probably eyeing it even now. A gentleman would have looked away, but then, she wasn't entirely certain he was a gentleman.

"Now," he said when they'd reached the top of the path, "what's all this, then?"

Cassandra's hand was at her throat, though normally the climb didn't leave her so breathless. "Simply what I said, my lord. I shouldn't be speaking with you like this. If anyone sees us—"

"Who will see us?"

She laughed, but without mirth. "It's been a long time since you've lived in a village, sir. Don't you know that everyone talks about you and whatever you do?"

"Yes, I do, blast it." He ran a hand over his hair, looking distractedly out to sea, and then caught at her hand. "Then we'll go to the Hall."

"No!" Pulling her hand free, she linked her fingers together. Absurdly, she missed the warm strength of his hand on hers. "You don't understand, sir. I can't go with you."

Nicholas jammed his hands into his pockets again. "Isn't your life your own, then, Cassie?"

"No. No more than yours is."

His wry glance acknowledged the truth of that statement. "Yet, this is your afternoon free—"

"But I am a governess, sir. I must be very careful how I behave and who I'm seen with, else I might lose my position."

He frowned. "Would they really dismiss you for so little a thing?"

"Being with a man, unchaperoned? Certainly they would." She smiled suddenly. "Especially since Miss Lamb has set her cap for you."

"The devil she has! Why?"

"Because you're the earl." And the most attractive man Cassandra had ever in her life met. She was fast remembering just why she had cared so desperately about him when she was a girl.

"Blast it. I didn't ask for this."

"Such a terrible fate," she said, lightly. "Wealthy, titled, and sought-after."

Nicholas waved his hand in dismissal. "Not what I had planned for my life." He looked down at her, his eyes keen and sharp. "Not, I think, what either of us planned. How in Neptune's name did you end up as a governess?"

"I need to support myself," she said, in that same light tone.

"What of your family?"

"Gone. At least, my parents are, and my sisters have their own problems."

"They're married?"

"Yes."

"You're not. Why?"

"I didn't take." She gazed off over the field, scattered with dandelions and daisies. "I must go, my lord—excuse me, Captain. It really would not do for me to be seen with you."

"I understand, I think. Come. I'll see you home."

"No." She pulled back from his hand, wanting his touch and fearing it at the same time. If she let him touch her, would she ever be able to leave? "No, that will only make matters worse. Good-bye, Captain."

"Cassie," he called, as she picked up her skirts and hurried across the field. "Just one thing."

She turned. "What?"

"Do you have the same day free every week?"

"Yes, Thursday afternoon."

"The beach. Next week."

An odd look flitted across Cassandra's face and then she turned, almost running from him. He watched her go, smiling, free at last from the tendrils of last night's nightmare and the resulting restlessness that had sent him down to the beach to watch the waves. There were compensations to this new life. He didn't know what had happened to turn his lively, red-haired Cassie into a colorless governess, but he was certain she was the same underneath, unable to resist a challenge. She'd be at the beach next week, no matter how she had protested today. He couldn't wait.

"Miss Aldrich, tell us again about when you were a little girl and the earl rescued you," Catherine said, interrupting Mary as she read from her primer.

Cassandra sighed and took off her spectacles, pinching tiredly at the bridge of her nose. "No. We're not done with lessons."

"Please? It's ever so much more interesting than this story. And we can learn from it."

"I don't consider it an educational story, Catherine. Mary, please resume reading."

"You could tell us about the navy. That's educational."

In spite of herself, Cassandra's lips twitched with amusement. "No."

"Please? I'll do my sums without arguing. I promise."

"Please?" Mary chimed in.

Cassandra threw up her hands in despair. "Oh, very well, you little monsters. Though I've told it to you enough."

"You were twelve years old," Catherine prompted.

"Yes. My sister Athena was fourteen, and Ophelia was seventeen."

Catherine's brow wrinkled. "You had funny names."

"My father was a scholar. He named us after characters in Greek mythology. Which you would know, Miss Catherine, if you would read as you're supposed to."

"So the earl came to your village," Mary said.

"He came home on leave. Mind, now, he wasn't yet the earl, of course," Cassandra said, getting caught up in the story in spite of herself. "He was only eighteen." Younger than she was now.

"Was he your beau?" Catherine asked.

"She was only a little girl, like us," Mary said scornfully.

"So?"

"No, of course he wasn't my beau," Cassandra said. "I was skinny and had terrible red hair that was always tangled. He liked my sister Ophelia better."

"Is that when he started calling you Red?"

"Mm-hm." And how angry that had made her, even then, that he hadn't looked past her carroty hair to the girl inside, who would happily have died for him. How it had hurt, that the man who was her hero preferred her pretty blond sister instead. Too often she felt out of place in her village, in her own home, the only redhead in a family of cool blondes, the only girl to share her father's scholarly interests. Shy, sensitive, she devoured every book about foreign lands to be found in her father's library, and daydreamed about someday traveling to them. Mr. St. John, though, had done more than daydream. He'd actually seen such places. Before she'd even met him, Cassandra was convinced he was a hero.

"May I come in, Miss Aldrich?" a voice said at the door.

Cassandra looked up, groaning inwardly. "Of course, Mr. Lamb," she said, and George stumbled in, throwing himself down into a chair. The second oldest of the Lamb children and the only son, George had somehow

43

managed to escape the arrogance and vanity that made Penelope so unpleasant. He had never spoken to Cassandra with anything less than respect or kindness. Too kind, perhaps. The doglike devotion in his eyes as he gazed at her made her groan to herself again. Here was a problem, indeed. "Is there something we can do for you?"

George stretched out his legs. "No, nothing. Got bored, you know. M'father wants to teach me farming."

"I see." She turned back to the girls. Perhaps if she ignored him, he would go away. "Please continue reading, Mary," she prompted.

"Is this what you do all day?" George said, cutting across Mary's voice. "Bloody boring."

"Mr. Lamb, please. Your language."

He looked stricken. "Sorry, Miss Aldrich. Forgot where I was. Won't happen again."

Cassandra eyed him, and then rose. "I really think you should leave, Mr. Lamb. You are disrupting the lessons."

"Don't make me go, Cassandra. I'll sit here quiet as a mouse."

"Oh, gammon," Catherine muttered, and Cassandra's lips twitched.

"I really can't allow it, sir. Please."

George rose to his feet, his lanky frame towering over her. When he gained some maturity he would be an attractive man, but he would never be for her. She wished he would only realize it. "Miss Aldrich, on your afternoon free, may I—"

"Cassandra, I need to ask you—George, what are you doing here?" Beatrice asked, breezing into the schoolroom and dropping into a chair.

George turned red. "Nothing. Must go. Sorry for bothering you, Miss Aldrich," he said, and fled.

Beatrice looked after him in amusement. "Has he been making a nuisance of himself?"

Cassandra sank down at the table. "Oh no. He merely stopped in to see how Catherine and Mary are doing."

The look Beatrice gave her was skeptical. "Mm-hm. I think he has a *tendre* for you, Cassie."

Cassandra cast a quick glance at the younger girls, who were listening avidly. "I doubt that very much."

"Does it bother you?" Beatrice lounged back, tucking her legs under her. "If you talked to Father, he'd do something about it."

Cassandra shook her head, smiling a little. Beatrice meant well, but she was a bit naive. If Cassandra complained, she knew she would be blamed for George's behavior. In matters such as this, the woman was the one at fault. Such was the way of the world, as she had learned too well. "It will be all right. Soon he'll notice someone more suitable, and he'll forget about me."

"Well, I don't know who," Beatrice said with devastating frankness. "The vicar's daughters? Uh." She shuddered, and Cassandra was hard-pressed to hold back a smile.

"Tell me about the frock you'll be wearing at the dinner party. Is it all you hoped for?"

Beatrice immediately brightened. "Oh yes, and I do wish you could come, Cassandra. Especially since you know the earl." For the next few moments she chattered on about the dinner party the Lambs would be giving for the earl. Cassandra smiled and nodded in the appropriate places, but her mind was far away. Down at the beach, where she had met Nicholas. Had he really almost kissed her? No, of course not, it had to have been her imagination, no matter how it stayed in her mind. She knew quite well how Nicholas saw her. To him she was still the little

45

girl he'd called Red. If she were a guest at the dinner, though, she could meet him as an equal. If only she could put up her hair, don the sea green muslin gown that had been her favorite, what a surprise he would receive. She was, however, only the governess, and that was all she ever would be. On the night of the dinner party she would be confined to the nursery wing with her charges, and Nicholas probably wouldn't even notice she was missing.

Next week, though. Cassandra's fingers tightened on the primer. Next week, and her afternoon free. Going to the beach was out of the question. Of course. It smacked of an assignation, and that was something she could not allow. Once she had been foolish beyond permission, but no longer. Now she was sensible, discreet, proper, all the things she needed to be, all the things she never had been. If in reality she longed to take off the hated mobcap and toss her spectacles away, well, no one had to know that. She may have learned not to act foolishly. Apparently, though, she hadn't given up her dreams.

Beatrice at last rose to leave. Cassandra took a few moments to settle the girls down and quiet their questions, and then began to teach them the intricacies of conjugating French verbs. It was just as well she had to concentrate, or heaven knew where her mind would go. All that thinking, and she had yet to decide. Would she go to the beach, or wouldn't she?

Chapter 4

Nicholas strode across the rolling emerald turf, heading for the path that led down to the beach. Blast it, here it was Cassie's free afternoon, and he was late. Blasted builders had kept him with all that had to be done to restore Sutcliffe Hall to anything approaching its former splendor. Thank Neptune his uncle had left a good legacy. Nicholas had managed to save a bit, and he'd earned more than his share of prize money at sea, but restoring the Hall would have beggared him. Besides, it wasn't exactly how he'd planned to spend his money.

Reaching the top of the cliff, he stopped and looked down at the beach, squinting instinctively as he had learned to do at sea. Huh. Not there yet, unless she was out of his sight. Or unless she had left. It was already four bells of the afternoon watch—two o'clock, he corrected himself. Another thing to remember, to tell time in land-lubber terms. Life was much simpler at sea. Finding Cassie again was the only thing that made his present life tolerable.

Strange he felt this way. If he'd thought of her at all over the last ten years, and he had, he'd remembered the funny, bright little girl who hung on his every word and had always been able to make him laugh. Certainly he'd never expected to see her again, or to react to her as he had. Probably, he thought, setting off down the path, it was because he felt adrift in this new life, and she was familiar, an anchor for him. Probably.

The path twisted and turned, and at last the beach was in sight. Nicholas saw the two youngest Lamb girls first, making him hesitate. Blast. Cassie had brought chaperones. He had no doubt that was their purpose for being there. Apparently she'd meant what she'd said last week, about being careful not to be seen alone with him. "Ahoy!" he called, and the children, standing just beyond the edge of the waves, turned to look at him as he came closer, their eyes huge. "Are those mermaids I see?"

The girls stared, and then, looking at each other, broke into giggles. "Silly! We're not mermaids," Catherine said, and Mary nudged her none too gently in the ribs.

"He's the earl, Cat!" she hissed. "You shouldn't talk to him that way."

"Well, Miss Mary," he said, smiling down at her, "when a seaman comes across two pretty sea sprites—"

Catherine giggled again. "You are silly! But I like you."

"Thank you, ma'am." His face grave, except for his eyes, he executed a faultless bow. That seemed to remind the girls of their own manners, for they both dropped hasty curtsies. "Surely you're not here alone, sprites?"

"No, Miss Aldrich is with us. You talk funny, sir."

"Catherine!" Mary protested.

"Well, he does. I didn't think earls talked like that."

"This earl does." He smiled. "Where is Miss Aldrich?"

Catherine waved her hand toward the cliff. "Over there, somewhere. Why do you talk like that?"

"From being at sea." His voice was absent as he scanned the small beach. Now where could she be—

48

there, just stepping out from the shelter of a boulder. He raised his hand in salute and started toward her, and then stopped, utterly still, transfixed. If the little girls were sea sprites, then the woman coming toward him was a siren, whose call no man could resist.

She was beautiful. Quite stunningly, gloriously beautiful. The hair that was usually hidden under a prim, ridiculous mobcap now streamed past her shoulders, thick and wavy and fiery red in the sun, like molten silk. Fire, the great enemy at sea, but which he would welcome now. It tempted a man, that hair, to sink his fingers into it, to wrap it around him, to feel the tendrils bind him close. It made a man long to see it, spread in soft satin waves on a white linen pillowslip. His white linen pillowslip.

Nicholas swallowed hard, stunned by the image and the resulting surge of heat within his body. But this was little Cassie. Not so little, now, though, not with that hair, not with her face finally free of those blasted spectacles. Not a little girl at all. Her features had lost the roundness of childhood and had the sculpted, delicate lines of a cameo; her skin was fair, unmarred by so much as a freckle. She was a beauty, his Cassie, just as he had once foretold, and he suddenly wanted her very badly.

He took a step toward her and she stopped, as if just now becoming aware of his presence. Delicate color surged into her cheeks, her throat, and he wondered if she blushed all over. Interesting thought. "Ahoy," he said, his voice thick. Blast. Of all the ridiculous things to say. But then, he never had been in the petticoat line. The women he'd known in the various ports of the world, the casual, easy acquaintances, quickly made and as quickly forgotten, he could deal with. Cassie, though, was far more than casual. Far more.

"Ahoy," she called back, and walked toward him.

49

Goodness, she hadn't known that Nicholas was here. She realized now, though, that she had heard voices for a few moments, and that her absorption in sketching the marine life she'd found in a little pool had prevented her from recognizing his. To step out from behind the rock to see him had been a shock, but then to see the way he looked at her—well, it quite took her breath away. It was out of her dreams, the focused, intent gaze a man gave a woman who attracted him. Which was nonsense. How could she, plain Cassandra Aldrich, with her carroty hair and prissy gray gown, ever interest a man like the earl? She had almost been relieved when he spoke so casually. Almost.

"I didn't know you were here," she said, her head up, her face serene. "I didn't think you were coming."

"Didn't you?" He walked toward her as well, until they were only inches apart. "Then why did you bring them?" he asked, jerking his head back to indicate the girls.

Cassandra's eyes slid away from his. " 'Tis a beautiful day. I thought they should get some fresh air."

"On your afternoon free, Cassie?"

"Yes."

"Dangerous thing to do. They'll expect you to take the girls all the time."

Cassandra raised her chin. "It isn't the first time they've been with me on my free day, and no one has expected any such thing."

"No?" He stood and simply looked at her, and she felt the color rising in her face again. Drat the man. Must he always make her feel so addled?

"No. Catherine, Mary." She turned away from him. "Do step back. The tide is coming in."

"May we swim, Miss Aldrich?" Catherine called.

"No, 'tis too cold."

Nicholas's eyes were bright. "Do you swim, Cassie?"

50

"Sometimes, yes," she said briskly, and moved away, refusing to be discommoded yet again by him. Opening her sketchbook, she sat down on a rock and set to work assiduously with a charcoal.

Nicholas stood for a moment before joining her. There was no room on the rock for him, so he simply dropped to the sand, sitting cross-legged. "I didn't know you drew," he said, reaching for the sketchbook.

"My lord, please—"

"Cassie." He placed a finger on her lips and, startled, she drew back. "We agreed you wouldn't call me that, remember?"

"Yes."

He smiled quickly up at her and then returned to the sketchbook. "This is quite good," he said in surprise as he came to a drawing she had done earlier, of the girls standing by the water. In spite of the gray and black of the charcoal, she had somehow managed to convey the sense of space and light so peculiar to the sea. "Do you paint, too?"

"No, not anymore."

That made him look up. Of course she wouldn't paint. When would she have the chance, even if she could afford the materials? Somehow the injustice of it made him angry. "Pity. You're good. Did your father teach you?"

She smiled, taking the sketchbook back. "Hardly. Papa was many things, but not at all artistic. My mother taught me first, and then later I had a drawing master. She was glad I had at least one feminine accomplishment."

Idly, he sifted sand through his fingers. "She talked to me about you once, you know. Your mother, I mean."

"She did? When?"

"Just before I left. She was worried about you. Said she feared you'd turn into a bluestocking."

Cassandra's mouth quirked. "Yes, well, she did worry about my studying so much. Strange, isn't it? She seems to have been right."

"Not really."

"What do you mean?"

"I think she feared you'd never attract a man."

"My lord!"

"She was wrong, of course. I told her I thought you'd grow up to be a beauty."

"You're funning me," she said in an uncertain voice.

"Would I do that, Cassie?"

"Yes."

"Not this time." His face softened. "You are beautiful, you know."

"I—" she began, but was spared the necessity of answering that remarkable statement by the sound of childish voices. She didn't know if she were relieved, or vexed, to see her charges.

"Lord Lynton!" Catherine cried. "Miss Aldrich told us you rescued her."

Nicholas glanced toward Cassandra, who was blushing again. "Rescued you?"

Cassandra bent her head. "From your nephew, Peter."

"Huh. That maworm."

"My lord!"

"Cassie, we agreed—well, he is a maworm," he said. True enough that they'd agreed not to be so formal. She couldn't very well call him by anything but his title, though, with the two girls looking on. He wouldn't put it past either of them to know exactly what it meant if she didn't. Blast! Must he do his courting before an audience?

"How is Peter?" Cassandra asked, and when Nicholas didn't answer, looked up. "My lord?"

"Hm? Oh." He looked at her face as if he'd never seen

it before, as if it were all he'd wish to see for the remainder of his life. By Neptune, was he courting her? "He's well, last I heard. He's a vicar."

"Is he really?"

"Why not? He's certainly narrow-minded enough to be a sky-pilot."

"Excuse me?"

"A minister," he said, realizing he'd used seaman's cant again. No, of course he wasn't courting her, he thought, continuing his internal dialogue. He had no desire to get leg-shackled. What he felt for Cassie was something else, though he wasn't sure what.

"What a thing to say, sir," she chided. "I meant that with his brain I thought he'd do something else. Politics, perhaps."

"Not enough money. And, to tell you the truth, too hard to get started. He never liked anything that was work."

"Miss Aldrich said he used to tease her," Catherine said.

"Now, girls, we don't wish to bore the earl with old stories," Cassandra said, quickly.

"But you always said he was splendid, the way he rescued you."

"Catherine!"

Nicholas chuckled. "Been telling tales, Cassie?"

"Oh, good heavens." Cassandra gave the girls a hard look, and they smiled back, not a whit abashed. "Oh, very well. I told them about the time you came to Norton."

"To see my sister. I remember." He grinned. "I was on leave, and very full of myself, as I recall."

"Oh no," Cassandra protested. "I thought you were very nice."

He grimaced. "Nice."

"Well, you were." She turned to the girls. It was Nicholas's turn to be discomfitted, and that tickled her. "It was like this. My father was the rector for the village, and he took in students. He allowed me to sit in on the classes. I was the only girl." And here, as elsewhere, Cassandra was different, and, because of that difference, alone.

"I don't know why," Catherine said. "Why you would wish to study."

"I liked it. And I was good. So was Peter. He and I had a rivalry to see who could be the best. Most of the time it wasn't too bad, but once in a while—well. Everyone was excited at the thought of a naval hero visiting the village."

Nicholas shifted uneasily beside her. "Cassie."

"Well, we were."

"I'm no hero."

"Nonsense. In any event, Peter was in alt, bragging and strutting. Oh, he was unbearable that day." She smiled. "I had talked my mother into letting me have a pink dress—can you imagine, with my hair!—and I was wearing it that day with a clean apron. Papa let us out early from lessons and we all went out to wait for the earl. And that was when the trouble started."

"Peter started bullying you," Catherine prompted.

"Yes. Well, you see, he hadn't done well at lessons at all, and I'm afraid Papa gave him a severe setdown. To make matters worse, I was the one who answered the questions Peter couldn't."

"I don't see what's so wrong with that," Nicholas said, unexpectedly.

"Don't you? Oh well, it bothered Peter. First he started teasing me about my hair—"

"Does that really bother you?"

"It did, then. And it got worse. Pretty soon all the boys were taunting me. It was terrible." For a brief moment her eyes were haunted by memory. "Then I'm afraid I did a terrible thing."

"You hit Peter," Mary said.

"I couldn't think what else to do! All the boys were around me and I couldn't get free, and it was all I could think of. A mistake, of course. Hitting never solves anything," she added, primly.

"Because he hit you back," Catherine said. "And that's when the earl came along."

"Yes." She smiled at Nicholas, who studiously avoided her gaze. "I'm sorry, my lord. Is this too embarrassing for you?"

"You may as well go on." He stretched out his legs. "Since you're enjoying it so much."

"Yes. Well, Peter did hit me back. And just when I was afraid that all the boys were going to start in, from out of nowhere came this hand that plucked Peter away. It was the earl. The other boys ran away, and he gave Peter such a dressing down I don't think he ever forgot it. I almost felt sorry for him."

"You forgot to say he looked splendid, Miss Aldrich," Catherine said. "You told us before that—"

"Yes, well, of course he looked splendid to me, he was saving me. And that is how I met the earl before. That's all." She smiled and sat back, her hands folded in her lap. It wasn't all, of course. She'd told no one, not even the girls, how much Nicholas's actions had meant to her. Oh, he had looked splendid, tall even then and seeming so grown-up to her, in his blue jacket with its round brass buttons, and the trousers that were a blindingly bright white. Never would she forget looking up and seeing him striding into the group of boys surrounding her, scattering them and grabbing Peter by the collar. It was the first time she had fallen in love.

"Did Peter bother you after that?" Nicholas asked, and she came out of her thoughts. The first time she'd loved, and the last.

"No. Catherine, Mary, why do you not look for shells? 'Tis getting late and we'll need to be leaving soon."

Something in Cassandra's voice must have told the girls there'd be no more tales forthcoming, for they dashed off without protest. Silence fell between the two adults. "Do you really dislike being teased about your hair?" Nicholas said, finally.

"What? No, of course not. I did, once, but no one teases me now."

"Probably because no one ever sees it."

"Oh, unfair," she said, but without heat.

"Don't you know?"

"What?"

"Nothing." How beautiful her hair was, he wanted to say, but somehow the words wouldn't come.

"We really must be going soon." From one pocket she pulled the mobcap, wrinkled now, and bundled her hair into it. From another, she produced the spectacles. Before she could put them on, however, Nicholas reached out and took them from her.

He squinted through them and drew back. "These are clear glass," he said, looking at her accusingly. "They're not even real. You don't need to wear them."

"No," she said, calmly, holding out her hand. "Let me have them, please."

"Blast it, Cassie, why do you wear them?"

"Captain, please. My spectacles."

Nicholas looked at her for a moment, but the tone of authority had its effect. Reluctantly he watched as she took the spectacles and perched them on her nose, transforming her from a beauty to a plain, mousy governess.

56

Something twisted inside him. "Why do you do it, Cassie? Why do you dress as you do?"

"I have to. 'Tis part of my position."

"Bilgewater. No one would expect you to wear spectacles you don't need."

" 'Tis my choice."

"Huh. What are you hiding from, Cassie?"

"I'm not hiding from anything."

"Spectacles, a mobcap, that awful dress—it's like a disguise. It's criminal to hide yourself the way you do."

"I'm not hiding! No one would hire me before I started wearing them."

"Oh." So that was it. He may have been at sea for a long time, but he hadn't completely forgotten the way the world worked. No woman would hire a governess so ravishingly beautiful as Cassie. Still, he couldn't help thinking there was more to her disguise—for that was what it was—than that. "I still don't understand why you're a governess at all."

"I need to make a living. Catherine! Mary!" She rose. " 'Tis time to go."

"But, by Neptune, were all the men in London blind?"

"The past is past, Nicholas!" She made a slashing motion with her hand. "I don't wish to discuss it anymore."

"I'm sorry," he said after a moment, feeling more awkward than ever. "If there's anything I can do—"

"Thank you. I'm quite content now, sir."

"If you say so." He began walking with her across the sand, toward the girls. "At least you're in a good home."

"Yes."

"They treat you well, Cassie?"

"Well enough."

"Good God." He stopped. "This blasted dinner party they're giving for me. You'll be there, won't you?"

"No, of course I won't. It wouldn't be proper."

"Proper." He looked at her in almost comical despair. "By Neptune, what will I do?"

"Don't worry, Captain." She smiled at him. "You'll be the most popular man there."

"That's what worries me. If you were there, Cassie, at least I'd have someone to talk to. The thing is," he went on, as they began walking again, "I've been at sea too long. I don't know how to go on in polite society."

"You'll learn. Besides, being who you are, they'll forgive you much."

"Cynical, Cassie?"

"No. Realistic. I learned a lot when I was in London." She clamped her mouth shut at that, looking away.

"Did you?" And just what, he wondered, had she learned? "I suppose you would. By Neptune, that's a thought!"

"What in the world?" she exclaimed, as he grasped her upper arms and turned her to face him.

"I need someone to teach me how to go on."

"Yes, well, grabbing a woman like this isn't the way."

"You could do it." He grinned at her, suddenly at ease. "I want you to show me."

Chapter 5

Catherine and Mary chose that moment to run up. "What are you going to show the earl, Miss Aldrich?" Catherine said.

"Nothing," Cassandra said, and quickly reached for her hand. "Come, girls, 'tis time we were getting home."

"She's going to show me how to go in society." Nicholas fell into step beside them, and Cassandra stiffened even more. "Do you think she can do it?"

"Oh yes." Catherine gave him a sparkling smile. "Penelope won't like it above half."

"Catherine," Cassandra said in a strangled voice.

"Miss Lamb wouldn't like it if I were less than a gentleman, now, would she?"

"Penelope doesn't care, long as you're the earl."

"Catherine," Cassandra said again, and tugged at her hand. "My lord, I am sorry. Catherine tends to be pert, and I fear I encourage her. Apologize to his lordship, Catherine."

"Why?" she asked.

"As I recall, Red," Nicholas said, "you used to be rather pert yourself. What is your answer?" He stopped before her, blocking her access to the path. "Will you help me?"

"No."

"No? Just like that?"

"It wouldn't be proper."

"I'm getting tired of hearing that word, Cassie."

"Please stand aside, my lord. We must return home." When Nicholas didn't move, she at last looked up at him. He was regarding her with an odd light in his eyes. "Please."

"I'm not joking about this, Cassie. I really do need someone to help me."

The glint in his eye, so familiar, said he was teasing, but there was a note of sincerity in his voice. It was that which scared her, more than anything else. She could not afford to have any involvement with Nicholas, no matter how innocent. Not for her reputation, and not for her heart. "Find someone else," she snapped, and pushed past him, dragging the girls with her.

"Cassie," he called, but she hurried up the path, away from him. Blast. Made a mull of that, he had. Or had he? Smiling, he turned away and prowled toward the water. Maybe not. When he'd made what he knew was an outrageous proposal, he'd seen a brief gleam in her eyes, answering his. The old Cassie, the girl he'd once known, was still there, buried under layers of propriety. He would, he thought, turning and heading for the cliff path himself, very much enjoy working through those layers to find the woman underneath. Very much.

The day for the Lambs' dinner party in honor of the earl drew closer. At odd moments, when her mind should have been occupied with the twins' lessons or one of her other myriad tasks, Cassandra would find herself, thinking about the dinner, and about the dismay on Nicholas's face when he learned she wouldn't be attending. At such moments, she felt a pang of regret for what she had lost. Had everything worked out well, she could have met him as more nearly his equal, instead of as a servant, clearly inferior to him. Never mind that that didn't seem to bother him. He himself had said he didn't understand society. His continued insistence on seeking her out was proof of that. She couldn't continue to meet with him, no matter how much she might wish to. It would be worth her position, were their meetings to be discovered.

Beatrice burst into the schoolroom several days after the afternoon on the beach, just one day before the party. "My parents are having a dreadful row," she proclaimed, throwing herself down into a chair. "It's all your fault, Cassie."

Cassandra looked up in surprise. "Me? What did I do?"

Mary dropped her primer. "Is Miss Aldrich in trouble, Bea?"

"Not yet." Beatrice smiled reassuringly. "Mama will want to speak to you, though."

They knew about the interval on the beach, Cassandra thought, her heart sinking. "Is it about the earl?"

"Yes, how did you know? Oh, you must have heard he paid us a call."

"No, I hadn't." Cassandra sank into a chair. Surely Nicholas wouldn't betray her.

"Mama's in a tizzy about it. Of course she can't very well refuse him, after all, he is the earl, but it's such a surprising thing he asked."

"Asked?"

"Yes." Beatrice frowned at her. "I thought you knew."

61

"What did the earl ask?"

"Why, he wants you to attend the dinner party, of course."

Cassandra let out a laugh. "Oh, of course. Don't be absurd, Bea! How could I do such a thing?"

"So Mama said. But he insisted." She grinned. "Penelope is ever so mad."

"You're serious." Cassandra stared at her. "He really did ask for me."

"Yes, silly, didn't I say? Mama doesn't want to ask you, but Papa does. I think he'll win this time."

"Good heavens." Cassandra stared blankly ahead. This was an unlooked-for complication in a life suddenly fraught with problems. Oh, what had happened to her calm, placid existence? "I won't go, of course."

"Don't be silly. Oh!" Beatrice's eyes grew round. "Oh, how dreadful of me. You haven't a gown, have you?"

"Yes, I do have something, but—"

"Oh. Then that's all right." She reached over and grabbed Cassandra's hand. "Oh, it'll be ever so much fun to have you there! I've always thought you should be included in our affairs."

"But I'm only the governess," Cassandra protested weakly. It would be fun, said a wicked little voice inside her head. To wear a pretty frock again, to pin her hair up so that tendrils of curls floated around her face, to laugh and talk and flirt, just as she once had. To flirt with Nicholas. Her heart speeded up at that thought. Impossible, she told herself. Absolutely impossible. "No. I cannot come."

"Cassandra—"

"I cannot, and pray do not tease me about it, Beatrice. I've made up my mind. I will not attend the dinner."

"Aldrich," a voice boomed at the door, and Cassandra

started. She looked up to see Mrs. Lamb. "What did I just hear you say?"

At the sound of that thunderous voice, everyone in the room rose and curtsied. Cassandra curtsied lowest, her head bent. "Mrs. Lamb," she murmured. "Miss Beatrice was just telling me of the earl's request."

"And you dare to refuse it, girl?" Mrs. Lamb stalked into the room, arms akimbo. "You dare to say no to an earl?"

"Ma'am, it would not be fitting—"

"I shall be the judge of that, Aldrich. If the earl wishes you to attend the dinner, then you will." She frowned, looking momentarily confused. "I trust you understand?"

"Yes, ma'am.

"I should hope so." Again that confused look flitted across her face. "I will expect you downstairs with the family tomorrow night."

Cassandra curtsied again. "Yes, ma'am," she said, and Mrs. Lamb turned and stomped out.

Catherine let out a whoop and ran to Cassandra, hugging her. "Oh good, oh good, you're going to the party!"

"Catherine, please!" Cassandra sank back into her chair, though she didn't push the child away. Oh Lord, she thought, putting a hand to her eyes and biting the inside of her lips to keep from laughing along with the others. The look on Mrs. Lamb's face! Surely commanding Cassandra to attend the dinner party had been the last thing in her mind when she'd come upstairs. Cassandra could almost feel sorry for her confusion.

"Oh my." Beatrice was still giggling. "When Mama realizes what she's done she'll be furious. It's your fault, Cassie."

"But I said I didn't want to go."

Beatrice giggled again. "I know. How dare you refuse

63

an earl, Aldrich?" she said, sounding so like her mother that Cassandra at last let out a laugh.

"I know. 'Tis rather like a royal request, is it not? Oh dear." She sobered. "I fear this will make matters a trifle difficult, though."

"Don't be so pea-brained. 'Tis only a dinner, and I'm sure you attended grander events during your season. Besides"—Beatrice looked thoughtful—"I do believe the earl has a *tendre* for you."

"Oh no!" Cassandra exclaimed, just as Penelope burst into the room.

It was strange for someone so emotionless to do such a thing, Cassandra thought later, but that was the only way to describe it. Penelope was, as usual, impeccably coiffed and gowned, today in ice blue muslin, but her cheeks burned a mottled red, belying her cool image. "You—you encroaching little hussy!" she declared, advancing on Cassandra with her hands balled into fists.

"Penelope!" Beatrice exclaimed, getting to her feet. "What an insulting thing to say—"

"Be quiet. Aldrich, how dare you insinuate yourself into the earl's good graces in this way?"

"I didn't," Cassandra protested.

"Oh no, not you. Butter wouldn't melt in your mouth, would it? Well, I'm onto you, miss! You've set your cap for the earl, haven't you? And all the time you sit there looking so innocent. I will not have it, do you hear me? I will—not—have it!"

"Who are you to talk to me like this?" Cassandra had to stand on tiptoe to meet the other girl's eyes, but she managed, letting her anger blaze out. All the frustrations she'd stifled, all the slights she'd ignored, returned, fueling her anger. "The earl has asked for me. If you're so unsure of yourself that you cannot handle that, then perhaps you'd best look to your own life before you interfere in mine!"

"Unsure!" Penelope shrieked like a fishwife. "I am a beauty! Everyone says so. I am the reigning Incomparable and men swoon for me, and my admirers are too many to count—"

"Then why haven't any of them come up to scratch?" Cassandra challenged, and dead silence fell over the room.

The hectic color in Penelope's face faded to pale, pale ice. "You'll regret that," she said, her voice deadly soft. "I swear to you, Aldrich, you'll regret that." She spun around, her skirt swishing about her, and stopped at the door. "By the bye. Mama was all for letting you go when this happened, but Papa convinced her to give you another chance." Her eyes were small and cold and gleamed with satisfaction as she saw that shot go home. "So don't make any missteps, Aldrich, or you'll be out of here quicker than that!" She snapped her fingers at Cassandra and stalked away, leaving a stunned silence behind.

Cassandra, shaking, fell into a chair. One more mistake. Dread coiled in her stomach. Dear God, she hadn't done anything wrong, and yet here she faced being unemployed. Likely without a character from the Lambs, either. What would she do, if she couldn't find work? She would be very careful, but she doubted it would do her any good. Penelope would find a way to make her leave. Perhaps it would be best if she went now, of her own accord.

"You can't go!" Mary's arms shot around her neck and clung. "You can't, you can't, you can't!"

"Hush, Mary," Cassandra soothed, though she felt far from calm, and pulled the little girl onto her lap. "I'm not going anywhere."

"We won't let you go." Catherine tugged at her arm. "We'll make them make you stay."

"Oh, Cat." Cassandra freed her arm and put it around Catherine, smiling at her. "Thank you, darling, but it won't come to that. I intend to be very careful."

"You had better be," Beatrice said, and Cassandra met her somber eyes. "When Penelope wants something—"

"I know." Cassandra made her voice deliberately brisk. She had no doubt that Penelope had meant every word. Just now, though, it was more important to calm the twins. "Hush now, this does no good." She disentangled Mary's arms from about her neck and rose, putting her hands on both girls' shoulders. "We can't worry about what may happen in the future."

"Perhaps you should talk to my father, Cassie."

"Why? It won't do any good." If Penelope decided she wanted Cassandra gone, what chance would Cassandra have against her? "Besides, I've faced worse." Much worse, heaven knew. If she did lose her position, she could always go to one of her sisters. Difficult though that might be, it would certainly be easier than what she had had to face six years ago. "Come, girls. I think we need a walk to blow the cobwebs away."

Catherine's face brightened. "No more lessons?"

"For now, no. It will be all right, Bea." She smiled at Beatrice. "Trust me."

"I hope so," Beatrice said, sounding less than convinced.

"It will be. Come. Let's get our cloaks and go out."

It would be all right, she told herself, feeling better once she was out in the fresh air, loping along under a weak sun. All it would take would be one wrong word, one misstep, and she would be gone, dismissed by arbitrary malice. Yet she would manage. She would survive. If she had learned nothing else, she knew that. She was strong. She had to be. There was just one problem. If she left here, she would never see Nicholas again.

"And remember, Aldrich," Mrs. Lamb said, turning at Cassandra's door, "you are to dress in a manner befitting your station."

Cassandra, standing with her head bent and hands folded before her, nodded. "Yes, ma'am." Mrs. Lamb gave her one last look and swept out of the room, and Cassandra, at last left alone, collapsed upon her bed. Such a lecture as she had just received, on the behavior expected of her at tonight's dinner party. Mrs. Lamb was furious at actually having to allow Cassandra to mingle with the gentry of the neighborhood. A strange situation, that; would she be another guest, or simply the Lambs' governess, there to make the numbers at the table even? Certainly the fact that the earl had asked for her personally would not be mentioned. It was not something the Lambs would want generally known.

Well, she knew how to behave, Cassandra thought, rising and going to her wardrobe. She would be quiet and not call attention to herself; she would not take part in any conversation, and she would excuse herself immediately after dinner. As to her dress. Cassandra's smile was wry. That was easy. She no longer owned anything remotely stylish.

Except. Reaching into the wardrobe, she pulled out a gown of sea green muslin, not at all a governessy frock. Her favorite, and the only one she'd been unable to leave behind when she had begun her new life. Oh, she remembered this gown, and all the promise it had once represented. She'd worn it for the first time to a ball in London, the color highlighting her hair, the soft muslin floating about her as she danced. She had felt beautiful that night, magical, surrounded by an eager coterie of admirers who had been attracted by her unusual looks. Beautiful, and invincible. How very young she had been.

The gown could no longer lay any claim to being stylish. The waist was too high for the current fashion, and the skirt was untrimmed by either ruffle or rouleaux. Still, for a moment she imagined herself in it, imagined the look in Nicholas's eyes when he saw her. He would see, then, that she was more than just a plain, faded governess, that there was fire in her still. He would, perhaps, see that she had grown up and was no longer the little girl he had once teased. And then—.

And then what, Cassandra? What would he do, swoon at her feet or instantly propose marriage? Of course not. He would smile at her, call her 'Red,' and then turn away with Penelope on his arm, leading her into dinner. And Cassandra, who had been anticipating this night with a mixture of delight and terror, would be left to follow, garbed in a several-years-old gown of gray jaconet.

It was that which made her push away from the wardrobe and walk with determination toward her bed, to lay the green muslin gown down with great care. Standing only in her shift and stockings, she washed, shivering with the coldness of the water and the boldness of what she planned to do. The green gown slipped over her head, laced up the front, and there. She was ready to defy the Lambs.

Oh, my heavens. Her mirror was small and pitted, but it showed enough to make the first doubts come creeping in. The gown didn't fit quite the same as it had. The emerald green ribbon that tied beneath her breasts gave it a youthful air that she thought sat ill with her maturity, while the bodice—well, she filled that in a way she hadn't six years ago. For a moment she quailed, and then, her mouth locking in a stubborn line, took a brush to her hair. It had been a long time, but she still remembered how to twist it into a knot atop her head, and then to smooth it, so that it lay in a long curl on her shoulder. Neat, and out of the way. Heaven knew that her looks would never be à la mode, but she certainly looked far different from the mousy, retiring governess everyone would be expecting.

A bell sounded downstairs, and she raised her head sharply. Heavens, she was late! The girls had been fractious this afternoon, leaving her little time to prepare, and now she must hurry. There was no time left to change, even if she wanted to. Quickly now, because she knew she would be scolded if she was late, Cassandra ran down the stairs, slowing only when she reached the landing above the hall. It wouldn't do to come tumbling down the stairs and thus call attention to herself. Any more than she was going to get, she thought, glancing quickly down at her bosom. The gown had been a mistake, and her reasons for choosing it now seemed foolish.

Taking a deep breath, she rounded the turn of the stairs and started down. Only then did she realize that the murmur of voices she had been hearing came from the hall, and not the drawing room. They must have assembled there to go into the dining room: Mr. Lamb, looking bemused, and Mrs. Lamb, furious; Penelope, her eyes narrowing to slits, while George's widened; Beatrice, grinning in approval; various neighbors, looking surprised; and Nicholas. *Oh, Nicholas.* Without quite intending to, she stopped, caught by his gaze.

He might talk about being a fish out of water, but he certainly didn't look it tonight. His shoulders looked broad, rather than bulky, in an evening coat of black superfine, while his linen, in contrast, was a snowy white. No country tailor had made those clothes; the knowing eye Cassandra had developed during her season discerned Weston's hand in the tailoring. His hair was brushed back, a burnished gold, and his legs were muscular and long in fine black pantaloons, but it was his eyes that caught her. As blue as the sea in a tropic clime, she thought, just the slightest bit dazed, and was that a spark of admiration she saw there? It couldn't be. Whatever it was, though, it warmed her soul.

"Aldrich," Mrs. Lamb said, her voice sounding strangled, and Cassandra came out of her reverie. Oh heavens, she had drawn exactly the kind of attention she had hoped to avoid, with her inadvertent grand entrance. Her position was dependent on the goodwill of the people below. She feared she had just made the mistake that would cause them to dismiss her.

"I'm sorry I'm late," she said breathlessly, hurrying down the remaining stairs. "I do beg your pardon. Mr. and Mrs. Lamb. And, my lord." She turned to curtsy to Nicholas, and rose, to see him regarding her with twinkling eyes.

"You look fine as fivepence, Red," he said, easily.

Cassandra's eyes sparkled. Drat the man! What she had thought was admiration in his eyes had obviously been ridicule. Oh, she had been wrong to wear this dress, a young girl's dress, when she was obviously past her last prayers, but he needn't tease her about it.

"Where had you that dress, Aldrich?" Penelope said, coolly. For the first time in her life Cassandra was grateful for her presence. To have answered Nicholas as she desired would have been disastrous. "Somewhat out of style, is it not?"

"I had it during my season," Cassandra said, her head

70

down, fighting anger and an absurd hurt that caused tears to prickle at the back of her eyes. She had worn this gown for Nicholas, and he didn't care.

"I say, I didn't realize you had a season, Miss Aldrich," a boyish voice said, and she looked up with some surprise at Charles Gregory, the son of the Lambs' nearest neighbor. Just down from Oxford, he was looking at her with all the admiration she had hoped to see in Nicholas's eyes. "There's the bell for dinner. May I escort you in?"

"Thank you, Mr. Gregory." Putting her hand on the arm he proferred, she stepped back as the procession formed to go into the dining room. As she had expected, Nicholas was escorting Penelope, and, as she'd thought, Mrs. Lamb swept by her with a hissed promise of future retribution. It was going to be a long, dismal evening.

Cassandra stayed quiet during dinner, keeping her head down, trying very hard to ignore the admiring looks George, seated across from her, sent her throughout the evening. How foolish she had been to dress like this; how foolish to think that she would fit in, when she was only the governess. She wished she'd worn her spectacles. Without them, she felt defenseless and vulnerable. When Mrs. Lamb at last rose to lead the ladies to the drawing room, signaling the end of dinner and leaving the gentlemen to their port, she sighed with relief. Her ordeal was over.

"No need to be so formal," Mr. Lamb said, stopping Mrs. Lamb at the door. "Thought we might have a hand or two of cards."

Mrs. Lamb gave him a fulminating look. "Penelope has been practicing on the pianoforte for tonight, Mr. Lamb."

"She can play later." He rose, tossing his napkin on the table and turning to the butler. "Carey, have tables set up in the drawing room."

It was Cassandra's chance to escape. "Pray excuse me," she murmured. "I need to see to the girls."

"Now, Miss Aldrich." Mr. Lamb smiled at her. "We need you to make up the tables, you know."

"Oh no, sir, I don't think—"

"As I recall, you used to enjoy whist, Red," Nicholas said behind her, reaching for her arm. "You'll be my partner."

"My lord, I can't," she protested, but too late. He was already leading her toward the drawing room. Penelope, making do with Mr. Gregory, followed, her eyes looking daggers at Cassandra. She should have been annoyed, or at the least apprehensive. Instead, the feel of Nicholas's hand on hers filled her with a strange exultation, erasing the discomfort of the evening. Never mind that he had likely asked her only because he felt comfortable with her. For the next hour, she would have the pleasure of his company.

All four players at the table were competent, and so play was brisk. After one last glare at Cassandra, Penelope settled down, smiling at Nicholas, to her left, and telling him of her London season. Cassandra concentrated on her cards, filled again with that glee, this time at Penelope's choice of topic. Nothing, she knew, was calculated more to bore Nicholas than town gossip and prattle.

"What was it like at Trafalgar, sir?" Mr. Gregory asked after a time.

Nicholas's face tightened. "It was a battle," he said briefly, squinting at his cards, and then playing one. "The builder your father recommended is doing a good job on the Hall. Dashed ugly place, though. I'm told there are at least five different styles of architecture and God knows how many additions. Excuse me, ladies."

"It sounds most fascinating," Penelope said in her cool little voice. "You must show us around sometime."

"Ahem. Well, yes. When it's done." He shifted in his chair. "Actually, I was thinking I'd like to invite everyone on my boat."

Cassandra looked up. He might be too modest to discuss his exploits in the navy, but this was a different matter. "You have a boat, my lord?"

"Yes. Bought it last week, as a matter of fact. A real beauty, named the *Spray*. About forty feet, narrow in the beam, and sloop-rigged. Just the thing for the waters around here."

"It sounds lovely." There was a notable lack of enthusiasm in Penelope's voice.

"Aye, she's trim. You like sailing, don't you, Red?"

Cassandra studied her cards. "I haven't sailed in years."

"Really, sir," Penelope put in, her smile tight. "Must you tease Miss Aldrich with that ridiculous name?"

"She doesn't mind. Do you, Red?"

Cassandra looked up again, to see him smiling at her across the table. Suddenly the hated nickname took on a different meaning, a shared jest between them. "No," she said, smiling. "I don't mind at all."

"I believe we take this hand, Miss Lamb," Mr. Gregory announced, laying down his cards.

"So we do," Penelope said, shooting Cassandra a look of sparkling malice.

"You let me down, Red," Nicholas chided, and again she smiled at him. This time he smiled back.

"Well." Mr. Gregory rose. "Would you care for some refreshment, Miss Lamb? Miss Aldrich?"

"Thank you, no." Cassandra rose, also. "I'm afraid I must excuse myself. I need to return to the children. Good

73

night, my lord." She curtsied, said her farewells to the remaining guests, and at last escaped. Heavens, such an evening! It hadn't ended at all badly, though. If only Nicholas weren't the earl, and thus so far above her—but that was a dangerous thought. She had learned, painfully, not to expect more from life than she already had. She would tuck the conversation with Nicholas away in her memory, and treasure it.

Nicholas sat back, a little frown between his eyes as he watched Cassandra leave the room, while beside him Penelope prattled on. There was a relaxed atmosphere in the room, as other tables finished their games, and he noticed George Lamb slip out into the hall, behind Cassandra. She'd changed, his Cassie, become prim and proper, but the spark was still there inside her. By Neptune, when he'd seen her come downstairs in that dress, his throat had gone dry and his heart had started to pound. He understood, though, why she felt compelled to hide her beauty. The shallow girl next to him was obviously eaten alive with jealousy, while the son had ogled her all night. Nicholas's eyes narrowed. Just where had George been going when he left the drawing room?

"Excuse me," he said abruptly to Penelope, and rose. Something havey-cavey was going on. He intended to find out what it was.

Chapter 6

In the hall, Cassandra drew the first deep breath she'd allowed herself all evening. There, it was over, and it hadn't been so bad as she'd feared. That she'd probably receive at least a thundering scold from Mrs. Lamb was something she wouldn't think about. It had been pushed to the back of her mind by the memory of Nicholas's smile.

As she started to climb the stairs, the door behind her opened. "Cassandra," a voice said, and she turned, startled.

"Mr. Lamb," she said, her face going wary as George walked toward her. "Is something wrong?"

"Not at all." He stopped, looking up at her where she stood on the second stair, his face shining. "You look dashed pretty tonight. Wanted to tell you, that's all."

"Thank you, sir. Now, if you'll excuse me—"

"Will you come down from the stairs, Cassandra? There's something I want to talk to you about."

"Sir, I can't," Cassandra began, and realized with a start that his eyes were at a level with her bosom, which he was eyeing dazedly. Good heavens! Hastily she stepped down. "Only for a moment, though. I need to see to the girls."

"But, Cassandra." His eyes, large and liquid, reminded her of a puppy. "Can you not spare a moment for me?"

"Well—"

His fingers reached out to touch her hair, and she jerked back. "I saw the way you looked at me at dinner."

"Sir, you are mistaken."

"You did. Don't deny it. Oh, Cassie!" He lunged forward, trapping her against the oak paneling of the stairs. "Ever since I've come down from Oxford I've thought of you and wanted you and now I know you want me, too!"

"Mr. Lamb—"

"It's all right, I mean you no harm. I want to marry you. I'll talk to my parents about it, and they'll see it's right, I know they will. Please, Cassie. Please say yes."

The situation was so ridiculous that Cassandra would have laughed, had she not felt so threatened. He was so very young, and so earnest. She didn't want to hurt him, but if he persisted in this way it would only mean disaster for her. "Mr. Lamb, please," she said in her most severe tones.

"George," he corrected. "Call me by my name, Cassandra.

"Mr. Lamb, let me go. Now."

"Cassandra—"

"There you are, George," Nicholas said from behind him, his voice easy. Neither of them had heard him come into the hall, so quiet had his step been. Cassandra took advantage of George's distraction to slip away from him. "Care to blow a cloud with me?"

George looked dumbly at the cheroot Nicholas held out, his expression showing how torn he was. On the one hand, the earl was his hero. On the other, he had at last summoned the courage to pour out his feelings to Cassandra. An embarrassing situation for a man to be caught in. "I—yes, of course," he stammered. "I'd be honored, my lord."

"Good." Nicholas smiled; only Cassandra noticed that the smile didn't quite reach his eyes. "Is there someplace in the house we can do so without disturbing the ladies?"

"Outside, I fear, sir. Mama does not allow smoking in the house."

"Outside it is, then. A fine night, too." George blanched. It was, in fact, cold and drizzly. "I'll join you there in a moment, shall I?"

"I—" George looked from Cassandra to Nicholas, helpless. "Yes, my lord," he said, and, looking miserable, trudged out the front door.

Cassandra let out a nervous laugh. "That was terrible of you, my lord."

"Nicholas," he corrected, placing a gentle finger on her lips. "My name. Say it."

She gazed up at him, mesmerized, her lips tingling from his light touch. "Nicholas," she said, wondering irrelevantly why the men tonight would not let her keep her distance.

"Are you all right, Red? He didn't hurt you?"

"Quite all right, sir. He was a bit more pressing this time, but he didn't mean any harm."

"This time?" he said, sharply. "There have been other times?"

"He's very young, Nicholas." His name came easily from her lips. She loved saying it. "I try to stay out of his way. I usually succeed."

Nicholas's face darkened. "I'd like to thrash him."

"Oh, please don't. 'Twill only call more attention to me. He means no harm."

"If you don't want to attract attention, why did you wear that dress?"

Cassandra's eyes lowered. "I know. It was too bad of me."

"That's not what I meant at all, Red," he said, just as the door opened and George came back in.

"Nasty night out, sir. I think I'll forgo that smoke, if you don't mind," he said, and Cassandra stifled another giggle. His hair, which had been so carefully arranged early in the evening, now clung to his head in lank strands, and his neckcloth was decidedly limp. She could almost bring herself to feel sorry for him.

"I must go," she murmured. "Good night, my lord. Mr. Lamb." With that, she picked up her skirts, and at last fled.

George started forward. "Perhaps there is someplace else we could have that smoke," Nicholas said, placing a firm hand on George's arm.

"Oh. Oh, of course, sir." He glanced up the staircase, his face abstracted.

Nicholas stared hard at him. "Leave Miss Aldrich alone, Lamb."

"What?" George turned to him, startled. "I don't know what you mean."

"I think you do. It must be obvious to you she doesn't welcome your attentions."

"She's an angel," he said, fervently. "I'd never hurt her."

"She's not to be bothered." Nicholas's voice was soft, but there was something about it that made George shuffle his feet, like a schoolboy caught in mischief. "Is that clear?"

George swallowed, hard. "I say, I know you're the earl

and all that, but to tell a man what to do in his own house—it's just not done."

"She's not to be bothered," Nicholas repeated. "You'll regret it if she is." His eyes bored into George's, and the younger man was the first to turn away. "Now." Nicholas clapped George so hard on the back he stumbled. "Let's go have that smoke, shall we?"

The sailing expedition was set for three days hence. In what Mrs. Lamb called a great gesture of generosity, Nicholas had invited the entire Lamb family to come along, down to the smallest girls. That meant that the girls' governess must come along as well, to make certain they behaved. Penelope's eyes narrowed at that, but there was nothing in the wording of the invitation she could protest. Oh well, at least the two brats would be out of her way. As for Aldrich. Penelope's huge blue eyes narrowed yet further. Aldrich was a problem. At least, though, she wouldn't be wearing anything so daring as that green gown. Imagine Aldrich owning something like that, so obviously London-made! No, she'd be back in brown stuff and mobcaps and eyeglasses, irredeemably plain. Penelope tossed her curls, knowing just the effect that motion produced. Why should the earl look at Aldrich at all, when he had the most noted beauty in the county present?

Her confidence ebbed a bit when the Lamb party reached the quay in Fairhaven where the earl's boat was berthed. Her father, holding her arm, looked at the boat and adjudged it magnificent, but all Penelope could see was how very small it was. She had no great conception of distances, and when the earl had spoken of his boat it had sounded large and luxurious. Surely this thing was too small to go out upon the waters of the Channel? Penelope nearly demanded to return home, when she caught sight of Aldrich and promptly changed her mind.

Cassandra, the twins on either side of her, was carefully picking her way down the steep hill that led to the harbor. Oh, what a magnificent boat! In her mind she'd pictured the little dory in which Midshipman St. John had once taken various nieces and nephews and neighborhood children out upon the Severn, when she was a child. Of course she'd realized that his new boat would be much larger, but she hadn't expected it to be such a beauty. It was a yacht, long and sleek and graceful, with two masts and a sharply raked bowsprit, and a highly polished wheel. In the sun the brasswork glistened and the highly varnished rails shown. Even the paintwork on the hull, black with a yellow stripe, like one of His Majesty's warships, looked pristine. Atop one mast a banner floated in the wind, the standard of the Earls of Lynton. An odd feeling, of pride, joy, and anticipation, gripped her, and she grasped the twins' hands harder.

"The earl took me out on a boat when I was not much older than you," she told the girls as they reached the quay and they walked along it. "It was a wonderful experience."

"Lucky you." Catherine eyed the boat with undisguised excitement, while Mary, more reticent, pressed back against Cassandra, her eyes huge and wondering. "Can we go on it?"

"We must wait for the earl. Ah, there he is."

The same odd mixture of emotions surged in her again, mixed with another, more unfamiliar ache as she watched Nicholas. He was emerging from the covered cockpit forward on the boat, which apparently led below.

80

"Ahoy," he called, easily, raising his hand, and it seemed the most natural thing in the world to answer in kind.

"Ahoy!" Cassandra called back, smiling, and saw his eyes crinkle.

Penelope shot her a frosty look. "Good morning, my lord."

"Good morning, Miss Lamb. Mr. Lamb." Nicholas leaped nimbly from the boat's rail to the quay, making nothing of the green water that lay between, and smiled at them all. Was it Cassandra's imagination, or did his gaze linger on her? "I'm glad to see you here. Mrs. Lamb didn't want to come?"

"Good morning, my lord." Mr. Lamb pumped his hand enthusiastically. "A fine day, and a fine boat. No, Mrs. Lamb had duties at home and felt she couldn't get away."

Nicholas nodded, a knowing little gleam in his eyes, as if he were aware of Mrs. Lamb's true reaction. "I'm sorry to hear that, but I think I can promise everyone an enjoyable time. Please, go aboard. I've some things to see to on shore."

Penelope hung back, delaying her father's eager approach to the gangplank. "Surely you don't do all the work yourself, my lord. You must have a crew."

"Aye." His smile was polite. "However, a good captain checks everything over himself. And no one takes the wheel but me." He gestured toward the gangplank. "Do go aboard."

It was the voice of authority, of a captain, or an earl. Cassandra stepped back as Penelope swept by her, her head held high, her bonnet tilted at just the precise, rakish angle. Oh, to dress like that, so that Nicholas might notice her instead, she thought, and looked up to see him regarding her.

"Do you like her?" he asked, with just a trace of anxiety in his eyes.

"Miss Lamb? Oh! Oh, the *Spray*. Yes, of course I do, my lord—Captain." She smiled at him, and he grinned back. "She's trim."

"Aye, that she is. Saw her in Portsmouth when I returned and couldn't resist, since I knew I was going to be landlocked."

"She reminds me of American ships I've seen. In pictures, of course. I believe they're called Baltimore clippers?"

"Aye. Came up against one or two in my time. But how do you know about such things, Cassandra?"

"I've read a book or two." Indeed, she'd read more than that. She had, in fact, grabbed every book about ships and the sea she could find, and every newspaper account of a naval battle, hoping to learn all that she could so that if, by some chance, Nicholas ever returned, she could impress him with her knowledge. It had been as if she could bring herself closer to him by doing so. Foolish thought. "We should be going aboard," she said, surveying the three older Lamb daughters in their light muslins and stylish bonnets. They presented a charming picture, grouped on the padded benches in the stern.

"George didn't care to come?" he said, detaining her just as she turned away.

"No. He claimed a prior engagement. If you'll excuse me, Captain—"

"Afraid to go on the boat, the pantywaist."

Cassandra turned her head sharply to the side, biting her lips to hold back her laughter. Oh, he was corrupting her! Several weeks ago such a statement would have shocked her. "Captain—"

"I like it when you laugh, Cassie. Seems like you haven't done so in a long time."

"Oh dear." She wiped at her eyes, aware that Catherine and Mary were staring at her curiously. "George has been very quiet lately."

"He was scared," Catherine put in. "When we told him about your boat he went all white."

"Good." Nicholas's smile was grim. "Man couldn't even appreciate a good cheroot."

"Why?" Cassandra asked, in spite of herself. She had been curious about the outcome of the incident after the dinner party.

"Took one puff and turned green," he said, chuckling, and then raised his head, sharply. "Wind's changing. Best we be off now. Ladies?"

"Thank you, sir. Come, girls." Cassandra shepherded the twins toward the boat, aware that Nicholas was watching her. She didn't look back to confirm it, but she knew. She could feel it.

Nicholas leaped back aboard, scorning the gangplank, and soon the deck was a hive of activity. Cassandra kept a firm grasp on the girls as they sat against the side of the boat, out of the way, and explained to them everything Nicholas and the crew were doing. That man, there, was casting off the lines that held the boat tethered to the quay. Yes, it was funny the way the boat moved underneath, but that was because of the waves. That man, there, was making sail, that is, he was pulling on a line that hoisted a sail up to one of the masts. That little triangular sail, forward, was called a jib; the earl had told her that many years ago. And the earl himself was at the wheel, his feet planted apart, standing easily and watching the sails as the boat came about from the quay. Cassandra's fingers itched for a pencil, to commit the scene to paper, the man of the sea so clearly at home on his vessel. She felt the exact moment when the sails filled with the wind, and the boat took on a life of its own, skimming across the waves into the English Channel. It was, quite simply, the closest thing to flying she could imagine.

"This is splendid!" Amanda's bonnet was already askew, her hair already loose, but her eyes were shining. "What a glorious day! The earl said we would have a luncheon later."

"We are going very fast," Penelope said. Her face was white and set, and her hands were clenched in her lap. Oh dear. Cassandra devoutly hoped she wouldn't be ill.

She looked down at her own charges. "Girls," she said, and they looked up at her with shining eyes.

"Miss Aldrich, may we go over to talk with the earl?" Catherine said.

"No, you may not, and you know better than to ask."

"But he won't mind, really. He's—"

"Busy steering the boat. If he wishes to speak to you, Catherine, he will."

"Oh, bother." Catherine leaned back against Cassandra, her lips set in a mutinous pout, and then brightened. "Oh! Then may I go downstairs and see what's there?"

"There are staterooms below, Miss Catherine," Nicholas said, looming above them, shading them from the sun. Cassandra looked past him to see that he'd lashed the wheel with a rope, keeping them on their course, and he followed her gaze. "I'll keep that there till we come about. The boat sleeps eight," he went on, "and it has a complete galley."

"What's a galley?"

"A kitchen." He smiled at them. "Are you enjoying yourselves?"

"Oh yes!"

"And you, Cassie?"

"Yes, thank you, my lord." She looked past him to Penelope, who, in spite of her pallor, was glaring at her. The fact that he had singled her out at the dinner party was bad enough. If he continued to do so here, however, it could lead to serious trouble for her. Oh, why could he not see that things were no longer as they once had been? He was doing her no favor, showing her such attention. As soon as she could, she had to point that out to him.

Once away from land the boat picked up speed, as the wind freshened and the sails filled. Cassandra tucked cloaks more firmly about the girls and wished she had the courage to pull off her bonnet, to let the wind whip through her hair. What a feeling it would be, of freedom and adventure and life. Freedom, however, was the one thing she didn't have, and adventure, she had learned, was overrated.

"Ready about," Nicholas called from the wheel. Cassandra remembered what that meant, and she put her hands on the girls' shoulders, bending them over. The boat sailed on a course called a tack, not a straight line, she explained to them, because of the wind. At the end of each tack the boat's sails would have to be swung over, thus turning the boat onto the opposite tack. One had to duck if one didn't want to be hit on the head by the boom, the long spar at the bottom of the sails.

"Hard alee," Nicholas said. The boom swung harmlessly over Cassandra's head, the boat heeled nicely, and then settled into her new course. Penelope, Cassandra noted, did not look at all well. Not seasick, but rather, scared, her face set and her hands gripping each other so hard the knuckles were white. Mr. Lamb, standing by Nicholas at the wheel, hadn't noticed; neither had Amanda or Beatrice. "Stay here," Cassandra said to the girls in her sternest voice, and carefully crossed the tilting deck to sit next to Penelope. "Are you all right?"

"No, I am not!" Penelope hissed, quickly looking up at Nicholas's back and then glaring at her. "I'm scared! And much you care."

"I do."

"Hmph. When you sit there like a brazen hussy, smiling at the earl and praising this infernal boat."

"Miss Lamb, perhaps you'd feel better if you went below."

"And leave him to you? Oh no. Did you think I really wanted to come today? Did you?"

Cassandra glanced at Nicholas. Penelope's voice was growing shrill, and she hoped he hadn't heard. "Miss Lamb, I simply meant—"

"Oh no. Once I knew you were coming, and God knows why he keeps asking for you, I knew I had to come. You may fool everyone else, Miss Butter-Won't-Melt-In-Your-Mouth, but you don't fool me. I know you're after the earl!"

"Is something wrong?" Nicholas said, quietly, and Cassandra looked up at him, wondering how much he had heard.

"Miss Lamb is unwell," she said. "I thought perhaps she should go below."

He shook his head. "She's better off topside. Sorry to hear that, Miss Lamb, but you'll be glad to know we'll be dropping anchor soon for luncheon. Shouldn't be so rough going back, with the wind behind us." He smiled. "You'll soon get your sea legs."

"Of course, my lord." Penelope managed to smile and bat her eyelashes at Nicholas. How did she manage to act so flirtatious when she was obviously feeling so wretched,

Cassandra wondered? She herself would never be able to do so.

A short time later the *Spray* dropped anchor in a serene cove, off the chalk cliffs and sandy beach where Cassandra had twice met Nicholas. She wondered if he had chosen the spot on purpose, though a glance at his face told her nothing. The bandy-legged man she had seen in the village and who, she had learned, had been to sea with Nicholas, acted as steward, serving the luncheon. They all fell to it with a will, the sea air having sharpened their appetites. Even Penelope's spirits improved; she allowed as to how she might be able to manage a sliver of cheese and a drink of lemonade, and she conversed with Nicholas quite as if they were in a drawing room. After luncheon Nicholas showed the more adventurous around the boat, and then it was time to depart. Penelope was not the only one who regretted that. Once they returned to Fairhaven, Cassandra thought, her afternoon's adventure would be over.

The wind picked up on the way home, and what had been a smooth, easy sail became more challenging. Nicholas and the crew were made to look sharp, changing tack as necessary and trimming the sails. As the bow rose and fell with the waves, most conversation ceased aboard the *Spray*, which was living up to her name as she plowed through the waves. "Think there's a storm coming in, my lord?" Mr. Lamb asked, looking not one whit concerned, though his daughters no longer seemed to be enjoying themselves.

"This bit of wind? Hardly." Nicholas held the wheel easily, moving with the boat as if he were a part of it. "Channel's usually rough, you know. Are you all right, Cassie? And the girls?"

"Yes, my lord." Cassandra's voice was demure, but her

eyes were sparkling and her cheeks flushed. This was glorious, glorious freedom such as she hadn't known in so long, and the wildness of the sea called forth an answering wildness in her. It was a real effort for her to sit still and not laugh aloud with the pleasure of it, but she kept her face composed and her arms around Catherine and Mary. Even here, the conventions of her life fettered her.

A gust of wind struck the boat broadside, making the *Spray* heel, the rail opposite Cassandra dipping beneath the water. Penelope shrieked and clutched at her father, but Cassandra reacted instinctively, as Nicholas had once taught her, as some of the crew were doing. Scrambling up onto the rail, she leaned back, perilously far out, over the water, to act as a counterbalance. The wind caught tendrils of hair that had escaped from underneath her bonnet, and this time she did laugh, for the joy of being alive. For the joy of being herself, Cassie, and not plain Miss Aldrich, the governess.

Catherine and Mary shrieked again, grabbing Cassandra around the waist and holding on for dear life. "Miss Aldrich, Miss Aldrich, you'll fall out!" Catherine wailed, just as the wind eased and the *Spray* righted herself.

"I'm perfectly safe, Catherine." Cassandra's voice was calm as she slid back down to the bench, as if nothing had happened. Her wildness had passed with the wind, though the exhilaration remained. "See?" She hugged the little girls. "I'm here."

"You might very well not have been," Mr. Lamb said, and Cassandra looked up to see everyone regarding her with varying expressions, ranging from amazement to disapproval. Penelope's face looked odd; Cassandra couldn't quite make out what she was thinking. Her exultation faded. Oh dear, what had she done?

"Quick thinking, Red," Nicholas said, grinning at her.

Was that actually admiration in his eyes? No, it couldn't be.

"Papa." Penelope's voice was weak and querulous. "I want to go home."

Mr. Lamb patted her hand. "We are, Penny. Soon."

"No, Papa. Now." She turned her face into her father's shoulder. "That was horrid, Papa. Horrid!"

"Perhaps you'd be more comfortable below, Miss Lamb," Nicholas said, and Mr. Lamb rose, a supporting arm around her.

"A good idea, sir. You'll let us know when we reach Fairhaven?"

"Of course." Nicholas inclined his head as the two passed, and his eyes met Cassandra's, silently communicating his opinion of what had just happened. Cassandra bit her lip to keep from smiling, and looked away.

"What a poor honey," Catherine said, scornfully.

"Now, Catherine," Cassandra chided. "Your sister was frightened. Many people are, of the water."

"Well, I'm not. And you aren't, either."

"No." Cassandra's eyes met Nicholas's. There were many things that frightened her, but the sea was not among them.

It was a tired, subdued party that disembarked at Fairhaven, in contrast to the gaiety of several hours earlier, Penelope, pale and quiet, clinging to her father's arm. Only the twins, with the resilience of childhood, seemed untouched, though their fractiousness and squabbling told Cassandra that both were tired. Soothing them with words and gentle hands, she hurried them toward the Lambs' carriage, giving Nicholas only the briefest of farewells. They were ashore again, and life was back to normal.

Cassandra settled back in the carriage, her arms about

the girls. For the first time in a very long time she regretted the limits she had set about her life. They had kept her safe, kept the outside world at bay; but they also kept her locked in. She had little choice. She did have to earn her way, and that meant behaving in a certain manner. Still, she felt stifled, suffocated, only half alive. There was another person inside her, the real Cassie, crying to be free, no matter the scandal, no matter the consequences. How she could be herself, and still hold on to her position, Cassandra didn't know. She knew only that, aboard Nicholas's boat, she had undergone a sea change. Nothing would be the same again.

That wretched Aldrich! Penelope plumped her pillows behind her and sat up in bed, arms crossed on her chest, fuming. Though it was late, she couldn't sleep for the anger churning within her. It had been a dreadful day, dreadful, not at all what she had planned. There she had been in her prettiest frock of pale blue, with the charming lace-edged parasol to match, and the earl hadn't even noticed. Worse, once she was on the boat, she couldn't use the parasol, unless she had wanted to lose it to the wind. Dreadful boat, with no place to sit comfortably and no awnings to shade her delicate complexion. And the earl, instead of sitting and talking with his guests as was only proper, had instead seemed more interested in sailing. Penelope wasn't certain she could forgive him that.

The man was a dolt. In London every man had been smitten with her beauty. Every one. Not the earl, however. He never flirted with her, never paid her the compliments to which she was accustomed. He seemed far more interested in her sisters, and in Aldrich.

A frown marred the soft, white skin of Penelope's forehead, but she was unaware. That dratted Aldrich! From the first she had coveted his attentions, the hussy. Look how she had got herself invited to the dinner party, and to today's excursion. Everyone thought Aldrich was so quiet, so retiring, but Penelope knew better. Under that unassuming exterior lay a heart as calculating as any to be found in a London drawing room. Penelope was certain of it. Why else would the dratted woman be casting out lures to the earl?

It had to be stopped. Penelope absently began to gnaw at one perfectly oval fingernail, stopping herself just in time. It was a measure of her agitation that she was reverting to that old habit, and she knew who to blame. Aldrich. Aldrich was at fault for all that had gone wrong since the earl's arrival. If Aldrich weren't there, surely the earl would pay court to her, instead. Aldrich, then, would have to go.

Penelope sank lower on her pillows. Yes, Aldrich must go, and she knew just what to do to ensure that. A cold, calculating smile crossed her face, a smile that none of her swains had ever been allowed to see. Her plan would work, she was certain of it. She would at last be free of her rival, and the earl would be hers.

Chapter 7

Nicholas whistled as he dismounted and swung up the stairs to Sutcliffe Hall, something he never would have done at sea. Whistling was bad luck there. It brought on storms and all manner of bad things. Not on shore, though. Silly, the freedom he felt to indulge in this particular habit, but there it was. Life ashore had its advantages. No longer was he bound by a military hierarchy that stifled and frustrated him; no longer did he deal in fighting and pain and war. If he sometimes missed the excitement of battle, or the tranquillity of a sunset at sea, there were compensations. There was the power he held, because of his title, to decide what needed doing and to do it, without interference. There were the new friends he had made, and the sense that, for the first time in his life, he just might belong somewhere. When he needed to get away, he had the *Spray*. Most of all, there was Cassie. Life, he reflected, walking into the Hall, was good.

He was met by chaos. Nothing unusual in that. Since the builders had begun work, everything was topsy-turvy. There was something different about this confusion, though. He saw no builders, but counted at least one footman and several maids, along with his housekeeper, running back and forth across the scarred oak floor. Must do something about the floor, he thought absently, laying his hat on a table, since no one was there to take it. "Kirby!" he bellowed in his best quarterdeck voice, and the activity ceased, as if his staff were all green hands and he were indeed the captain. Then everyone commenced talking at once, from Mrs. Feather, his housekeeper, down to the smallest maid. Nicholas held up his hands for them to stop. "Where is Kirby?" he shouted above the hubbub.

"Here, my lord." Kirby lurched toward him. "And proper glad I am to see you, too."

"My lord?" Nicholas stared at him. "Since when do you call me that?"

"Sorry, Cap'n. I just be that glad to see you. We got a problem, Cap'n."

"Oh?" Nicholas turned and gave his staff a look that made them all scatter. "What sort of problem?"

"While you was gone, Cap'n, someone delivered somethin' for you."

"What, man? Spit it out. I'd like to know what the devil is happening in my own home."

"Well, Cap'n—all right. But don't say I didn't warn you."

"Kirby—"

"Yes, Cap'n. Someone brought you—those."

Kirby stepped aside, pointing dramatically. Nicholas looked toward the stairs, and blinked. Sitting on the bottom stair were two tiny girls. Both wore white dresses; both had long, dark hair; and both were regarding him with huge, dark eyes. Except that one was a bit larger than the other, they were identical; the smaller one had her thumb firmly in her mouth. "What the devil, Kirby?"

"Ah, Cap'n Maidstone, Cap'n. Remember 'im? He left 'em."

"Left them! When?"

"Several hours ago, Cap'n. Tried to find you, but you was out on the *Spray*—"

"I know, I know." Nicholas pushed his hand through his hair and continued staring at the girls, who stared right back. "Did he say anything?"

"No, Cap'n. Said you'd know what it was about and left you a note. Then left."

"Blast and the devil take it," Nicholas began, and then stopped. He couldn't curse, much as he wanted to, in front of children. "Give me the note. And get Mrs. Feather back here. She'll know what to do with those— those—"

"Children, Cap'n."

"I know what they are!" Nicholas glared at him and stomped into his study. What the devil was Maidstone about, to leave two children with him?

A moment later, he had his answer. Groaning, he sank his head into his hands. What the devil Cassie would think of this, he didn't know. That it was his own fault didn't help matters at all.

He remembered David Maidstone, though he hadn't thought about him in ages. They'd been midshipmen together, and then lieutenants. In the heat and noise and terror of their first naval engagement, so many years ago, Nicholas and Maidstone had made pledges to each other. Should one die, the other would communicate the news to his family, and take charge of all his possessions, until they could be disposed of properly. In subsequent years Nicholas, making other friends and rising through the ranks, had forgotten that promise, but Maidstone apparently hadn't.

Nicholas looked again at the note, frowning over Maidstone's crabbed, almost illegible writing. He was off to America, he wrote, transporting Wellington's seasoned troops to fight against the upstart Yankees. Problem was, he had these two little girls. Mother was dead; anyway, she'd been Spanish, and his family would never have accepted her. Maidstone knew he could rely on his old friend to look after his girls for him, until he returned from America. Nicholas was the best of good fellows, and he remained Nicholas's obedient servant, etc., etc., Captain David Maidstone, R.N.

"Kirby!" Nicholas bellowed, and Kirby tumbled into the room, having been waiting for just this summons. "Did that cork-brained sapskull say anything to you at all?"

"No, Cap'n. Just that you'd know what it was all about and that he was going back to Portsmouth. Said he was sailing with the tide."

"Damn and blast. Have my horse saddled. I've got to catch him."

"Cap'n, he'll be gone—"

"Blast it, man, what are we supposed to do with his daughters? I've got to stop him."

Kirby followed Nicholas into the hall. "You won't make it, Cap'n. He'll be gone."

"Maybe not. There are always delays. You know that, Kirby." He glanced out the open door, where the bright sun of late afternoon turned the lawn a rich emerald. "Thank God it stays bright late. Maybe I'll even make Portsmouth tonight."

"Maybe, Cap'n." Kirby stood back as Nicholas mounted his horse. Already the cap'n sat his mount with more ease. Kirby's spirits rose a bit. If anyone could salvage this situation, it was the cap'n, Kirby thought, going back into the house as Nicholas rode away with a spurt of gravel. After all, what were they supposed to do with two little girls?

Penelope walked into her room and stopped short. "What are you doing here?" she asked, irritably, crossing to her mirror.

"Waiting for you." George smiled up at her with the eager hopefulness of a puppy. In his riding gear he looked out of place in the delicate armchair, one booted leg swinging to and fro over the arm and scuffing the oyster-colored satin. "Thought perhaps you'd like to go riding."

Penelope looked at his reflection. "Heavens, no! Why would I want to do that?"

George scowled. "You've changed since you had your season, Penny. You used to be a bruising rider."

"Well, I am not going riding with you today." She leaned forward, wetting a fingertip and taming a wayward curl. "This is our at-home day, or have you forgotten? I fully expect the earl to pay a call."

George snorted. "Well, you're out there. Saw him riding hell for leather out of here yesterday afternoon."

Penelope turned in surprise. "You did? Why did not you say so?" She flounced down onto the tufted vanity stool, pouting. "How dare he go when he knew I wanted to see him! And where did he go?"

"Don't know. Didn't stop to tell me." George grinned. "Set your cap for him, have you?"

"Of course I have." Penelope turned back to the mirror, searching for nonexistent blemishes to her appearance. Perfect. But then, she expected nothing less. "I'd make a splendid countess, don't you think?"

George snorted. "You? Don't be stupid."

"Well, I would!"

"He don't want you. You ask me, I think he's interested in Miss Aldrich."

Penelope went very still, her hands clenching into fists. That Aldrich! So it wasn't her imagination. "He wouldn't so demean himself."

George shrugged. "Seems to like her."

"He's being polite," Penelope snapped. "I must admit, though, that Aldrich looked rather well at dinner. I thought you noticed, too."

George's eyes were soft. "She did look pretty."

"Mm-hm." Penelope picked up a comb, looked critically at her hair, and then set it down again. "I will say one thing for Aldrich. She's smart enough not to try for an earl. She'll set her sights a little lower."

"What do you mean?"

Penelope smiled sweetly. "Why, brother dear, haven't you noticed how she looks at you?"

"No, by Jove, does she?"

"Oh yes. She likes you, George."

"I thought she might," he mused. "But she always pushes me away, Penny."

"Of course she does, stupid. Haven't you figured her out yet? She wants marriage." Penelope applied a light dusting of powder to her face and then sat back, pleased with the results. "Do close your mouth, George. You look like a fish."

"Do you really think she'll marry me?"

"Of course she would. However, Mama wouldn't countenance it, you know."

"I am a grown man. I can make my own decisions."

"Of course." Penelope rose. "I must go. Our guests will be arriving at any moment."

"Are you sure of that, Penny?" George's voice stopped

97

her at the door. "Do you really think Miss Aldrich is interested in me?"

"Trust me, George. A woman knows these things. Of course, she won't make the first move. That's up to you."

"Mm." George furrowed his brow in concentration.

Penelope bit back a malicious grin. "Think about it, brother dear," she said, and swept out of the room, well satisfied with the afternoon's work.

Several days later Nicholas returned, alone, to the Hall. He looked tired and dusty as he swung off his mount, handing the reins to a groom. Kirby met him at the door. "No luck, Cap'n?"

"None, blast it." Nicholas handed his hat to Kirby. "Blasted horse threw a shoe just this side of Worthing and that slowed me down. By the time I got to Portsmouth, Maidstone had just sailed." He glared at Kirby. "Don't you dare say you told me so."

"No, Cap'n."

Nicholas thrust his hand into his hair. "I need a bath. God only knows what we're going to do with two little girls."

"Mrs. Feather's taken them over, Cap'n, and seems right happy about it. They're taking little things."

"I'll write to Maidstone's family about them, for all the good it will do. Where are they now?"

"Belowstairs, with Mrs. Feather. Maybe his family will take 'em, Cap'n."

"I hope so," Nicholas said, and headed for the kitchen.

"My lord!" Mrs. Feather started up from the kitchen table, looking a bit flustered, as he came into the room. "I didn't know you were returned home. I'll just—"

Nicholas waved a hand. "Sit, ma'am." He liked Mrs.

Feather. Since he had hired her she had begun restoring order to the house, and she was friendly and competent. Best of all, she had taken on the two little girls, who sat at the table with mugs of milk and identically wary expressions on their faces. "How do you go on?"

"Very well, sir."

"I hope this new responsibility isn't too much for you."

"Oh no, my lord, they've been perfect angels." She turned and smiled at the girls, mimicking a curtsy. "Now, Elena, Juanita, make your curtsy to the earl like I taught you."

"That's not necessary," Nicholas protested, but both children scrambled down and bowed with the clumsy grace of childhood. They weren't beautiful children, with their straight dark hair and solemn eyes, but, Nicholas reflected, Kirby was right. They were appealing. "Which girl is which?"

"Juanita is the older. Their mother was Spanish, my lord?"

"Yes." He spoke in an undertone. "According to Captain Maidstone's letter, she died just a few months back. He didn't want to leave the children in Spain, but he didn't think his own family would take them, either. They didn't approve of his marriage, you see."

"Poor little mites, to lose their mother, and so young. No wonder they're so quiet, then. Why, do you know they've hardly said a word since they came?"

"Haven't they?" Nicholas went down on one knee. Elena moved closer to her sister, and both looked frightened, but they held their ground. Good stuff in them, Nicholas thought. "Buenos dias, señoritas," he said, softly.

Elena's face brightened and she began to babble, a mixture of Spanish and baby talk, so that Nicholas, whose grasp of the language was rudimentary, was hard-pressed to keep up. Juanita, still wary, kept her distance, but even she answered his haltingly phrased questions. Soon both children were talking, Elena chattering happily away.

"There's your answer, Mrs. Feather," Nicholas said, rising. "They only speak Spanish."

"Fancy that!" Mrs. Feather stared at the girls as if they were a rare species of bird. "Fancy knowing a foreign language already, and them so young."

"Ahem. Yes." Nicholas fought to keep the laughter from his voice. "I'll leave them in your care, ma'am, if you don't mind? Until I hear from their family."

"Oh no, my lord, I don't mind at all. But, my lord," she said, stopping him at the door, "what if their family doesn't want them?"

"I don't know, Mrs. Feather," he said, and went out.

That was a problem, Nicholas thought as he climbed the stairs to his room. It was all very well taking temporary charge of the children, but what if no one else wanted them? Maidstone could be gone for years. Nor was it unheard-of for a naval officer to be killed in battle, as Nicholas knew too well. In that case, he would be left with the care of two little girls who weren't the least bit related to him, and what he would do with them, he didn't know.

But Cassie would. He raised his head as the answer to his dilemma came to him. Cassie, of course. Should've thought of her sooner. He couldn't go charging up to Lambton Manor and demand to see her, but if things went as they had she would be at the beach on Thursday. Then he would ask her.

Yes, he thought, easing back into a chair and groaning as his tired muscles protested. For the first time since

100

taking up his title, he felt content. He'd ask Cassie, and everything would be all right.

Thursday dawned gloomy, with quick showers of rain, so that Cassandra despaired of ever being able to leave the manor. Life had been difficult lately, with both Penelope and Mrs. Lamb being openly hostile. Cassandra suspected that it was only by Mr. Lamb's intervention that she had kept her position. Complicating matters was George's sudden strange behavior. He'd always been a bit of a nuisance, but lately he'd taken to appearing in the most unexpected places, just outside the schoolroom, perhaps, or around the curve of a staircase. What he wanted he never said, but Cassandra had a sinking suspicion she knew. Thus she had learned to be on her guard at all times. Many things could be forgiven her, but not an affair with the son of the house, even if it wasn't something she wanted.

By noon the rain had let up. After a hurried lunch Cassandra bundled Catherine and Mary into their cloaks and out into the cool, gray day. Joyous at being out, the two girls ran ahead along the cliff path, shouting and singing. Cassandra's pace was more sedate, though her heart was beating fast. She was going to see him again, Nicholas. No matter that she was too far below him ever to mean anything to him. His friendship had become the most important part of her life. As difficult as things were at Lambton Manor, she would endure. Only by doing so could she ensure that she would be close to him.

"Miss Aldrich! Look at the earl!" Catherine shouted, pointing across the field. Cassandra stopped. There he was, his head, uncovered as always, gleaming a dull gold even in the dimness of the afternoon. His normal rolling gate, however, was slower than usual. Cassandra put her hand to her mouth to stifle a sudden laugh. Oh dear! Held in Nicholas's arms and clinging to his neck was a small girl, while another lagged along beside him, holding to his hand. Nicholas had apparently gained some new admirers.

"Good afternoon, sir," she said, when he was within hearing distance. "I see you brought company."

"I didn't have much choice." This close Nicholas showed signs of strain that hadn't been there before: a certain look in his eyes, a grimness to his lips. Everyone in the neighborhood had heard about the arrival of the children at Sutcliffe Hall, and were engaged in lively speculation about them. One look at the girls was enough for Cassandra to discard the most common rumor. They bore entirely no resemblance to Nicholas and could not possibly be his children. "They wouldn't let me go without them," he went on.

"Yes, they do seem rather attached to you." Cassandra smiled at the little girl in his arms, who took one look at her and promptly buried her head in his shoulder. "Or is it only that you wished to bring your own chaperones?"

"Duennas, more like. They speak only Spanish, you see." Nicholas bent his head and said something to the child, his accents musical, in spite of the halting pace of his speech. Cassandra was entranced. So, apparently, was the child, who at last looked up and gave Cassandra a quick, shy smile.

"But they're lovely children. What are their names?"

"This is Señorita Elena Maidstone, Cassie, and Señorita Juanita. And I don't doubt," he added, "that you've heard all kinds of stories as to how I ended up with them."

Cassandra cast a quick glance at Catherine and Mary,

listening with rapt interest. "Let us go down to the beach, shall we? You may tell me about it there."

Once on the beach Catherine and Mary took charge of the younger girls, taking them on a search for shells and other treasures the sea might have given up. In the mysterious way children have of communicating, they were all soon playing happily together, and even Elena seemed to have forgotten Nicholas's presence. Cassandra and Nicholas sat on the rocks, watching. How extraordinary this was, she thought, sitting straight, her hands folded in her lap. They might almost have been parents, watching their own children at play.

"They're beautiful children," Cassandra said to escape the pain of that thought. "Are they Spanish?"

"Their mother was," Nicholas said, and went on to explain the circumstances of his unexpected guardianship.

"But what a terrible thing to do!" Cassandra's eyes were flashing indignantly when he had finished his tale. "To leave two babies in the care of a stranger."

"I'm hardly a stranger, Cassie." He grinned. "One thing about it, the matchmaking mamas are looking at me differently."

"It's not funny. Poor little mites. When Captain Maidstone returns, you may be certain I'll give him a piece of my mind."

Nicholas grinned. "That I'd like to see, Red."

"Pray don't tease," she said, irritably, wrapping her arms around herself and leaning away from him. Men! They could be the most inconsiderate creatures alive. She had to admit, though, that Nicholas appeared to be doing the best he could for the girls. How very strange. Nicholas, with children.

From the corner of her eye she cast him a quick glance,

though he was looking away from her. She didn't know this man, not really. In all his years in the navy, stopping at all those foreign ports, he must have met many women. What kind of woman attracted him? So far he had shown no partiality to any of the young ladies of the neighborhood, not even Penelope, though that she ascribed to his good sense. Sooner or later, however, someone would catch his eye. He would marry and have his own children. Lowering thought.

"They're well behaved, but I don't know quite what to do with them," Nicholas said, breaking into her thoughts. "My housekeeper is taking care of them just now, but it's wearing her out. She's not young, and she does have other duties. And girls. What do I know about girls, Cassie? I could deal with boys, but girls?"

"They need a mother," she said, calmly, hiding the pain of that thought.

"Aye. They do." He turned to look at her. "I've thought about this, Cassie. There's every chance Maidstone won't return. What will I do with them, if I don't have a wife?"

Cassandra strove to make her voice light. "You'll have to find one. For an earl, that shouldn't be a problem."

"Think I've already found her. Cassie." He reached out and covered her hands with his, grasping them hard. "Will you marry me?"

Chapter 8

The words rang in Cassandra's ears, the words she had been dreaming about since she was a child. Never, though, had she thought to hear them under such circumstances. "How dare you!" Snatching her hands away, she jumped to her feet. "How dare you ask me such a thing."

"Cassie." Nicholas rose, his hand outstretched and his face puzzled. "What is so wrong—"

"Ooh! You don't even realize. That just makes it worse." She stalked a few paces away and then turned on him. "Look at me, my lord. At me! I am a person. I have feelings. If you want someone to care for your children, then hire a governess!"

"Cassie, I didn't mean to insult you—"

"No, of course not, no one does. To them I'm just Aldrich, the governess—"

"But, Cassie, you are a governess. I thought—"

"Catherine! Mary!" Cassandra spun away. "Come. We're going home."

"Blast it, Cassie, I didn't mean—"

"Come, girls. Now!"

The girls came toward her reluctantly, dragging their

feet in the sand. "But, Miss Aldrich, we were just starting to find some good shells," Catherine protested.

"They'll have to wait for another day."

"But, Miss Aldrich—"

"Catherine Louise Lamb, I have had quite enough of your back talk! We're going home."

Catherine looked quickly up at her, and then back down at the sand. Cassandra used that tone of voice rarely, but when she did it was to be obeyed. "Yes, ma'am."

"Say good-bye to Juanita and Elena, now, and to the earl."

"Cassie." Nicholas stood awkwardly, his charges hanging on to him, looking frightened. "Cassie, I'm sorry."

Cassandra didn't look at him. "Good day, my lord," she said, and turned, leaving Nicholas to stare after her and wonder just what he had done wrong.

The rain began again just as they reached the manor, and continued for the remainder of that day, and the next. A fitting setting for her mood, Cassandra thought, glancing out her narrow window at an evening made darker by the clouds. She had gone through bad times in her life, but never had she felt quite like this. And all because Nicholas had asked her to marry him.

It had been a difficult two days since she had left him on the beach. The girls, upset at being deprived of their treat, were quarrelsome and rebellious, paying little mind to their studies and misbehaving until Cassandra, driven to distraction, sent them to their rooms. Beatrice and Amanda hadn't helped matters by coming to the school-room to ease their boredom, and ending by squabbling. Nor had Cassandra appreciated Penelope's brief visit to inform her that Mrs. Gregory was giving a musicale for the earl and that Cassandra was definitely not invited. Thank heavens no one else in the house had seen fit to invade her domain. Thank heavens this long, long day was nearly over.

Not bothering to remove her shoes, she stretched out on her bed, tracing the spidery cracks in her ceiling. Nicholas had asked her to marry him. Her childhood dream had come true, but not in the way she had hoped. He didn't want her for herself, as his wife. He wanted her because he needed someone to look after his unexpected charges, and she had been at hand. It hurt. Oh, it hurt, with a pain that was unique in her experience, striking deep to her soul and lodging there. For just a moment, before the import of his words hit her, she had felt only joy, and the pain was the worse for it. How she would deal with it, she didn't know.

There was a knock on her door, loud but somehow tentative. Sighing, Cassandra rose, straightening her cap. "Yes, yes, I'm coming," she said as the knocking sounded again, and reached for the door handle to see George standing on the threshold. "Mr. Lamb?"

He smiled at her, a boyish, crooked smile that she found exasperating. "Hullo, Cassie. May I come in?"

Cassandra stood in the doorway, blocking his entrance. "No, sir, I think not. 'Tis late."

"I know. It's why I'm here."

"Because it's late?"

"Dash it, Cassie, I never get to see you alone, otherwise. You're always busy with one of my sisters. Please let me in."

"No, sir, I cannot."

"Please?" His smile pleaded. "Only for a moment."

"Mr. Lamb." His voice had risen, making her uneasily

aware of the others who slept nearby. She couldn't afford any sort of a fuss. "Oh, very well. But only for a moment, mind."

"Thank you, Cassie." The faint scent of brandy trailed after him as he ambled in. "Small room, this."

Cassandra stood with her back to the door. "What is it, Mr. Lamb, that couldn't wait until morning?"

"George. Can't you at least call me by my name? Ugly name." He sank down onto her bed. "Always hated it."

An awful suspicion was growing in Cassandra's mind. "Mr. Lamb, you're drunk."

"Devil a bit," he said, cheerfully, slouching. "Just a little well to live, that's all. Come talk to me, Cassie. You can do that, can't you? Just talk to me?"

"Mr. Lamb—"

"Please? And then I'll go. I promise."

Cassandra glanced at the door. There was no hope for it. She wasn't strong enough to push him out bodily, and going for help would only make matters worse. Everyone would put the worse possible construction on George's being in her room, and she had little doubt as to who would be blamed. "Oh, very well. But this is most improper, you know."

"Not to worry." His smile broadened. "You know, Cassie, you should leave your glasses off more often. Dashed pretty without them."

"What is it you want, sir?"

"Come sit with me, Cassie." He patted the side of the bed. "Please."

"I think I'd best stay here, sir."

"But all I want to do is talk."

"Mr. Lamb." Cassandra had had enough. "You keep saying that, and yet you say nothing to the point. I am fast running out of patience. Please say what you came to say and leave, or I will summon your father."

"Don't do that!" He looked alarmed. "It's my job to talk to him."

"Mr. Lamb—"

"Dash it, Cassie, won't you listen to me? I love you."

That stopped her. She stood in the middle of the floor, hand paused halfway to her throat, and stared at him. This was worse than she had expected. "Oh, George. You do not."

"I do," he insisted. "I tell you, Cassie, I love you."

"But you don't even know me." Sitting there peering owlishly up at her, he looked like nothing so much as a small boy. He was very young. She remembered all too well what it was like to be so young and in love, and to have that love tossed back in one's face. "George, I'm sorry," she said, as gently as possible. "I don't love you."

"The devil you don't." He abruptly straightened, staring at her. "You do so!"

"No, George. I don't. I'm sorry."

"You have to! I love you, Cassie."

"I don't love you, George. I never will."

"Don't you think, if you gave it time—"

"No." Cassandra's voice was firm. The time for gentleness had passed. "Please, sir, you really must leave."

He rose, his hands out in supplication. "But you have to love me, Cassie. I love you. I want to marry you."

Good heavens! Two proposals in two days, and the wrong man professing love. "It would never work, George. Even if I did love you, your parents would never allow it. For heaven's sake, I'm five years older than you."

"Hang the age difference. Hang my parents." He stood, his hands flexing into fists, but there was such deep misery in his eyes that Cassandra felt no fear. "I love you."

"But I don't love you," she repeated, hoping this time he would listen.

"There's someone else, isn't there?" he demanded, staring at her. "Isn't there?"

Cassandra sighed. "Yes, George. There is." Nicholas. Not that that would ever come to anything.

"Damn it. I knew it." He took a turn about the room and then stopped, his back to her. "Well. That's it then, isn't it. I'll leave then, Miss Aldrich."

"Thank you."

"But, you know, I don't understand." He paused at the door. "Penelope told me you loved me."

Cassandra's hands clenched. So Penelope was behind this. "She's wrong. I think Miss Gregory is fond of you, though."

"Jennifer?" He brightened. "Do you really think so?"

"She looks at you in a certain way. And she is pretty."

"Yes, by Jove, she is." He stared blankly ahead, and then looked down at her. "I say, Miss Aldrich, you won't tell anyone about this? Wouldn't want it to get around, what a cake I made of myself."

"It will be our secret," she promised, and because he looked so like a small boy in need of solace, reached up to kiss his cheek. He turned his head, leaning it against hers, and, at that moment, the door to her room burst open.

"Look!" Penelope's voice declaimed in shrill accents. "I told you that she lured him in here, didn't I? I told you what she was. Now maybe you'll believe me!"

George exclaimed in surprise and Cassandra pulled away, but too late. Penelope stood in the doorway, flushed

110

and triumphant, an indignant Mrs. Lamb behind her. "Penny, it's not what you think—"

"Be quiet, George," Mrs. Lamb ordered. "I know exactly what it is. Well, Aldrich?" She faced Cassandra. "What have you to say for yourself?"

"It wasn't what you think, ma'am." Cassandra's head was raised, her eyes meeting the other woman's directly. She was fighting for her very life. "Mr. Lamb had a problem he needed to discuss with me."

"Problem! Yes, it's a problem for you, isn't it?" She gazed at her, her eyes narrowed. "My daughter was right. You are no good. I will not have you near my children any longer."

"But, Mama," George protested. "I want to marry her."

"Oh no," Cassandra groaned.

"Marry! So that's your game." She glared at Aldrich. "Thank heavens we caught you in time. Now. I am not an unkind person. I could turn you out tonight, but I will not. However, you will leave this house tomorrow. Is that clear?"

Cassandra looked from one to the other, from Penelope's malicious smile, to George's open-mouthed, foolish-looking dismay, to Mrs. Lamb's wrath. There was no help for it. "Yes, ma'am," she said, her head lowered. Her fate was sealed. She had been caught again in a compromising position, and she would pay in scandal.

"I'm sorry, Miss Aldrich." Mr. Lamb, sitting behind his desk, didn't look up at Cassandra where she stood before him in his study. "What happened last night leaves me with no choice. I'm afraid we'll have to let you go."

Cassandra looked fixedly down at the floor and nodded, not trusting her voice. She hadn't slept the previous night, after what had happened. Knowing what was coming made the reality no easier to bear, however. Once again her life was in ruins, and all because of a man's thoughtlessness.

"I realize it wasn't your fault," he went on, his voice heavy. "If it were up to me I'd send George away and—but what's done is done."

"What George feels is calf love," she said, her voice a mere thread.

"I'm aware of that. Still, you see my position. I'm sorry." He rose. "Do you have someplace to go?"

"Yes." Her sister would not be happy to see her, not after another scandal, but what choice did Cassandra have? She wasn't likely to find another position after this.

"Good. I'm sorry I can't give you a character, but—"

"I understand, sir. Thank you for your kindness." Dropping a curtsy, she turned and fled the room, before she disgraced herself by breaking down. Matters were quite bad enough as it was.

In the hall, her portmanteaux waited, holding all that she owned in this world. Except for that, and the Lamb's coachman, who would take her to the inn to catch the stage, the hall was empty. It was no more than she'd expected, but it hurt. She wouldn't have the chance even to say good-bye to her charges, or to the older girls, who had become her friends. She'd never see them again. She'd never see Nicholas again.

No, she wouldn't allow herself to think of him. He had never been meant for her. She would tuck him back into her memory where he belonged. There was a new life for her to make now. Standing here moping did no good.

Squaring her shoulders, Cassandra picked up the

smallest portmanteau and walked, for the last time, out of Lambton Manor.

"And of course, my lord, you know Mrs. Lamb," Mrs. Witkin gushed, clinging to Nicholas just a bit tighter as she brought him around her drawing room, introducing him to everyone.

"Of course," Nicholas said easily, showing none of his discomfort. He was used to this by now, to being shown about by the hostesses of the neighborhood rather as if he were a prize bull. What, he wondered, had they done for excitement before his arrival? "How do you do, ma'am?"

"Very well, my lord." Mrs. Lamb simpered up at him. Penelope, by her side, dropped into a very deep curtsy, making Nicholas hastily look away. Penelope's dress was cut much too low for an afternoon spent taking tea at a neighbor's, and when she curtsied like that—by Neptune! What was wrong with him? He'd always enjoyed looking at a woman's attributes before.

"Do come and sit by me, my lord." Mrs. Witkin led him over to a sofa, across the room from the Lambs. He felt at once relieved, and trapped. "You must tell me how you are finding life in our quiet neighborhood. I am certain it does not compare with being in a battle at sea."

Nicholas's lips twitched. Only in the particulars, he thought. With Mrs. Witkin beside him and Mrs. Lamb occasionally glaring in their direction, he felt rather as if he were caught between two ships of the line. "It is different," he agreed. "Hardly dull, though." Before she could question him more closely on his plans for the future, including, perhaps, his hopes for marriage, he launched into a detailed account of the work being done on Sutcliffe

Hall. By the time he was done, Mrs. Witkin's eyes were glazed, filling him with a mixture of remorse and glee.

"Very interesting, my lord," she said, faintly. "And what of your two poor orphans?"

"They are well, ma'am, thank you for asking." Nicholas's voice was carefully noncommittal. "I had a letter from their father. He expects to return from America in a few months."

"You must be glad of that, my lord."

"Yes." Nicholas sipped at his tea, well aware that few people in the neighborhood really believed that the girls had a father. Other then himself, that was. It was annoying. The gossip was bad enough, but did they really think he was the sort of man who would desert his own children and their mother? Cassie hadn't thought so. Warmth filled him as he remembered her reaction to the children, and her staunch support of his actions. She was the one person who saw him as he was, as Nicholas, not the earl, and she wanted nothing to do with him.

He hadn't seen Cassie since that afternoon on the beach. Her reaction to his proposal still baffled him. Seemed to him their marrying was a perfectly logical and reasonable idea. It wasn't just so he'd have someone to look after the children, as she'd implied. After all, with any luck they'd be gone in a few months, while marriage was forever. He liked her, blast it! He thought she liked him. He also thought she'd be glad for the chance at a new life, the life he would offer her. What woman wouldn't? Certainly not the other eligible girls in the neighborhood. Cassie, however, was different. She always had been. Maybe that was why he was so drawn to her.

". . . and of course, you'll need someone to look after them," Mrs. Witkin was saying. "She would have been perfect for the post. She was so good with the Lamb girls. Pity she disgraced herself."

Nicholas snapped to attention. "Who, ma'am?"

Mrs. Witkin glanced across the room and leaned conspiratorially toward him. "Why, Cassandra Aldrich, of course. Haven't you heard, my lord?"

Cassie. Something had happened to Cassie. "No. What?"

"It is the most delicious scandal. I had it from my cook, who had it from a footman at the Lambs, that Miss Aldrich was found with Mr. Lamb last evening."

Nicholas drew back. "I don't believe it."

"Oh, 'tis true." Jennifer Gregory, conventionally pretty in sprigged muslin, leaned forward. "She always did cast sheep eyes at George Lamb."

"Jennifer." Mrs. Gregory scolded, but her eyes were avid. "It doesn't do to spread tales."

"George. Do you mean the son?" Mrs. Witkin frowned at her. "I had heard Joseph was involved."

"No, no, my maid told me it was Mr. George Lamb. She probably thought she could snare him into marriage."

"When did all this happen?" Nicholas asked, surprised his voice sounded so normal.

"Last evening, my lord." Mrs. Gregory leaned forward, tittering. "I hear she's sitting outside the Crown and Anchor right now, waiting for the stage."

"Is she?" Mrs. Witkin broke in. "Well, of course they had to let her go, after doing such a thing."

"Yes, of course. It does serve her right. Servants should be punished when they reach so high above themselves."

"Exactly. I always say—my lord?" She stared up at Nicholas, who had abruptly risen. "Is aught wrong?"

115

"I am afraid I must leave, ma'am. I've an appointment with the builder at the Hall."

"Oh, surely he can wait—"

"I'm afraid not. I'm late as it is." Nicholas bowed. "If you'll excuse me," he said, and strode out of the room.

Shocked silence followed in his wake, and then delighted speculation, as conversation broke out among the people in the room. Why, he had turned absolutely white when he had heard about the Aldrich woman. Hadn't he known her in the past? Perhaps they had been conducting an affair, though that meant Aldrich really was aiming above herself. Life had become vastly exciting since the earl's arrival. Everyone was avid to know what would happen next.

Blessedly unaware of the furor his abrupt departure had caused, Nicholas vaulted up into the seat of his curricle and drove off, with hardly a word to the groom who had held his horses. Cassie, and George Lamb. No, he wouldn't believe it. He remembered well that scene in the hall of Lambton Manor the night he had taken dinner there. If Cassie had welcomed George's advances—well, he'd swear never put out to sea in any kind of craft again. That was how certain he was of Cassie's virtue. No, George had forced himself upon her, and that thought lent urgency to Nicholas's actions, making him hunch over the ribbons and drive his team faster. If she was hurt—by Neptune, Lamb would pay if he had hurt her! The important thing now, though, was to find her.

The road to the village seemed longer than it ever had. What time did the stage come in, he wondered? And where was it headed? He might find himself in a chase across England, to find Cassie. To bring her back. She was the only thing that had made his life here at all bearable. Without her, he didn't think he could go on.

Fairhaven was at last in sight. Nicholas, more experienced at driving now, eased up on the ribbons, but still he drove onto the High Street at a smart pace. There was the Crown and Anchor, with no sign of the stage in sight, thank Neptune. And there, sitting on a bench in front of the inn, her head bent, was a woman. Cassie.

Nicholas brought the curricle to a stop in the innyard and jumped down, carelessly tossing the reins to the ostler who ran forward. All his attention was on the small, forlorn figure in gray. She hadn't even raised her head at his approach. Dear Lord, she must be hurt. That thought made him slow, made him bite back the harsh, hasty words relief had brought to his lips. He would have to be very gentle with her.

"Cassie," he said, crouching down before her, and she started, raising her head. For a moment she returned his gaze, her eyes lusterless, and then bent her head again.

"You heard," she said, her voice as dull as her eyes.

"Aye. At least, I heard something. Did he hurt you, Cassie?" Concern made his voice urgent. "Tell me. Did he?"

"No. You shouldn't be here, my lord. It won't help your reputation."

"Hang my reputation. He didn't hurt you?"

"No. Nothing happened, my lord, in spite of what you may have heard."

"Nothing?"

"Nothing."

Nicholas rose and stood looking down at her bent head, puzzled. In all the time of their acquaintance he had never known Cassie to be so listless, so dispirited. "So why are you sitting here feeling sorry for yourself?"

"I am not feeling sorry for myself!" she exclaimed, snapping her head back to look at him. For the first time

117

color returned to her cheeks and life to her eyes. In spite of himself, Nicholas smiled. "Oh, laugh all you want, my lord." She rose, gathering her belongings together. "I know what everyone is saying about me. Now, if you'll excuse me, I'm going inside to wait for the stage."

"A very good idea." Nicholas grasped her arm. "We can't talk out here."

"What are you doing?" Cassandra stared up at him, trying to free her arm from his grip. "Unhand me, sir."

"Hush, Cassie. You are overset."

"Overset!"

"Cassie, the village is watching."

That silenced her. With a shrug, she let him lead her inside. The innkeeper came toward them, managing somehow both to sneer at her and to bow respectfully to Nicholas. Cassandra didn't think she had ever been so mortified in her life. Why was Nicholas doing this to her?

Before she could protest further, the innkeeper was leading them down the hall to a private parlor. A maid whisked in to serve them tea and fresh, hot muffins, and then they were alone, silence ringing between them.

Nicholas sat at the table across from her. "Did you eat this morning?"

"I—I'm not hungry, my lord." She raised dazed eyes to him. "Oh, Nicholas. Don't you know what you are doing?"

"Feeding you luncheon. You have a long journey ahead of you, I'll wager. You need to keep up your strength." He leaned back, watching her. "Where are you going?"

"To Norton." She didn't meet his eyes, but instead concentrated on pouring out the tea. He was right. She did need to eat, though how she would swallow anything, she didn't know. There was a persistent ache in her stomach, a stubborn lump in her throat. "To my sister's. After that, I don't know."

"What happened, Cassie? Tell me." He leaned forward. "All of it."

Cassandra hesitated, and then plunged in. This morning she would not have thought she had an ally in the world, but here was Nicholas, watching her, concern darkening his eyes to turquoise. He couldn't do anything for her, not really, but being able to talk to him, to know he cared, was enough. Seeing him again was enough.

"I don't understand," he said when she had finished, leaning back. "You say nothing happened. George says nothing happened, and yet you've been let go. What is the fuss?"

Cassandra raised her teacup and was surprised to find that, at some point, she had drained it dry, and that she had devoured a muffin. She must have been hungrier than she thought. "Don't you know, my lord, that when something like this happens the woman is always blamed?"

"But, blast it, you didn't do anything!"

"I tempted him. No, I really didn't," she went on, at his startled look, "but that is what everyone assumes. And of course he mustn't be allowed to contract a mésalliance. Therefore, I must be punished."

"It's stupid. It's unfair. It's—"

"Oh, stubble it! Don't you know what will be said about this tête à tête of ours?"

"It's hardly that, Cassie."

"They'll say I enticed you into Lord knows what kind of goings-on. They'll say you either were a fool, or that you knew a good thing when you saw it, and what a sly dog you are!" She set her cup down with a bang. "The woman is blamed, and the man becomes a hero."

"Blast it, Cassie." He pushed his chair back and paced around the room. "This can't be. There are women who deserve that kind of reputation—"

"Are there?"

"Of course there are. They—"

"But you don't really know that, do you? How do you think a woman earns a bad name? From a man, of course."

Nicholas peered at her. "Cassie, what man hurt you?"

"No man." Her voice was frosty. "A woman must always be above reproach, while a man can do anything. Is that not the way of the world?" She looked up at him. "You asked me, once, why I wear spectacles I don't need, and a mobcap. Don't you know? To protect myself. To make myself as plain as possible, so that men won't think me fair game."

"Didn't work, did it?" Nicholas said, mildly, sitting across from her and ignoring her look of outrage. Something was going on here, something more than the incident of the night before. What had happened to Cassie to make her so bitter? "Since you admit they're only for show, take 'em off."

"My lord—"

"Take off those blasted glasses and that bonnet, Cassie. I want to be able to see you."

Cassandra hesitated, and then reached up to untie her bonnet strings. A moment later the hated spectacles lay discarded on the table, and she was sitting back, her hands folded primly in her lap. "Well?"

"That's better. Now." He reached for the teapot. "Let's decide what to do about this. Why didn't you come to me?"

"There's nothing you can do, my lord."

120

"Oh?" He looked at her from under his brows. "Have I ever let you down before?"

She lowered her head. "No. Of course you haven't."

"I won't start, now. So, what can we do?"

"Well." She took a deep breath. "I need to find another position.

"Exactly." He set down the teapot with an emphatic thump. "What you need is someone who'll take you on without a reference from your last employer—I assume the Lambs didn't give you a character?—and then give you one when it's time for you to leave."

Cassandra simply looked at him. Without her glasses she looked much younger, more vulnerable, and yet there was knowledge in her eyes that didn't belong to one so young. "That would be nice. Where, pray tell, am I to find such a paragon?"

He grinned. "Why not me?"

"What!"

"Why not?" He leaned toward her, that wayward strand of hair falling over his forehead. "I need someone to take care of Juanita and Elena. You've seen that yourself. Thought I could get by with just Mrs. Feather, but she told me last night they're too much for her. They got into the flour yesterday." He shuddered. "You've never seen such a mess."

Cassandra bit back a smile. "I don't see that it's a solution, though, sir."

"Hear me out. I need you, Cassie. The girls need you. Juanita has bad dreams at night."

"Nicholas—"

"And since I hope their father will be coming for them soon, you won't have to put up with me for long."

"I still don't think—"

"There's one more thing, Cassie." His face sobered. "A man in my position needs a wife."

Cassandra straightened. "Oh no, my lord, I can't—"

"So I was thinking that you could help me find one."

Chapter 9

Different emotions chased across Cassandra's face: surprise, shock, and finally, chagrin. Nicholas, leaning back, kept his face straight by a great effort. Didn't like that, did she? Claimed she didn't want to marry him, but looked like she didn't want anyone else to, either. The thought filled him with immense satisfaction. "You know I'm not in the petticoat line," he went on. "Being at sea all those years, I don't know how to do the pretty. You could teach me."

"I'm hardly an expert on proper behavior," she said, her voice sounding strangled.

"You've had a season. More than I've had. Blast it, Cassie!" He rose again to pace the room, wheeling sharply to face her. "They're all after me, all of 'em. The Lambs, Reverend Carlisle's daughters, everyone. I don't know what to do. You've got to help me, Cassie." He braced his hands on the back of the chair and stared at her, his gaze compelling. "You've got to."

"I—" Cassandra's eyes fluttered away. "What will people say?"

"I am the earl," he said, with more than a trace of an aristocrat's arrogance. "They won't dare say anything to me. To you, either. I'll see to that. Anyway"—he waved his hand in dismissal—"you worry too much about that."

"Someone has to," she retorted. " 'Tis all part of proper behavior."

"See?" He grinned at her. "You're teaching me already. This will work out fine. Come." He picked up her bonnet and shoved it onto her head; the spectacles went into his coat pocket. "We'll return to the Hall. You can start today."

Cassandra struggled against his hand on her arm, pulling her to her feet. "Have you run mad? I can't go there with you."

He fixed her with the stern, blue gaze that had intimidated many a luckless midshipman in his time. "Why not?"

"I can't. It's not proper."

"Forget about being proper for a moment and think about what's right for you. Think about what you want to do." He put his fingers under her chin, forcing her eyes to meet his. "Blast it, Cassie, where has being proper got you? Take a chance, for once in your life."

Cassandra's eyes gazed at him steadily, unblinkingly. He had thought that, without the spectacles, he would see her better, know her better, but he was wrong. He had no more idea of what was going on in her head now than he ever had. "Please release me, sir. I do not like to be coerced."

Nicholas snatched his fingers away. "Cassie, I didn't mean—"

"You are right." She concentrated all her attention on pulling on her gloves. "I do need a position. I believe I will accept your offer, my lord." She looked up at him again. "But only until the children's father comes for them."

"Capital!" Grinning, he swooped down and planted an

exuberant kiss on her lips. "I knew you wouldn't fail me, Cassie."

"My lord!" Cassandra fell back, her eyes huge, her hand to her mouth. "What was the meaning of that?"

"Just a kiss, Cassie."

"Just—! Oh no, my lord." She whirled around, tying her bonnet strings. "If you think that will be part of my duties—"

"Cassie." He laid his hand on her shoulder, and she stilled. "Of course I don't think that. I'd never think such a thing of you."

She turned, studying his face, her eyes still wide and very uncertain. "Then, why—"

"Gratitude." He grinned. "You're rescuing me from a devil of a coil, you know."

"Oh." Again varying emotions chased across her face. Among them he thought he saw disappointment. Good. "I see. I understand. But it must not happen again, sir."

"Of course." He feigned surprise that she would think such a provision necessary, to hide his exultation. It had worked. He wasn't going to lose her. At least, not yet. As far as when Maidstone's children left—well, he'd think of something then. "Hate to think what those little imps have been up to since I've been gone. Come, let's get back to the Hall." And, with his hand on her elbow, he ushered her out of the inn, and into his life.

It was a nine-day's wonder. Cassandra Aldrich, who had been so summarily dismissed from service with the Lambs, now was ensconced at Sutcliffe Hall, governess to the earl's two little foreign girls. At least, that was what she was supposed to be. Those who were privy to the reasons for her departure from Lambton Manor, and that included nearly everyone, had their doubts. Governess, indeed! Looked like the new earl was as bad in his way as the old, they said, and those with daughters of marriageable age began to reconsider him as a match. Still and all, he was the earl, and nothing would be served by offending him. They would wait and see. For now.

In the day nursery of Sutcliffe Hall, Cassandra stood, hands on her hips, and looked around, frowning. On Nicholas's orders she had put away the spectacles and the mobcap, but still, with her dull, shapeless gown and her tightly bound hair, she looked very much a governess. If Nicholas didn't like it, that was his problem, she thought, continuing the internal argument that had begun when she'd left the inn with him. She had accepted his offer because she needed a position, and for no other reason. None. Never mind that she had been swayed by the hint of hopelessness deep in Nicholas's eyes, or by that unexpected kiss. She was here to be a governess, and that was what she would be.

Across the room, Juanita and Elena sat at a table, chubby legs dangling from chairs that were too high for them, and worked diligently at the drawing she'd set them to. Occasionally they would talk to each other in Spanish, and occasionally one of them would look at her with wary, uncertain eyes. She had two major tasks before her, to win their trust and to teach them at least a smidgeon of English. Fortunately they were young and would learn quickly. Whether they would overcome their reserve with her was another matter. Poor little mites, they'd had so much upheaval in their young lives, and it showed. They clung together, holding the rest of the world off, with Juanita already assuming the duties of a protective older sister. Captain Maidstone had much to answer for.

Cassandra frowned again, and Juanita, looking up at

126

just that moment, hastily applied herself to her drawing again. "It's all right, *querida,*" Cassandra said, using one of the few Spanish words she knew, and smiling. "I'm not angry with you." She pulled out a chair and sat across from them. "It's this room. 'Tis so gloomy, no wonder you never smile! But there, we'll do something about that. Look at it." She waved her hand. "Such a hideous color the walls are, that awful green, and they're dirty, too. And this table will have to go. It's much too big for you. I'll speak to the earl about it, shall I? And you can help me fix it up. Would you like that?"

Juanita gazed at her unblinkingly and then returned to her work. Cassandra sighed. This was going to be difficult. "I think we'll start by getting you some new clothes. Some new—" Her mind searched fruitlessly for the word. She would have to ask Nicholas to teach her Spanish. *"Nuevo* clothes." She indicated her own dress, and though she suspected the children didn't understand a word she was saying, Elena gifted her with a shy, sweet smile. It lifted Cassandra's spirits immeasurably. "Yes. New clothes. You need frocks you can play in without worrying about ruining them. I think we'll go to the village later and choose some fabric for you. As for the room. Elena, would you like to hang up your picture? Hang it up on the wall."

She reached for Elena's childish scribble of color upon color, and the child drew back, suddenly possessive. Oh dear. She had forgotten again how frightened they must be. "Like this, Elena." Rising, she crossed to the wall and pantomimed hanging a picture there. Both girls watched her solemnly, but suddenly Elena scrambled down, painting clutched in her fist, gabbling in a language all her own. With demanding arms she held the drawing up to Cassandra, her eyes, huge and liquid brown, pleading.

"Why, I think that's a fine idea, Elena. Let me just find

127

some tacks. Do you want to help? That's right, hold it in place." Cassandra pressed in the map tacks she had found and at last the picture hung, a little crooked and at child's height, but bright and cheerful. "Very good, Elena." She crouched, to bring herself more to the child's level, and searched her mind for the words. *"Muy bien."*

Elena smiled again, not shyly this time, but a genuine smile of happiness. *"Ojo,"* she said, poking a stubby finger at Cassandra's eye.

Cassandra drew back. *"¿Ojo?"*

"Ojo."

"Oh. Oh! Eye." She pointed to Elena's eyes. "Eye."

"Eye," Elena said, testing out the sound.

"¡Muy bien! Juanita?" Cassandra smiled up at Juanita, who was watching them warily, and pointed to her eye. *"¿Ojo?"*

Juanita seemed to be considering the matter. "Eye," she finally said.

"Oh, very good! I'm so pleased with you both."

"Señora." Juanita's voice was hesitant as she pointed to her own nose. *"¿Nariz?"*

"Nose," Cassandra said and patiently repeated it until the girls could say it on their own. In this way she took them through the features of the face, teaching them the English words and making a song of them, until everyone, even Juanita, was giggling.

"Muy bien. Very good," she said at last, leaning back against the wall. At some point she had sat down on the floor, and both girls had joined her there, their solemn faces alight. It was a start, Cassandra reflected. She might never win more than this, but at least now she knew she could teach them.

"Señora," Elena said, and to Cassandra's immense sur-

prise crawled up onto her lap, a heavy, but satisfying weight. *"Señora muy linda."*

There was a noise at the door, and Cassandra looked up, to see Nicholas standing there. She was suddenly acutely aware of her crumpled dress and the disarray of the room. "My lord," she said, gathering as much of her dignity as she could. "We were having an English lesson."

"Oh? Is that what you call this?" Nicholas sauntered into the room, his height making Cassandra feel at a distinct disadvantage. "You've made headway."

"Yes, some. Although we're far from understanding each other yet."

"Mm." Nicholas crouched down, and for one crazy moment Cassandra felt as if they were a family. *"Señora muy linda."*

Cassandra gave him a quizzical look. "That is what Elena said. What does it mean?"

"She said the lady is very pretty." He smiled. "She is."

"Oh, nonsense." Looking everywhere but at Nicholas, she sought for a diversion. "Elena." She indicated the drawing tacked to the wall, and instantly Elena, who had seemed nearly asleep a moment before, jumped up, gesturing excitedly toward her drawing. Nicholas let her grab his hand and pull him over to the wall, answering her with such seriousness that Cassandra felt her eyes sting. How good he was with children. He really should have a family of his own. Thank heavens, though, that she would be far away when that happened. She didn't think she could bear to see it.

Nicholas turned, after helping Juanita hang her drawing as well. "Is this how you plan to decorate this room, Cassie?"

Cassandra, standing now, concentrated on smoothing the wrinkles from her gown. "Actually, sir, we were discussing that very thing. At the least, the walls could use a coat of paint."

"So they could." Nicholas grimaced as he glanced about the room. "Dreary place, isn't it?"

"Indeed. I would also like to make the girls new frocks."

"Have the dressmaker do it. Have some made for yourself, while you're at it."

"No, my lord. I cannot. My gowns are perfectly suited for a governess."

"There was more to our arrangement than that, Cassie."

Cassandra straightened her spine. If he seriously thought she would help him find a suitable bride, he was in for a sad letdown. "My lord."

"Cassie. Haven't I asked you not to call me that?"

"Yes, you have," she said, after a moment spent struggling with herself. He was her employer. He was also more than that. "Very well, Captain."

"Cap-tain," Elena said, very clearly and very precisely. Nicholas and Cassandra looked at each other and laughed.

"I can see we'll have to be careful what we say around these two, Red."

Elena looked up at Cassandra. "Red?" she said.

"Roja," Nicholas explained.

"¿Roja?" Elena looked up at Cassandra and let out a giggle. *"¡Roja!"*

"Oh, lord. Now what have you taught them?"

"Your name, Red." He grinned at her. *"Muy linda Roja."*

"Oh, nonsense," she said again as the girls giggled, but her face was pink, with embarrassment, and, she admitted, delight. How radically her life had changed. Instead

130

of being desperately in need of work, she had found something that came perilously close to feeling like family. It wasn't, of course, and it certainly wouldn't last, but for now she would cherish it all. For now she was content.

That Nicholas intended to hold Cassandra to her other duty, that of teaching him proper behavior, became entirely too clear that afternoon. "You'll dine with me tonight," he said in a tone that brooked no argument when she and the girls encountered him after taking some exercise outside. "And don't wear one of those sacks you're always in. Wear that green thing you had on at the Lambs."

Cassandra protested at this high-handedness, but his answer was a stern, direct look that made her swallow her remaining words. Apparently when Nicholas made up his mind to something, there was no denying him. And so, here she was, standing just outside the door to the drawing room and smoothing down the skirt of her green muslin gown with damp, trembling fingers. Really, this was most irregular. What in the world could he want with her? Never mind the nonsense he had spoken in the nursery this morning; never mind that kiss at the inn, the kiss she couldn't seem to forget. She was no beauty. She was, instead, what she was suited to be, what fate had ordained for her. She was a woman who cared for other peoples' children. That she sometimes yearned for more, a husband who would love her, and children of her own, was beside the point. It was not to be. Nicholas was not for her. She must be much on her guard against such dreams and wishes.

Taking a deep breath, she reached for the handle of the door. Nicholas rose as she came into the room, and she dropped a brief curtsy, rising to see him looking at her assessingly. "You look very well, Red. But what did you do to your hair?"

Cassandra's hand flew to her hair and found nothing amiss. "Why nothing, Captain. It is the way I usually wear it."

He scowled. "That's what I mean. You should wear it loose."

"It wouldn't be suitable, sir."

"Suitable." He crossed the room to a table that held several decanters. "Is that another of your words?"

"I suppose it is, sir."

"First 'my lord,' now 'sir.' Sherry?" He held up a decanter.

She hesitated. What could one glass hurt? "Yes, thank you. And what else am I to call you?" she went on as he crossed to her, handing her a fine cut crystal goblet filled with amber fluid. "You are my employer."

"As you keep reminding me." He held his glass up in a brief salute as he sat, before drinking. "So I think it's about time you earned your keep."

"I thought I was, sir."

"What about the rest of our bargain, Cassie?"

"Oh dear."

He grinned. "So you haven't forgotten."

"No, but—"

"For example." He rose and strode to the fireplace, hands clasped behind his back, as if he still walked the quarterdeck. "Am I dressed properly for polite society?"

He was hoaxing her, she knew it, and yet Cassandra couldn't keep from studying him. There was nothing wrong with his ensemble, as well he knew. The coat of midnight blue superfine fit across his broad shoulders and back with enough ease for comfort, and enough closeness

132

for fashion. Clearly it had been fashioned by a master tailor. It also brought out the sea blue of his eyes, but she forced herself to ignore that. His linen, snowy white, was faultless, and if his neckcloth weren't tied intricately enough for a London ballroom, still it was acceptable. Then there were his pantaloons, biscuit colored and fitting quite closely to his thighs and calves. Lean, muscular legs, but she wouldn't allow herself to dwell on that, either. No, there was nothing wrong with his clothes. It was the man himself who was different. He was too alive, too vital for a fashionable drawing room, and that, she admitted, was what made him so attractive.

"You'll do," she said, staring into her sherry.

"Nothing you'd change? Not a fancier waistcoat, maybe, or higher shirt points?"

"No. You must know your clothing is quite acceptable."

"Thank you." His smile was wry. "I think."

Cassandra concentrated on her sherry, rather than look at him. Wretched man, couldn't he see how difficult this was for her? She opened her mouth to tell him so when the door opened and Kirby came in.

"Supper's ready, Cap'n," he said, and went out again without waiting for acknowledgment.

"Well." Nicholas held out his arm. "Cassie?"

"Thank you." Laying her fingers lightly on his arm and forcing herself not to notice the warm strength of it, she allowed him to lead her into the dining room.

The dining room was gloomy, though quite likely it had once been magnificent. Draperies of burgundy velvet hung at the windows, dusty now and shiny where the nap had rubbed off. The walls, painted a lighter red, were peeling in places, and the paintings were of quite explicit, and quite gory, hunting scenes. Not at all the kind of thing

133

to help one's appetite, Cassandra thought, stealing a glance at Nicholas. He was seated at the head of the table, while she was at his right, rather than at the foot. Such informality really wasn't proper, but for once Cassandra didn't give a fig for propriety. Her fingers still tingled where they had rested on his coat.

Kirby came in and set down bowls in such a slapdash manner that the soup sloshed over the rim. Nicholas caught Cassandra's frown just as he raised his spoon. "What?"

Cassandra lifted her own spoon. She knew better than to criticize Kirby, who seemed to have Nicholas's confidence. "You really should have more staff, Captain."

"Blast it." He laid down his spoon. "I know. But where do I start?"

"Ask Mrs. Feather for help. I'm sure she knows of local girls who would love positions here. Young men, too. You need footmen, you know."

"I know. And I've hired some, Cassie." He took a sip of wine, casting a furtive glance back at the door. "Trouble is, Kirby disapproved of them all."

"Kirby is not master here," she said, tartly. "Would you allow your ship to be run like this?"

"No, by Neptune, I wouldn't." Nicholas looked at her with new respect. "I'll see to hiring new staff tomorrow."

"Good." Cassandra at last took a sip of her soup, and found it cold and thin. "You might want to consider hiring a new cook first. And you really do need a proper butler."

"I know," he said, gloomily. "Kirby won't like it."

Cassandra laid down her spoon. Judging by the soup, the meal was not going to be appetizing. "Who is Kirby, sir?"

"He was my steward. Took care of everything for me,

meals, clothes, things like that." He paused. "He also saved my life."

Cassandra stared at him. "What? When?"

"During a battle." He smiled at her. "You don't want to hear about it, m'dear. Even I know it's not proper talk for polite company."

"Of course," Cassandra murmured, bringing her napkin to her face to hide her expression. In the past weeks she had grown so accustomed to thinking of Nicholas as an aristocrat that she'd forgotten what his life once had been like. She had forgotten the dangers he had faced, dangers that must have marked him in ways she couldn't even guess. No wonder he was so different from any man she'd known. That brought up a question. Did she really want him to change, to become polite and proper and polished?

"But, you see, this is just the kind of thing I need," he said. The enthusiasm in his voice grated against her misgivings. "You know what's needed to run a house. You knew the girls needed new clothes, things like that. Sort of thing a woman would notice. Guess I need a woman in the house."

"Then you should marry," she snapped.

"Aye. Aye." He pounded the table again with such enthusiasm that she regretted her hasty words. "I should. You'll help me there, too, Cassie?"

"We'll see." Cassandra's eyes were downcast, fixed on her soup, and so she didn't see the expression of satisfaction that crossed his face. She didn't like that idea at all. Good. Neither did he. True, he should marry. Someday. For now he couldn't imagine sitting this way with anyone but Cassie.

During dinner Cassandra hesitantly voiced her opinions on the dining room furnishings, and that gave him an idea. "Come take a look at the house," he said when they were through eating, taking her arm. "It's pretty bad. Maybe you can tell me how to fix it up."

"What have you had the builders working on?" she asked as they climbed the stairs to the floor where the family would have their private apartments.

"Roof, chimneys, dry rot. Things like that. Whole house was ready to fall down." He waved his hand in a gesture that encompassed more than just the corridor they were walking. "Place is like a ship that hasn't been seasoned properly." He stopped and opened a door. "The countess's rooms."

Cassandra stepped in, and stopped short. "Oh dear."

"Yes." Nicholas stepped in beside her. "What would you do in here?"

"I don't quite know," she said, looking around. The room was handsomely proportioned, square with a high ceiling and lovely long casement windows, but the furnishings were truly awful, old, heavy, and dark. Wardrobe, bed, dresser, all were massive; in addition, there were various chairs and tables scattered around, making the room seem cluttered. That nearly everything was red didn't help. There were red brocade draperies and a red coverlet on the bed, crimson damask wall coverings and Turkish carpet that was primarily scarlet. Worst of all was the enormous, gilt-framed painting of a nude of truly magnificent proportions, reclining on a red chaise longue. Cassandra took one look at that and glanced quickly away. "Oh dear," she said again. "Someone certainly liked red."

"Awful, isn't it?" Hands on hips, he surveyed the room. "Got to do something with it, Cassie. Place would give a person nightmares."

"Yes, I can see that."

136

"What colors would you suggest?"

"I?" she said in surprise, looking about the room again, and gave into temptation. If this were her house, her room . . . "Cool colors. Light colors, like blue and sea green and maybe a bit of peach. I'd get rid of all this furniture, and I'd put light muslin draperies at the windows. And pale walls."

"Done," Nicholas said, nodding his head once. "You'll take charge."

"What? I can't."

"You can." His eyes twinkled. "I dare you."

"Well, if you put it like that." She smiled at him, pleased with the idea. "Very well. As part of my job, mind."

"Of course. What, though, do we do with the painting?"

"You may have it in your room, if you wish."

Nicholas chuckled. "No, I don't wish. Tell you the truth, she intimidates me."

"Captain."

"Very well, Red. Feel up to taking on the rest of the house, too?"

"Why not?" she said, recklessly. After all, if she were going to pretend she was more to him than a servant, she might as well do it right.

"Good." He grinned. "One request. No red, especially in here." He grinned. "Clashes with your hair."

"As this isn't my room, that doesn't matter," she snapped, and went out. Nicholas, still grinning, followed, watching as she looked at the various guest rooms and gave her opinions. Aye, he wouldn't mind having Cassie in the countess's room. If he had to marry, he could do worse in his choice of a wife.

"Just one more thing I want to show you," he said.

They had returned downstairs, looked into his study, and proclaimed it usable, and declared the music room a disaster. "Here, in the bookroom. There's a secret door."

"Really?" Cassandra wandered in, slowly turning in circles and craning her head to take in all the shelves of books. "What a wonderful room. Dusty, but wonderful."

"Aye. It's back here." Nicholas reached up to a shelf at the back corner. "Third shelf, twelfth book in. There." He lifted the proper book and the shelf swung out, leaving a sizable opening.

Cassandra stepped through, into another room. "Oh. Oh!" She stepped back. "Good heavens."

Nicholas grimaced. "Sorry. Should have warned you about that. My uncle had strange tastes."

"So I see." She fled to the center of the bookroom, away from the next room and all it held. She had taken only one glance, but that had been enough, to see artwork that made the nude in the countess's room look innocent by comparison. In statues and paintings and tapestries, men and women cavorted in postures so abandoned that her cheeks burned just to think of it. "What is that room?"

"Called the Persian Room. Well, some of the pictures look Oriental. God knows where they came from." Nicholas grasped her elbow, leading her away. "I am sorry, my dear. I didn't think of it when I opened the secret door."

"Is there another way in?"

"Yes, from the hall, but we keep the door locked."

"I should hope so! Well. That will have to go."

"Cassie." He stopped. "Such fine works of art?"

"Pray do not tease. You cannot have a room like that, sir. Who else knows about it?"

He shrugged. "No one. The servants, probably."

Which meant that the entire neighborhood likely knew about it, too. Lowering thought. She could only imagine what they thought of it, and the earl. And, by association, herself. The circumstances of her being here were already extraordinary. This could only make matters worse. "Nicholas."

He turned. "Yes, m'dear?"

"Do you have any idea what people are saying about me?"

"It doesn't matter, Cassie."

She bit her lips, turning her head. He didn't understand. He never would. "Once you lose your good name—"

"You won't lose it over this. I promise you."

"People will think what they want."

"Aye. So why worry about it, Cassie?" He stood before her, his face grave. "Some people will never change their minds, no matter what you do. Doesn't it make sense to ignore them and get on with your life?"

"I was wrong." She peered up at him. "You do need to learn how to go on, Nicholas. Polite society never lets you forget a mistake."

"What mistake did you make, Cassie?"

"It doesn't matter. I dread to think what my reputation is now."

"Cassie. Look at me." His eyes were blue and sincere. "I promise you you'll come to no harm through me." He paused. "Do you trust me?"

There was something reassuring about the way he stood there, as if he had placed his solid bulk between her and the world. "Yes," she said, softly. "I do trust you."

"Good." He smiled, so that the corners of his eyes crinkled, making her heart turn over. Oh, he was a good man, and he was right. She could only live her life as best she could. Hiding her true self from the world hadn't saved her; nor had being proper. For now she would allow herself to listen to Nicholas. For now she would let herself feel safe, secure, protected, even though she knew it was an illusion. For now.

With new clothes to see to for the girls and fabrics to choose for the Hall, Cassandra finally persuaded herself to leave her newfound security. Thus she spent an enjoyable several hours the following morning at the linen draper's in the village, choosing sturdy broadcloth to make into new frocks for the little girls; striped satins for reupholstering sofas and brocades for draperies. She even succumbed to temptation and purchased several lengths of material for herself, blaming the impulse on Nicholas's command of the day before. The clerks were pleasant, treating her as they always had and not as if she were a fallen woman, and the other patrons, while curious as to her change in status, didn't snub her. Her fears of the evening before faded. Her reputation apparently was intact.

The sun at last broke through the clouds as she stepped out of the shop, eager to return to the Hall and tell Nicholas about her morning. Perhaps she would take the girls down to the beach for their outing today. Tugging on her gloves, she stepped out to cross the High Street, where the earl's carriage waited, and came face-to-face with Penelope.

Chapter 10

For a moment the two women stood, very still, staring at each other. It seemed curiously hushed in the street, as if all activity had ceased so that people could watch this encounter, until, with a little sniff, Penelope lifted her chin and turned away. Cassandra's hands clenched. She had been given the cut direct, and by a member of the gentry. Never mind that she and Penelope had never liked each other. The gentry were the ones whose opinions counted. They could make her life unpleasant if they chose. Well, let them! she thought, remembering the conversation of the evening before, and began to turn away herself, her head held high, when two small figures hurled themselves at her.

"Miss Aldrich!" Catherine caught Cassandra around the waist so hard that she rocked back, nearly losing her balance. "We've missed you. Why didn't you come to visit us?"

"Oh, Catherine. Mary." Cassandra gathered the two little girls close, feeling absurd tears prickle at her eyes. "I've missed you, too. How wonderful to see you again."

"You're not too busy for us?"

"No, of course not, whatever gave you that idea?"

"Mama said so. In fact, she said—"

"Don't tell her that, Cat," Mary put in.

"Why not? Mama said you'd be too busy with the earl to care about us anymore." Her eyes were wide and innocent. "I thought you were taking care of Juanita and Elena."

Caught between chagrin and amusement, Cassandra smiled. "I am. I've been teaching them English. They're very sweet. But I'll never forget you," she added, quickly.

"Miss Aldrich!" Beatrice and Amanda, just coming out of another shop, hurried over, their faces alight and their warmth going a long way toward easing the hurts Penelope had inflicted. Why Cassandra had expected anything else from her, she didn't know. Nicholas was right. Some people had narrow, closed minds.

"Beatrice, Amanda! We must go," Penelope called. "You know how Mama feels about mingling with unsuitable people."

"That's unfair!" Beatrice protested. "You know nothing happened between her and George, and I know that you—"

"Miss Beatrice, please," Cassandra murmured, embarrassed at having her private business proclaimed in the street. "It's all right."

Beatrice glared at her. "Well, I think what happened is awful, and I'm glad the earl gave you a position."

"Yes, and so romantic, too," Amanda chimed in. "Following you to the inn!"

"Yes, well, if you saw the mischief Juanita and Elena get into I'm not sure you'd think it romantic. They certainly needed someone to care for them."

"Then you won't be staying, once they're gone?" Catherine said, sounding subdued for once.

"No, Catherine." Cassandra smiled down at her. "I

142

fear not. Now." She disentangled herself from the girls' clinging hands. "I really must be getting back to the Hall, and you'll be late for your luncheon, too, if you don't hurry."

"You haven't changed." Beatrice smiled at her. "Still telling us what to do." She leaned forward suddenly and hugged Cassandra around the neck. "I'll come visit you, shall I?" she whispered in Cassandra's ear.

"I'd like that," Cassandra whispered back, and pulled away. "Now I really must be going."

"Beatrice!" Penelope's voice was sharper now as she turned from the carriage, where she had herded the twins, amid much protesting. "Come! We're leaving now."

Beatrice grimaced and pressed Cassandra's hand. "Don't let her bother you."

Cassandra smiled. "I won't, Beatrice," she said, and headed again for the carriage.

"Aldrich!" Penelope's voice was peremptory. "A word with you, if you please."

Cassandra's shoulders stiffened, and she turned, feeling at a distinct disadvantage in her old gray round gown and spencer. Penelope was as stylish as ever, in a walking dress of sky blue, with a Vandyke ruff at the neck and long, full sleeves. Upon her head sat the new Oldenburg bonnet, trimmed with a plume of feathers dyed to match. Cassandra had planned to order quiet, conservative clothes, but now decided she wanted a similar ensemble, except for the bonnet. It was too large for her small stature. "Yes, Miss Lamb?" she said, coolly.

Penelope's blue eyes burned with a strange fire, and her mouth was set, taking away much of her prettiness. "I will not have you accosting us on the street like this again. You are not our equal, and you'd do well to remember it."

"I wouldn't want to be your equal," Cassandra retorted.

"What, pray tell, is that supposed to mean?"

"I thank God every day that I'm not like you." Months of frustration, of having to swallow every slight, every insult, fueled her anger. She was making an enemy, but she didn't care. "You don't fool me, you know. I know why you're so opposed to me. You're jealous."

"Jealous!" Penelope gave a short, bitter laugh. "Of you? Don't be absurd. Why should I be jealous of you? You're plain. You have awful hair and terrible clothes and you'll never be more than a governess."

Cassandra's gaze was steady. "You're jealous because the earl has always preferred me over you."

"You little hussy." Penelope stared at her. "You schemed for this, didn't you? Well, if you think he'll marry you, you're sadly mistaken! No, when the time comes to choose a wife, he'll want someone suitable." Her smile was cool and smug. "He'll choose me."

"Not if I have anything to say about it."

"Don't interfere with me," Penelope said, sharply, "or you'll regret it."

"Penelope," Beatrice called from the carriage. "Are you ever coming?"

Penelope turned. "You can wait! And don't you forget what I've said." She stared hard at Cassandra. "I'll make you pay if you do anything against me."

Cassandra returned the look. "Good day, Miss Lamb," she said, and climbed into the carriage at last, effectively dismissing the other woman. As the carriage drove away she caught a glimpse of Penelope, her perfect features contorted with fury, and felt a fleeting sense of satisfaction. Very fleeting. She had learned firsthand how difficult Penelope could make her life when there had been only dislike between them. What would Penelope do now?

The carriage jounced over a rut in the road, making Cassandra reach out to grab the strap. She was shaking, she noticed dispassionately, looking at her hand. Surely she hadn't let Penelope upset her that much? Surely she had, though. What worried her most, however, wasn't the effect on herself. She had faced scandal before, and survived. No, it was Nicholas she was concerned about. By association with her, his reputation could very well be tarnished.

It wasn't fair! She gripped the strap tighter, angry now. Nicholas was a good man, and could do so much for the neighborhood. Already he'd put people to work repairing the Hall, and that very morning he'd told Mrs. Feather to begin interviewing staff. He was also knowledgeable and experienced, for all his protests to the contrary. He could provide leadership, a quality that had been sadly lacking in the neighborhood even before the old earl's death. Not, however, if he lost peoples' respect. Cassandra was already aware that Nicholas's unconventional ways had raised more than a few eyebrows, and that only his title had stilled any disapproval. Now, though, her presence in the Hall had added fuel to the gossip. Penelope had only voiced what most people were probably thinking: Cassandra was far more than a governess. Country people were by nature cautious and conservative. How long would they continue to respect a man who openly, or so it seemed, kept a mistress?

"Where is the earl, Kirby?" she asked as he opened the door of the Hall to her.

"Cap'n's down on the beach. But I wouldn't bother him if I was you." Kirby's face was wooden. In the past few days he'd made it abundantly clear that he didn't like her. Nor was he happy about the prospect of new staff. "He's in one of his black moods."

That made Cassandra stop on the drive, turning to face him. "I've never seen him in such a mood."

"No. He hides it." Kirby's eyes were sharp, much as Nicholas's sometimes were. "But he gets 'em, and you'd do well to stay away when he does."

"He won't mind seeing me."

Kirby snorted and stepped out on the drive. "You're as blind as all the others. Last thing the cap'n needs is a woman interfering. Look, he's not too easy to live with sometimes."

She frowned. "But I've always found him easygoing."

"Huh. You don't know him. But you're going to live here, you might as well know. He had the nightmare again last night."

"What nightmare?"

"Can't tell you that. Just you leave him alone."

"I wouldn't do anything to hurt him, Kirby," she said, and turned, walking away, ignoring the look of outrage on his face. Nicholas, having nightmares? How very strange, when he always seemed so even-tempered. But, she admitted, striding along, Kirby was right. She didn't know him, not as well as she would have liked. One thing she did know, though. She had to talk to him immediately. The longer she stayed at the Hall, the more seriously hurt he would be. She loved him too much to let that happen, even if leaving would destroy her.

Cassandra found him on the beach, standing at the edge of the waves and staring out to sea. There was a little frown between his eyes, and though the breeze ruffled his sun-streaked hair, he was motionless. He looked so handsome, and at the same time so distant, that her heart turned over. He had rescued her from unpleasant situations many times in the past. It was now her turn to help him.

"Captain," she called, and he turned. Instantly the frown disappeared from his brow and his eyes lightened, from dull, dark blue to azure.

"Cassie. Back from shopping already?" He grinned. "Didn't think I'd see you again for weeks."

Cassandra smiled in spite of herself, caught by his teasing. Oh, to have to leave this behind! How could she bear it? "I think you'll be pleased with my choices. Captain, there are some things I'd like to discuss with you—"

"Juanita and Elena were asking for you. They wanted to know where Roja was."

"Don't encourage them! That is a dreadful name."

"I like it." He looked at her more closely. "What is it, Red? You look upset about something."

"Oh no." She shook her head. This close to him she could see the signs of the mood Kirby had mentioned. His eyes were shadowed, his brow furrowed just a bit. The last thing she wished to do was add to his troubles. "I did meet the Lambs in the village."

"Penelope cut you?"

"Yes. How did you guess?"

"Sort of thing she would do. Don't worry, Red." He smiled. "I don't think most people here are so narrow-minded. And listen, Cassie. Last night we were talking of your other duties, remember?"

Cassandra's throat suddenly went dry. "Yes?"

"I want you to lock me up if I show any sign of proposing to Penelope."

That startled a laugh from her. "She'd love it if you did."

"Yes, but it's not me she wants, Cassie. It's the title." His gaze was suddenly serious. "You're not like that."

147

"Yes, well, that's beside the point."

"I'm not so sure." He gazed out to sea. "Things you said last night got me thinking."

"About what?"

"About people accepting a person, things like that." His feet shifted in the sand. "I'm important to everyone here because of my title." His voice was bitter. "And because I'm supposed to be a hero."

"I think you're being very hard on yourself, and unfair, too," she said, gently. "People are willing to like you, if you'll just give them a chance."

"You think so?" he said, skeptically. "I'll tell you something, Cassie. I feel all at sea here."

" 'Tis your home now, Captain."

"Such as it is." He laughed, without mirth. "My father always wanted me to stay on the land. Wonder what he'd think if he could see me now."

"Do you miss him?" she asked, wondering if this was the cause of his nightmare.

He shrugged. "Some, I suppose. He'd be the earl now, if he'd lived. We never got along. He was a country squire. Didn't know what to do with a son who wanted to go to sea. He thought I was a hellion." Again he smiled without humor. "Tell you the truth, I did everything I could to prove him right. Once, when we were in Bristol, I stowed away on a ship bound for India."

"You didn't!"

"Aye." His smile was real this time. "Caught holy hell for it, too, but it was worth it. All those years I watched the ships come and go, and I finally knew it was for me. My father never forgave me, though, for joining the navy."

"I'm sorry," Cassie said, after a moment spent absorbing this new picture of Nicholas. She, too, knew what it was like to feel like an outsider in one's own family. "I know what it's like. I used to dream of sailing, too."

He looked at her in some surprise. "Really?"

"Yes, always. My father took the Grand Tour when he was young, and he told me about it." Her eyes were soft. "I always wanted to go to Venice."

He smiled down at her. "Aye, you'd like it there." He shifted on the sand. "I'd sail for China. Be my own master."

"But you are."

"Not really. Not the way I wanted. See, I thought I'd go into the merchant trade. Own my own ship."

"Then you never would have come here," she said, and immediately realized how foolish she sounded.

"Aye, China," he went on, as if she hadn't spoken. "There's a fortune to be made on the seas, and adventure, too. Think of it, Cassie. Teas from China, tobacco and cotton from the Americas, sugar from the West Indies. Know what color the ocean is there? Turquoise. Crystal clear and calm and warm all the same. But that's the beauty of it, Cassie. The sea's the same wherever you go, and different. Different colors, different moods. She never bores you, and she never expects you to be what you're not. She demands the very best from you."

"And you miss it."

"Aye. Like the devil." He scuffed his toes in the sand. "Instead, I'm on the beach."

"You don't have to be."

He shrugged. "When I went to Portsmouth to try to catch Maidstone, there was a ship caught my eye. Remember you mentioned Baltimore clippers? Rig was different on this one, but she had the same sharp lines. Owner was considering selling. I almost bought her."

"Why didn't you? Surely you can afford to, now."

149

"Aye, and why not? I'm a rich man. I could own my own ship, skipper her without having to bow to any man. Aye." The smile faded from his eyes. "Except I have responsibilities here, Cassie."

"The old earl was rarely here," she argued. "Why can't you do what you want?"

"Look at the shape he left things in. No." His mouth tightened. "I'm stuck here."

He sounded so disconsolate that she couldn't resist. She slipped her hand through his arm, hoping the closeness would comfort him. "It isn't really so bad here, Nicholas."

"No." He looked down at her in some surprise. "It isn't. You've helped, Cassie."

"Have I? I'm glad." She couldn't leave. No matter what might be said about her, it was clearly her duty to stay at the Hall, at least until Nicholas found his feet. Without her, he would be so lonely.

"Aye." There was a peculiarly intent look in his eyes as he studied her face. "Do you know, Cassie, how much prettier you look with your hair loose like that?"

She took a step back. " 'Tis the wind. I assure you, it was neat a little while ago."

"I like it." He reached out to touch her cheek. *Pull back*, she warned herself, but she couldn't. There was something magnetic in his gaze, something that compelled her, and the touch of his calloused fingertips on her skin was somehow exciting and soothing at the same time. "Soft, so soft," he murmured. "You don't freckle, Red."

"No, I'm lucky that way. My lord—"

"I liked it better when you used my name." His lips hovered a mere breath from hers. "Say it."

"I can't."

"Say it, Cassie."

"Nicholas," she said, helpless to resist, and his head

150

lowered. Abruptly the danger she was in struck her, and she pulled back. She could not allow another kiss, not for her peace of mind. "Heavens! What is the time? The children will be wondering what has become of me."

"Cassie—"

"I really must go." Hastily she shoved her bonnet down onto her head and tied the strings into a knot she would later have to cut. "Good day, Captain."

"Cassie," Nicholas said as she walked away, and she stopped. "You won't leave."

"No." She gave him a quick smile. "I won't leave."

The drawing room at Lambton Manor, usually peaceful, resounded with the sound of a crashing chord. There. Penelope sat back on the stool in front of the pianoforte. She had finally, finally, played this newest sonata by Mr. Beethoven without an error. She had a long way to go before she perfected it, but she had at last mastered that tricky piece of fingering in the first movement. The rest now was a matter of hard work. This was something she could do, something she loved doing, almost more than anything else. She didn't have to look perfect to play the pianoforte; didn't have to have the right gown or shoes or jewelry. This was something that depended on her, her talent and her effort, and not her looks.

Flushed with accomplishment, she turned on the stool. "Mama, did you hear that? I finally did it!"

Mrs. Lamb, head bent over a piece of needlework, frowned. "I don't know why you must choose such a noisy piece of music, Penelope, and something no one can sing to. Why not practice that nice book of songs I ordered for you from town? I am persuaded the earl would sing, if you would only play for him."

"Oh, Mama. The earl told us he cannot carry a tune."

"He was being modest. You may be sure, Penelope, that there is no more charming sight than a young lady at the spinet, as long as she is playing something everyone may enjoy." Mrs. Lamb looked up, and her frown deepened. "Penelope, your hair is coming loose."

"Is it?" Penelope's hand flew to her chignon, to find that some strands had indeed worked their way free. But that didn't matter, couldn't Mama see that? This was what happened when she played, really played, losing herself in the music. One's looks didn't matter to a pianoforte. Only the skill of one's fingers.

"Really, Penelope, I despair of you," Mrs. Lamb went on, never once setting her needlework down. "The earl has been here now for weeks, and you have not yet made a push to attract him."

"I have, Mama. I've talked with him and smiled at him, just as you said—"

"But you have not brought him up to scratch, have you?" She sighed. "A London season, and terribly expensive that was, and not one proposal. And now, this."

Penelope looked down, biting the inside of her lip. Failure was sour in her mouth. "I tried, Mama. I really did."

"You did not try hard enough. Penelope, with your looks, you should be able to choose anyone you desire. I do not know why you haven't."

"I'm sorry, Mama." But she had tried. She didn't know why all of her suitors in London had gradually drifted away, to other, less attractive girls. Hadn't she always dressed in her best clothes, worn her hair in the most flattering way, smiled her prettiest smile? She had taken, she knew that. She had been a success, even if the name they had given her, the Ice Princess, still hurt. She had

152

TAKE ADVANTAGE OF THIS SPECIAL OFFER, AVAILABLE *ONLY* TO ZEBRA REGENCY ROMANCE READERS.

You are a reader who enjoys the very special kind of love story that can only be found in Zebra Regency Romances. You adore the fashionable English settings, the sparkling wit, the captivating intrigue, and the heart-stirring romance that are the hallmarks of each Zebra Regency Romance novel.

Now, you can have these delightful novels delivered right to your door each month and never have to worry about missing a new book. Zebra has made arrangements through its Home Subscription Service for you to preview the three latest Zebra Regency Romances as soon as they are published.

3 **FREE** REGENCIES TO GET STARTED!

To get your subscription started, we will send your first 3 books ABSOLUTELY FREE, as our introductory gift to you. NO OBLIGATION. We're sure that you will enjoy these books so much that you will want to read more of the very best romantic fiction published today.

SUBSCRIBERS SAVE EACH MONTH

Zebra Regency Home Subscribers will save money each month as they enjoy their latest Regencies. As a subscriber you will receive the 3 newest titles to preview FREE for ten days. Each shipment will be at least a $11.97 value (publisher's price). But home subscribers will be billed only $9.90 for all three books. You'll save over $2.00 each month. Of course, if you're not satisfied with any book, just return it for full credit.

FREE HOME DELIVERY

Zebra Home Subscribers get free home delivery. There are never any postage, shipping or handling charges. No hidden charges. What's more, there is no minimum number to buy and you can cancel your subscription at any time. No obligation and no questions asked.

TO GET YOUR 3 FREE BOOKS
ILL OUT AND MAIL THE COUPON BELOW

3 FREE BOOKS

Mail to: Zebra Regency Home Subscription Service
120 Brighton Road
P.O. Box 5214
Clifton, New Jersey 07015-5214

YES! Start my Regency Romance Home Subscription and send me my 3 FREE BOOKS as my introductory gift. Then each month, I'll receive the 3 newest Zebra Regency Romances to preview FREE for ten days. I understand that if I'm not satisfied, I may return them and owe nothing. Otherwise, I'll pay the low members' price of just $9.90 for all 3 books and save over $2.00 off the publisher's price (a $11.97 value). There are no shipping, handling or other hidden charges. I may cancel my subscription at any time and there is no minimum number to buy. In any case, the 3 FREE books are mine to keep regardless of what I decide.

RG0294

NAME

ADDRESS   APT NO.

CITY   STATE   ZIP

TELEPHONE
(   )

SIGNATURE   (if under 18 parent or guardian must sign)

Terms and prices subject to change. Orders subject to acceptance by Zebra Home Subscription Service, Inc.

GET
3 FREE
REGENCY
ROMANCE
NOVELS—
A $11.97
VALUE!

ZEBRA HOME SUBSCRIPTION SERVICE, INC.
120 BRIGHTON ROAD
P.O. BOX 5214
CLIFTON, NEW JERSEY 07015-5214

done something wrong, and she didn't know what. The worst part of it was, it was happening all over again. By all rights, the earl should have taken one look at her and been instantly enamored. Instead, he seemed hardly to know she existed.

"You have been groomed for this, Penelope." Mrs. Lamb held up two strands of silk, comparing the shades, and finally settled on one. "We have made certain you have all the accomplishments of a young lady, and that you are fashionable. You are our hope. You must make a good match."

Penelope stared fixedly at the floor. "Yes, Mama."

"You must make a firm effort to attach the earl."

At that, she at last looked up. "How can I, with that dreadful Aldrich living in his house?"

"Aldrich! Do not mention that name in this house! No." Mrs. Lamb's voice moderated. "She is much to blame, of course, but I am persuaded the earl wouldn't even have noticed her if you had done as you ought."

"Mama, I did all I could!"

"Did you?" Mrs. Lamb subjected her to the same cold scrutiny she had often given Cassandra. "You are very beautiful, Penelope. You have been since you were a child. However, you have not lived up to our expectations."

"No, Mama." Again, she bit the inside of her lip. It had been so much easier when she was a child, when it had been enough to be her father's darling, as bright as a new penny. When had it changed? Papa hardly talked to her anymore, and Mama harped constantly on her failures. The only thing certain in her life was her music.

Turning on the stool, she sought out more music, a piece by Mozart that invariably soothed her. She had just begun to play the first notes when her mother's voice interrupted her. "Penelope! I am still speaking to you."

Penelope's hands hovered for a moment over the keys, and then fell into her lap. "Yes, Mama?"

"You must attach the earl. Otherwise, I shall be very disappointed in you."

"Yes, Mama." At last she began to play, but the music gave her no solace. Her duty was clear. She had to capture the earl, for herself, and for her parents. She had to. And nothing, nothing, would get in her way.

Chapter 11

Life quickly settled into a pattern for Cassandra. She spent most of her days with the children, and was gratified to see them bloom under her tutelage. Elena, with all of a child's trust, wholeheartedly gave herself to Cassandra's care, following her around the house and clambering up onto her lap whenever Cassandra sat down. Juanita, more wary, was also more reticent, but she, too, was livelier and happier. Both girls showed a marked improvement in speaking English, while Cassandra was learning more and more Spanish. Here, she was content.

In other ways, however, her life wasn't so easy. The neighbors were cool, a result of the scandal, and that hurt. Worse than that, though, was Nicholas, and her reaction to him. Since that day on the beach she had managed to keep her distance from him. In her dreams, in unguarded memory, she relived again and again those few stolen moments when the attraction between them had been as fragile and as strong as silk thread, and as tangible, binding her to him, him to her. Again and again she wondered just what would have happened had she not pulled away; again and again, she decided she had done the right thing. Long ago she had learned that a kiss was not worth all the heartache it could cause. Not even a kiss from Nicholas, something she'd long dreamed about. In her less sane moments she regretted pulling back from him, wondering what it would be like if he really kissed her, remembering the brief kiss at the inn, and her reaction to it. When she was more herself, however, she was quite aware of the fine line she walked, and of the danger she faced. There must never be a repetition of that incident on the beach, no matter how much she might wish it. He was not for her. She would do well to remember that.

One day in late spring, after traveling to Dover for several days to meet an old friend, Nicholas bounded into the day nursery, where Cassandra was endeavoring to teach the girls their numbers. His vitality and enthusiasm brought a freshness into the room, and made him appear almost a boy. There was nothing boyish, however, about the lean planes of his face, the broad set of his shoulders. He was very much a man. Nor was there anything the least bit childish in her response to him. Unbidden the memory of that afternoon on the beach, when they had come perilously close to an embrace, returned. Cassandra felt her face turn red.

Nicholas sent her a quizzical look as he sat, and both girls clambered onto his lap, talking excitedly. "Well, *mi niñas,*" he said, hugging them. "*¿Como está?* Have you been behaving for Roja?"

"They've been very good girls," Cassandra said. "You're back earlier than I expected."

Elena, with the restlessness of childhood, had already climbed down and was waving her latest drawing, a scribble of color, in his face, while Juanita, apparently content, leaned against him. "Dover was damned—excuse me—dashed crowded. Everyone's there to see the sovereigns."

"Well, can you blame them?" Everyone in the vicinity

was excited about the imminent arrival of the Allied Sovereigns, the leaders of the countries which had banded together to defeat Napoleon. Besides Czar Alexander of Russia, King Frederick William of Prussia and Count Von Metternich of Austria were due to land soon at Dover, to begin a long visit to England. "It would be exciting to see them."

"Do you want to go?"

"Heavens, no. The girls are too young to travel such a distance, and I'd rather not leave them now." She smiled at Juanita, who was rooting inside Nicholas's waistcoat and had pulled out his pocket watch. "How did you find your friend?"

"Busy." He grinned. "Samuel's finding life ashore hard, especially working in the Admiralty. Truth to tell, we didn't have much chance to talk, he had so much to do to prepare for the visit."

"You should invite him here."

"Aye." He smiled down at Juanita. "That's a watch, *niña*, to tell the time. Not as accurate as a chronometer, but it will do." He opened the case, showing its inner workings to her. "Don't know what a chronometer is, eh? Well, it's a special clock, kept always to Greenwich Time. Use it to find latitude at sea. Actually, latitude's easy enough." He leaned back, and Juanita settled against him. "Ship's clock is set to local time, so by comparing it with the chronometer, you can find your latitude. Longitude's trickier. Have to shoot the stars for that."

Juanita looked up, her soft brown eyes huge. "Shoot stars? Bang?"

"No, not quite like that. With a sextant. It's shaped like this"—he indicated a roughly triangular shape—"and it has a mirror in its base—never mind, I'll show you one sometime. Here. Play with this."

"She's likely to break it," Cassandra murmured as he handed the child his watch. She had been vastly amused, and touched, by his little dissertation on navigation.

"Doesn't matter. Only a watch." His eyes darkened to slate. "Crew of one of my ships gave it to me."

"What? Then you really should take better care of it. It must mean a great deal to you."

"It means nothing," he said, flatly, and then his face softened. "She looks heavy. Aren't your arms tired?"

Cassandra shook her head. Elena had settled onto her lap, her thumb tucked securely in her mouth and her eyelids drooping. Her warm weight was oddly comforting. "No, I'm fine. And you're a fine one to talk."

"Aye." Nicholas glanced down. Juanita still had a grasp on the watch, her fingers playing with the chain, but she, too, looked drowsy. *"Pobrecita* Juanita," he said, laying his hand briefly on her head, and Juanita turned to give him a sweet, broad smile. Then, apparently feeling secure and cherished, she turned in his arms, her head butting under his chin.

Cassandra felt tears prickle at her eyes. "You're good with her."

"Not that hard." He looked down at the child and then back at Cassandra, and for a moment their eyes held. Odd, how cozy and right this felt, as if they were more than employer and governess. As if they were a family. A dangerous fantasy, but an appealing one.

"I should put them down for their naps," Cassandra said, her voice brisk.

"Aye. I'll carry her in for you. She's heavy, for such a little mite."

"Children are, when they sleep." She brushed her lips lightly over Elena's head, and then rose.

"You'd make a good mother, Cassie," Nicholas said, softly, following her into the night nursery.

"And you'd be a good father," she retorted.

"Aye. I would." He looked entirely serious, except for the twinkle in his eyes. "I'll have to think about marrying. You're supposed to help me find someone, remember?"

"You'll do well enough on your own."

"Just think. I could choose someone like Penelope—"

"No! I mean, you'd have more sense."

"Aye." The twinkle grew more pronounced. "You wouldn't be jealous, would you, Cassie?"

"Don't be silly," she said, not looking at him. The thought of his marrying someone else caused a peculiar ache in her heart; the image of him holding the woman's children, *his* children, caused that ache to increase in strength until it pressed at her eyes, making her want to cry. "I'm not jealous. Shh, *angel*." This to Elena, who had wakened when Cassandra put her on her bed, and was whimpering. "Sleep, now."

"Cassie, just one thing," he said, as they stepped back into the schoolroom.

Cassandra looked up from clearing off the table to see him tugging at his neckcloth, a sure sign that he was nervous about something. "Yes?"

"I invited Samuel—Captain Fairleigh—to the Hall when the visit is over. End of June, or thereabouts." He paused, clearing his throat. "Said he'll bring his mother and sister, and maybe some friends."

"Oh, Nicholas!" Cassandra set the books down with a thud. "A house party?"

"Well, er, yes."

"But the Hall isn't nearly ready for guests—"

"Builders are nearly done, and you've got the fabrics ordered, haven't you?"

"Yes, but—"

"We'll get it done."

"You mean I'll get it done. Oh, very well. I did promise." She busied herself with the schoolbooks again, so that she wouldn't have to look at him. Why did he have to look so appealing, standing there, smiling like a hopeful little boy? "Go away, Nicholas," she said, crossly. "I've things to do."

"There's one more thing, Cassie."

She looked up. "Now what?"

"I, er, need a hostess."

"No! Nicholas, absolutely not! What will people think of me?"

"Actually, I was thinking of Penelope."

"What!"

"Gammoning you, Red," he said. "Seriously, I do need a hostess."

"No." Her back was rigid. "You presume a great deal, my lord."

"Uh-oh." His eyes twinkled. "I've got you mad, haven't I, Red?"

"This isn't funny." She swept across the room and flung the door open. "I will oversee preparations for you, my lord, and I will make sure all runs smoothly, but nothing else. This is your idea. You'll have to manage by yourself."

"That's your final word, Cassie?"

"Yes. Now, please go, before you disturb the children."

"Well, I can't force you." He crossed to the door, grinning down at her. "I'll see you at dinner, Red."

"Good afternoon, my lord," Cassandra said, and, after one last look, he ambled out of the room.

Nicholas stood still in the hall for a moment, grinning at the door that she might as well have slammed, so quietly and firmly had she closed it. Cassie with her temper up was something to see, with color in her cheeks and a sparkle in her eyes. He liked it. Made her look prettier. In the weeks to come, likely he'd have more chances to annoy her, just to see her looking like that. Because, he thought, turning away and walking down the hall, if she thought he'd let her sit tamely in the background during the house party, she was mistaken. Cassie was going to be a part of his life.

Cassandra spent the next month in a state of hectic activity, overseeing renovations to guest rooms and staterooms, supervising staff, planning menus and activities. Nicholas casually informed her at dinner one night that Samuel Fairleigh was bringing some friends, a viscount, he couldn't remember the name, and some duke and duchess, Bainbridge, he thought. Cassandra's jaw dropped at that. Three members of the nobility in the house, and he saw fit to tell her only a week before the guests were expected? She was extremely cross with him over that, but he seemed only amused, the blasted man. And, there, she was picking up his language. If she weren't careful he'd corrupt her totally.

The work got done, of course. She still had her duties as governess, but those she minded not in the least. The children's ability to speak English was expanding rapidly, and both little girls were now open, affectionate, and demanding of her time. Most mornings found her facing work that completely filled her day; most nights she dropped exhausted into bed. She had never been happier in her life.

Nicholas, in the meantime, bought a ship.

Since that day on the beach with Cassandra, the day

after he had had the nightmare and had felt again the old despair, he hadn't been able to stop thinking about their conversation. Why not buy a ship, she had said, as if it were that easy. It wasn't, of course, and so he had told himself, but once the idea was planted it grew. Why not? He wouldn't be able to skipper it, but he could still own one, keep in touch with his dreams in that way. Maybe take a cruise on her someday, too. Aye. Why not buy a ship?

To that end, he traveled to Portsmouth, to see again what might be available. To his delight, the ship he had seen in the harbor over a month ago, the *Eagle*, was still in port, abandoned except for a watchman. Criminal waste, he thought, sweeping his eyes over the ship, even if the merchant trade was a hazardous and expensive business these days, with the American privateers roaming everywhere. With a ship like this, though, he would be able to outrun anyone. She wasn't, as he'd told Cassie, a Baltimore clipper; she was bigger, square-rigged, a three-masted brig, rather than a schooner. She had, however, the sharp lines of an American ship, and, he'd judge, decent cargo space. Better for what he had in mind than a clipper. A ship like this could go anywhere in the world.

After speaking with the watchman, he found the owner, a Captain Talbot, in a nearby tavern. Talbot was a large, unkempt man, in need of a shave and with a bitter twist to his lips. Aye, the *Eagle* was his, and a more cursed ship he'd never seen. Bought it in Jamaica, he had. It had been a prize captured by a British man of war, and later condemned for sale. After seeing the way the Yankees sailed their ships, Talbot had decided he wanted one. However, the damned thing didn't sail right. He couldn't get the speed out of her, and twice he'd nearly been overtaken by privateers. Talbot spat, tobacco juice arcing in a long stream toward a spittoon. Wasn't worth it anymore, not with the dangers and the cost of insurance. He was sorry he'd ever lain eyes on the cursed vessel.

Nicholas leaned back, nursing along his tankard of ale, his face pleasant but giving nothing away. He doubted the *Eagle* was cursed. If there were problems, the damned fool had brought them on himself. He'd noticed that there had been changes to the running rigging, and that heavy railings had been added topside. No wonder Talbot couldn't get the speed out of her the Yankees did. Nicholas was willing to concede that the Americans knew how to sail their ships, as well as build them, and that most British seamen couldn't do as well. He, however, was willing to try.

An hour later, after some earnest bargaining, Nicholas walked out of the tavern with the ownership papers in his hand. Talbot was so desperate to unload the ship that Nicholas had been able to bargain him down to a ridiculous price. He was now owner, and master, of the *Eagle*, and a better purchase he'd never made. He felt it in his bones.

Sending a note home, he took a room at the George Inn, and set about finding a skeleton crew to man his new ship. She'd need work, before going back to sea. Those railings would have to go, for one thing, and she needed new sails. He had no trouble finding a crew; the seamen he talked to were only too happy to sign on, if only to escape being impressed into the navy. Thus, several days after he'd made his purchase, he was on the deck of *Eagle*, steering her toward Newhaven, near to home, where the work would be done. He was at sea again, even if only for a little while. He was content.

At the Hall, he found when he arrived home, after several days spent supervising the repairs, everything was ready. The guests would be arriving sometime that day, which meant that Cassandra's work was done. She intended to devote the next two weeks to the children.

"But won't you be down for dinner?" Nicholas said. He'd missed her in the days of his absence, and he was bursting to share his news with her.

She turned at the door of his study. He had that helpless look on his face again, the one that had drawn her into doing so much work. She steeled herself against it. "We've discussed this, Captain. It's not proper for me to act as your hostess."

"I'm not asking you to. You always come down for dinner."

"The guests won't know that."

"So I'll tell them."

"And what will they think?"

"You care too much what people think."

"It matters, Captain."

"All right. What will people think about uneven numbers at the table?"

"Hardly an earth-shattering problem. Now, if you'll excuse me—"

"Blast it, Cassie!" He rose and came around his desk to her. "I need you there. Please?" he added, as she hesitated. "I've never been a host before."

"What about aboard ship?"

"Doesn't count." He paused. "Please?"

There it was, that helpless look again. "Oh, very well. But just tonight, Captain."

"Just tonight," he agreed.

So it was that, that evening, Cassandra donned her green muslin gown and styled her hair as she had in the past, with one curl over her shoulder. Not the first stare of fashion, she thought, gazing at her reflection, but it would do. After all, she was only the governess. Silly to feel so nervous. She had dined in exalted company before, if a long time ago, and she knew how to behave. Besides, it was just for tonight. After this, she need have little contact with the guests.

All the guests had arrived that afternoon, and had been shown to their rooms. Now, Cassandra was informed by the new butler, Hargreaves, nearly all were assembled in the drawing room. Cassandra thanked him, and went in.

The drawing room was the first room she had redecorated, knowing Nicholas would be using it for entertaining. Glancing around, she was pleased with the results. She had chosen a pale yellow damask for the walls, with creamy white paint for the plaster medallions and moldings. The color harmonized with the dark rose satin-striped sofa and the mahogany tables, which shone with beeswax and long hours of polishing. With much of the old furniture removed to the attics, the Turkish carpet at last showed to advantage. Outside the French windows, framed by gold draperies, the garden bloomed in the mellow light of late evening. Everything looked very well, she saw in that quick housewifely glance, and let Nicholas lead her to the guests, to be introduced.

Captain Fairleigh, Nicholas's friend, bowed over her hand and presented her to his mother, Harriet, a small, plump woman with alert, lively eyes, and his sister, Daphne, who had just made her come-out. The Duke of Bainbridge was a tall, handsome man, though Cassandra found his looks a shade too arrogant for her taste; his duchess was surprisingly young, very pretty, and rather pale. Both were dressed in mourning, as the duke's grandmother had passed on in the spring. Cassandra expressed her condolences and accepted a glass of sherry from Nicholas, feeling herself relax. There was no one high in the instep in this group. She would brush through fine. Of course, she didn't know about the missing guest, the viscount whose name Nicholas kept forgetting, but, since he was a friend of the Fairleighs, he was probably quite as amiable. She had nothing to fear.

The door to the drawing room opened. "The Viscount Byrne," Hargreaves announced, and Cassandra's glass shattered as she spun around to face the new arrival. It couldn't be, but it was. Basil Mayhew, Viscount Byrne. The one man in the world who could ruin her.

Chapter 12

He stood in the doorway for a moment, quizzing glass raised, studying the group, very much the dandy in his immaculate linen, high shirt points, and richly embroidered satin waistcoat. He was darkly handsome, in the Byronic mold, with a lock of hair falling strategically over his brow and a world-weary air that had attracted many a woman. He had also, Cassandra realized with a sinking heart, seen her, his eye looking greatly magnified and distorted through the lens of his glass. It was a nightmare come true. She had hoped, no, prayed, that she would never see him again.

"Cassie." Nicholas stepped before her, blocking Basil from view, and she looked dumbly up at him. "You've cut yourself."

"What?" She looked down at her hand, and noticed with odd detachment that it was bleeding. Strange. She had snapped the stem of her crystal goblet without realizing it. "So I am. How clumsy of me."

"Oh dear, that could be nasty." Harriet Fairleigh bustled over, holding out her handkerchief for Nicholas to wrap around Cassandra's fingers. "You should have that attended to. However did you do such a thing, my dear?"

"I—was startled. What a silly thing to do." She let Nicholas take the remains of the goblet from her; let him wrap the handkerchief around her hand. "I think I will have this seen to. If you'll excuse me."

"Cassie," Nicholas said, very low, but she ignored him and fled.

Sometime later Cassandra sat at her dressing table, staring blankly at her reflection. Her bandaged hand throbbed a bit, but she paid it no heed. Her green muslin gown was stained, perhaps beyond repair, with sherry and blood, and she had had to change. For once she was grateful that Nicholas had insisted she buy new clothes; she was now wearing a respectable gown of gray silk. It was far more suitable for a governess. Why she had ever aspired to anything more, she didn't know.

There was a knock on the door, and Nicholas stepped into the room before she could protest. "We're waiting dinner for you," he said, dropping into a chair facing her.

Cassandra put her injured hand in her lap, shielding it from his gaze. "I think you should go on without me. I don't quite feel up to dinner."

Nicholas reached over for her hand. "What happened, Cassie?" he said, softly.

"I—don't know. I didn't even realize I'd broken the glass." She laughed a little, though her eyes didn't meet his. "Silly of me."

"Mm. You're very pale."

"Yes, I know. It was the strangest thing," she said, suddenly voluble. "I never faint—I detest being such a poor honey—but I felt all over strange when I turned. Perhaps I turned too fast, the way you do when you're a child? To get dizzy? I did feel dizzy for just a moment. Perhaps I'm sickening for something."

He caught her chin in his hand, forcing her to face him. "Something has upset you. Tell me what it is."

"Nothing, Captain." She met that direct blue gaze without blinking. He, of all people, must never know. "I knew Viscount Byrne once, did you know that? Heavens knows what he must be thinking of me! I do not ordinarily act like such a peagoose. You are right. I really should go downstairs." She rose, pulling back from his hand. "Cook has prepared a splendid dinner, I should know, I made up the menu, and she'll be upset if it spoils. I should—"

"Cassie." He laid his finger on her lips, and she stilled. "Have I ever failed you?"

This was difficult. Oh, it was difficult. "No, Nicholas."

"Then tell me what has upset you and let me help."

"There's nothing wrong." She met his gaze straightly. "I promise."

"Hm." The look he gave her was hard, but she kept her head up. "Very well," he said at last. "I'll see you down."

"Thank you, sir," she said, and laid her hand on his arm.

Everyone was still assembled in the drawing room. Mrs. Fairleigh, whom Cassandra already liked, came over and fussed over Cassandra's hand, while the duchess inquired after her with real concern in her voice. Such nice people, Cassandra thought, squaring her shoulders and raising her head as Viscount Byrne crossed the room to her.

"Cassandra." He took her uninjured hand in his and bent over it. Cassandra was suddenly glad she was wearing a high-necked gown. "A pleasant surprise to see you here."

"Yes, it was a surprise, my lord."

"So formal, Cassandra?" He raised an eyebrow at her,

a trick she had once found devastatingly attractive. "When once we were such good friends?"

"But I am a governess now, my lord." Smiling, she slipped her hand from his. Only Nicholas noticed her wiping her palm against her skirt. "I can hardly address you by name."

"Ah yes, a governess." He glanced from her to Nicholas, and her hand clenched. No one else had commented on her presence; no one else had made any innuendo. "The last occupation I would have expected for you, Cassandra."

"One must live, my lord. I do apologize to everyone for delaying dinner," she said, stepping away from him. "You must be ravenous."

A chorus of protests greeted that, but Nicholas nodded his head at her. "Best we go in to eat," he said. "I have it on good authority that Cook will be upset if we don't. Ma'am?"

The Duchess of Bainbridge looked up at him and smiled. "That would be disastrous, wouldn't it?" she said, laying her hand on his arm and allowing him to lead her, the highest-ranking lady present, into dinner. The others fell in, leaving Cassandra to be paired with Captain Fairleigh, a distinct relief. Never before had she been so grateful for her lack of rank. After tonight she wouldn't face this problem again. She intended to stay as far away from the house party as possible.

Since there were only eight at table, dinner was informal. Nicholas had had the good sense to place Harriet Fairleigh at the foot of the table, rather than Cassandra. To her further relief, Basil was diagonally across from her, and the centerpiece hid her from his direct view. If she hadn't known better, she would have thought Nicholas had arranged this, though he was not normally so socially adept. Still, he seemed to be doing well enough, she thought, looking up quickly from her soup to see him talking with the duchess, to his right. It was just as well he'd started his excursion into social life with such a small, congenial group.

Throughout dinner the conversation was relaxed and comfortable. Cassandra listened with only half her attention to talk that would have interested her greatly at other times. The Duke of Bainbridge was in the Foreign Office and would probably be attending the peace congress, planned for later in the year at Vienna. He had a country house, of course, but he had liked the idea of spending some time by the sea. This was said with a glance toward his wife, who only smiled in reply. She, surprisingly, was American, and, with that country's informality, insisted people call her by name, Sabrina.

Harriet, too, talked comfortably of enjoying the sea, though she never had quite understood her son's attraction to it, while Miss Fairleigh, very quiet and shy for a girl who had had her come-out, stole occasional glances at Basil. She was, apparently, attracted to him. That last worried Cassandra, thought she didn't know quite what she could do about it.

Of all, however, it was Samuel Fairleigh who told the most interesting stories. As a liaison between the Admiralty and the staffs of the visiting sovereigns, he had witnessed firsthand the events in London over the past month. He described with zest all the activities, and the Prince Regent's futile attempts to entertain his guests. Futile, because Czar Alexander had turned supercilious and refused to stay at Carlton House, Prinny's residence, in favor of the Pulteney Hotel, where his sister, the Grand Duchess of Oldenburg, was already ensconced. There he had been greeted by an admiring crowd daily, whenever he stepped out. When he had at last consented to meet with his host, he had lectured Prinny on the merits of liberal government. Adding insult to injury, the grand duchess had insisted on attending a dinner given at the Guildhall in the City, that bastion of commerce, though such an event was traditionally for men only. She had compounded her offense by protesting when the national anthem was sung, saying she detested music. This prompted one disgruntled observer to mutter that if people didn't know how to behave, they should stay home.

Finally, the crowning moment of the visit had come at the opera, at Covent Garden. Prinny had taken his seat in the royal box and the house lights had just gone down, when who should walk in but Prinny's estranged wife, Princess Caroline. Instantly the audience had risen and cheered. The Princess, while no innocent, had become the darling of the Whigs, the opposition party, and was far more popular than her husband. To his credit, Samuel said, chuckling at the memory, Prinny carried it off well, rising and bowing as if the applause were meant for him. All in all, it had been a memorable visit, and the victory celebrations, planned for next month, promised to be entertaining.

"You should come up to town for them, Nick," Samuel said. "See something of England, now you're on the beach."

Nicholas glanced at Cassandra before answering. "Maybe. Right now there are things enough here for me to see to. Being ashore is hard enough to adjust to, without facing London. Besides," his face shone, "I've just bought a ship."

Samuel leaned over the table. "A trader? By God, Nick—excuse me, ladies—I envy you that. Tell me about her—"

"Now, Samuel," Harriet said from the foot of the table. "Please let's not talk of ships at table. Tell me, Miss Aldrich. Have you ever been to town?"

Cassandra looked up warily from the sweet, a trifle, for which she had no appetite. "Yes, but not for many years."

"Miss Aldrich and I were acquainted," Basil drawled, one of his few contributions to the conversation. "When she had her season."

"Yes," Nicholas said, giving Cassandra a glance, before turning back to the guests. "Been thinking of things for you to do. Can't exactly compete with London, but we're not completely dull."

"Actually, I'll be glad of the rest," Harriet said. "And the chance to work in a garden again. If you don't mind, sir?"

"Not at all. Cassie, you'll arrange it with the gardener?"

"Of course," Cassandra murmured, feeling everyone's eyes on her for just a moment. What must they think of her, when tonight Nicholas had made it so clear that she was more than a governess in this house? She doubted, though, that anyone would believe in the essential innocence of the friendship.

"The village is small, but worth a visit," Nicholas went on. "I also have a boat, if anyone's interested. No?" This was said with a smile at Daphne, who had made a face. "Well, one of my neighbors has offered the use of his stables, for anyone who wishes to ride. Afraid I haven't got around to that myself."

"Are there many neighbors, sir?" Harriet asked.

"Aye, and some good people, too. Don't doubt we'll all be invited to tea and such. Also, I was thinking of having some entertainments here. Dinner, certainly, and maybe a ball."

"A ball!" In spite of herself Cassandra stared at him. This was the first she'd heard of this idea. "When were you thinking of having that?"

"Next week, sometime. You'll know what to do, Cassie."

"Oh yes, my lord." And she'd give him a piece of her mind when she got him in private! She could feel her face burning. How dare he put her in such a position?

"Dare I assume you mean to make Miss Aldrich work all this time, Lynton?" Basil said lazily, lounging back and peeling an orange with an exquisitely manicured thumbnail.

"Of course not," Nicholas said. "Just that I don't know anything about arranging balls and such."

"And I am in service here," Cassandra murmured, causing Nicholas to give her a swift, puzzled look.

"I protest, Lynton!" Basil set down the orange. "To make Miss Aldrich work while the rest of us enjoy ourselves? It's hardly fair, man." He leaned back so that he could see Cassandra around the centerpiece. "You used to enjoy society, Cassandra. Surely you haven't changed that much."

"I have duties, sir."

"Surely Lynton would release you from them. Just for the fortnight."

"If it's what you want, Cassie," Nicholas began.

"No, it isn't!" She glared at him. She would not, would not! let him coerce her into joining this house party. "What about Juanita and Elena?"

"Your children, Lynton?" Basil drawled.

"My wards." Nicholas's voice was clipped. "Blast it, Cassie, I'm not saying you should neglect them, but Lynton's right. You should have a little fun."

"I am sorry, my lord." Cassandra stressed the last two

words, and saw belated contrition cross his face. "I cannot leave my duties."

"Life can't be all work, Miss Aldrich," Sabrina said. "Please do spare some time for us."

"We'd miss you, you know," Harriet put in. "Do please change your mind."

"After all, someone's got to keep Nick in line," Samuel said, his smile kindly.

Cassandra felt her resistance weakening. She had a profound distrust of Basil's motives, but everyone else was genuinely nice. And not one of them treated her as if they thought she was more than a governess. "Well—"

"Oh good," Sabrina said. "I am sure you will enjoy it, Miss Aldrich."

"Yes, but I cannot neglect the children." She looked up at Nicholas. "I'll join you only when they don't need me."

"Surely in the evening, Cassandra," Basil said.

She hesitated, and then bowed to the inevitable. "Yes, of course," she said, smiling. Nicholas sent her an unreadable look. She would, she knew, have to deal with him later. For now, all she could think of was escape. "I really must look in on the children. If you'll excuse me," she said, and fled.

Nicholas found her much later, sitting alone in the old scarred rocking chair in the day nursery, with only a sputtering candle to give any light. Though she still wore her gray silk dress, her hair was loose upon her shoulders, making her look very young, and very vulnerable. And very desirable. Quickly Nicholas closed his mind against that thought. He'd already done enough damage with his casualness, without adding this unwanted attraction. "Cassie?" he said, softly, and she looked up at him. In the dim light her eyes were huge, fathomless, and it suddenly struck him that he didn't know her at all. The woman he had thought of as a companion was as mysterious as any woman he had ever met. "Is all well?"

"Juanita had a nightmare." She leaned her head back against her chair. "Elena doesn't understand what has happened to her, but Juanita does. I don't know how much I helped. I couldn't understand what she was saying, poor lamb."

"I'm sure you helped. The girls love you."

"But I'm not their mother." She sighed. "Nicholas—"

"I know, I know." He dropped down onto a stool, his hand dangling between his knees. "Don't take a lash to me, Cassie. I know I behaved badly tonight."

"You just don't seem to think before you talk, Nicholas."

"I know. All the things you've been trying to tell me—I saw what you meant, tonight."

"Did you?" She raised her head. "Well, that's something, at least."

"I'll send that jackanapes packing if he's bothering you," he said, abruptly.

"Who?"

"Byrne. Man grates on my nerves. Never could stand dandies."

"He's stronger than he looks."

"Ha. Get him aboard a ship and he'd likely turn green."

Cassandra smiled. "Likely."

"Seriously, Cassie. If you want him to go, I'll get rid of him."

"You can't do that, Nicholas."

"Oh, can't I? It is my house."

"Don't be silly. He's a guest. It wouldn't be polite."

"Aye. One must be polite at all costs, is that right, Cassie? No matter how much it hurts?"

"Nicholas?"

"Oh, never mind." He rose and took a turn about the room. "If you want him to stay, he stays."

There was silence for a moment. "It isn't precisely that I want him to, but—"

He turned. "Yes?"

"Oh, nothing."

Nicholas waited. Bewildered as he might be by women, but he knew there was something very wrong here, and that it concerned the viscount. "Do you care about him? Is that it, Cassie?"

"Byrne?" She sounded surprised. "I suppose I once thought I did. I was very young."

"Oh." It wasn't quite what he'd wanted to hear. "Didn't he feel the same?"

"He's a dandy. Dandies hide their feelings behind a mask of boredom. Besides, I had no money."

"Under the hatches? Him, I mean?"

"Yes."

"I see." He took another turn about the room. "Must be why he's sniffing about Miss Fairleigh. There's money there."

"Do you think there's something between them?"

"Aye. Don't you?" he said, startled by the sudden urgency in her voice.

"I didn't know. Good heavens." She stared into the darkness. "That explains much."

Nicholas couldn't see how, but he decided not to ask. She wouldn't tell him, in any event. *Ah, Cassie.* If she would only turn to him, as she had when she was a child. If she would only let him hold her, comfort her. "You don't have to join the guests, if you don't want to," he said, abruptly.

"No, I'd like to. To be honest, Nicholas?"

"Yes?"

"I think I would enjoy being in company again. I like your guests. Most of them, at least. They didn't make me feel like your—"

"What?" he said, when she didn't go on.

"Servant."

"Blast it, Cassie, I wish you wouldn't call yourself that."

"And I wish you wouldn't call me 'Cassie' in front of the guests!"

"Blast it, Cassie. I wish—blast it, you're right." He stopped. "Should I call you 'Miss Aldrich,' then?"

"No, my name is appropriate. But I do think you should tell them that you knew me when I was a child, and just why I'm here. It would explain our friendship."

He stared at her. "Reputation is very important to you, Cassie, isn't it?"

"It's all I have," she said, simply.

"Blasted silly thing to say."

"Not in my position. How would you feel, Nicholas, if you lost your good name?"

Nicholas glanced away. He remembered all too well how it felt. "Very well, Cassie. Do my best not to embarrass you, I promise." He smiled. "You'll help with the ball, won't you?"

She laughed, and rose. "Oh, you are an impossible man! Yes, I'll help with the ball. But if you have anything else to surprise me with, I wish you'd tell me now."

"No more surprises." He gazed down at her. Her hair picked up the dim light and sparked flame, rivaling that of the candle; her eyes were dark, fathomless pools. Wine dark, like the sea, and as deep. She was, he realized with a stab of desire so sharp it was almost pain, a beautiful woman. "Too bad about your green dress."

"It doesn't signify. It was old. If you'll excuse me, Nicholas, 'tis late—"

"And your hand? Does it pain you?"

"Oh no. The cut wasn't deep. I'm sure it will heal." She looked up at him, and her eyes flickered. "Nicholas?"

"Cassie, you know if you need any kind of help, you can come to me."

"Yes, Nicholas. I do know that."

"You've always been very special to me, you know. Ever since you were a little girl."

"I'm not a child now, Nicholas."

"I'm aware of that," he said, and bent his head. She pulled back with a start, and he paused, waiting, waiting. Then, when she made no other movement, he lowered his head just that little bit. Their lips met, clung, hers pressing sweetly against his in a kiss that was infinitely tender, and yet sent fire blazing through his veins. He'd meant to comfort her, only that, but this was so much more than comfort, and when at last he drew back he saw his uncertainty mirrored in her eyes. "Ah, Cassie." With his thumb he lightly traced her lower lip, and she started again. " 'Tis all right. All right."

And with that, he gathered her into his arms and kissed her again, harder this time. She rose on tiptoe to meet him, her arms slipping about his waist, and he gathered her closer, his hands moving on her back as his lips moved on hers, exploring, touching, tasting. No woman had ever felt like this. No woman had ever tasted like this, sweet, so sweet. Sweetness and peace and home, somehow, and yet yearning, too. He wanted, needed, more. Instinctively his mouth opened over hers; instinctively she responded, and his tongue found safe harbor. Somewhere in the back of

179

his mind came the strange, fleeting thought that she had done this before, that someone had taught her how to kiss, but he let it go. It didn't matter. Cassie was in his arms, at last. He was home.

Abruptly she broke away from him, and he felt lost, a ship at sea without a rudder. "I must go," she gasped, and fled.

"Cassie," he called. He took a step after her, and then stopped. If he caught her, what would he do? Where would this lead? He was in dangerous waters, and he'd best proceed slowly. Sinking down onto the stool again, he stared blankly ahead. She had gone, leaving him with the ache of unsatisfied desire, and a vast confusion. Now what did he do?

In the morning Cassandra walked in the garden, Juanita clinging to her and Elena toddling ahead. She had spoken with Harriet, who was sincere about working in the garden and wore an old dress and apron. "Not much chance of doing this in town," she told Cassandra, pulling up weeds with blithe abandon. Cassandra smiled at her and walked on. She liked Mrs. Fairleigh. In fact, what she had told Nicholas last night was true. She liked most of the guests. She simply wished they would all leave.

Elena spied one of the estate cats, kept to keep down the mice, and, with a little cry, ran after the animal with amazing speed. Juanita followed, pulling away from Cassandra, who was obliged to hasten behind them. Her thoughts stayed with her, however. No question that life at Sutcliffe Hall wasn't exactly easy, even before the house party began. There had been the gossip about her, for one thing, and though that had died down, it hurt. More serious, and far more dangerous, was her attraction to

Nicholas. She'd felt it as a child; she felt it still. If she'd been honest with herself, she would have admitted that her real reason for taking this position was to be close to him. Now she had no choice but to face the truth. After last night, everything had changed.

Elena let out a sudden screech, and Cassandra ran, to see her sitting on the gravel path and holding up a finger. "*El gato* scratched her," Juanita reported.

"Oh, *pobrecita.*" Cassandra gathered Elena close. "Poor little *niña,* and wicked *gato.* Cat." She gave Juanita, who was looking solemn and a little frightened, a quick smile. "I think you'll be teaching me Spanish before I teach you English. *Pobrecita,* 'tis all right. Let me kiss it and make it better."

Kiss it and make it better. The phrase resounded in her head as she lightly touched her lips to the tiny scratch on Elena's finger. A kiss didn't always make things better. Sometimes it made them infinitely worse. Whatever had she been thinking of last night? She was no green girl. She had seen the look in Nicholas's eyes and had had a very good idea what he planned. Why hadn't she moved away, then, when she had the chance? Because she'd wanted the kiss, too, with every fiber of her being. She had wanted, just once, to be held by him, to be kissed by him. Oh, she was wanton, for all her attempts at propriety. Futile attempts. Had she not come to her senses in time, she might have allowed a great deal more than kissing.

And yet, was it really wanton of her? In the long hours of the night, when she had lain awake alternately reproaching herself and glorying in what had happened, she had at last admitted to herself that what she felt for Nicholas was a great deal more than attraction. It always had been. She was in love with him.

Boots crunched on the gravel, and she felt her cheeks

reddening. Nicholas. Well, she'd have to face him sooner or later, and learn how to live with all that had happened last night. Raising her eyes, she looked up to see Basil.

The color drained from her face. Last night's events had completely driven from her mind the threat this man posed. Now, though, dread and panic mixed in her stomach at the memory. She lurched to her feet, jostling Elena, and faced him.

He stood there, looking impossibly cool and collected, every hair in place, and his neckcloth tied in an incredibly intricate knot, his eyebrow raised. "Good morning." His eyes traveled over her from head to toe, and she flushed, knowing she looked disheveled. "Are these the brats you care for?"

"This is Miss Juanita Maidstone and Miss Elena Maidstone," she said, her lips tightening. Juanita and Elena hid behind her skirts, staring up at the elegantly dressed stranger. *"Niñas,* make your curtsy to the *hombre."*

His eyebrow raised higher. *"Niñas? Hombre?"*

"Hombre tonto," she said, lightly, and the girls giggled. Silly man, she had said. She could only pray that he didn't understand Spanish. "A mark of high honor, I assure you."

"Really." His voice was dry. "Charming children. If you like children. Can't you get rid of them, Cassandra?"

"No. They are my charges. In fact, we were just going indoors to start lessons. If you'll excuse us."

"We need to talk, Cassandra."

She stopped. "I don't believe we do, sir," she said, without turning.

"Oh, we do, Cassandra, we do, and I believe you'll want to hear what I have to say. Or have you forgotten that I once knew you very well?"

Cassandra slowly turned around. "What do you want?"

"Merely to talk."

"We've nothing to say to each other, sir."

"Oh?" His eyebrow arched again. "I believe we do."

"About what?"

"About our past." He paused, smiling, not a nice smile. "And our future."

Chapter 13

Cassandra stood very still. Here it was, then, the threat she had been expecting since last evening. Oddly enough, now that it had come, she was calm. Deadly calm. "We've no future, sir."

"It will take only a moment, Cassandra," Basil said. "I'm sure you'll want to hear what I have to say, after all we were to each other."

Cassandra glanced down at the children. Elena, still clinging to her skirt, was quietly singing to herself, but Juanita was staring up at them unblinkingly. With their youth and their limited knowledge of English it was hardly likely they would understand anything that was said, but it was certain that they understood tension. They had been through enough. "Very well," she said, her voice clipped. "But not here, and certainly not in front of the children."

He shrugged. "As you wish. Where, then?"

"I will meet with you in the music room, after luncheon. The children will be napping and I need to go there to make preparations for the ball."

Basil tilted his head to the side. "I wonder if Lynton knows what a prize he has in you?"

"This afternoon, sir," Cassandra snapped, and turned, stalking away. The children ran on chubby legs to catch up with her, Elena reaching up her arms to be lifted. Basil watched them for a moment, his face expressionless. Then he smiled, a smile completely different from the charming ones he bestowed on the ladies, and sauntered away, whistling and looking well pleased with himself.

It was a few moments before Nicholas stepped out from behind a rosebush, where he had suddenly ducked when he had realized that Cassie was talking with Byrne. Inadequate cover for a man of his size, but it seemed neither of them had noticed him. They'd been too involved in their discussion, and in each other. So. It was as he had thought. Cassie had some link to the viscount. He very much wanted to know what it was.

He had awakened this morning full of optimism and boundless energy, and a great desire to see Cassie. Last night's encounter in the schoolroom had stirred something to life within him, something he had thought long gone. Hope for the future. In her arms he had come alive again. All he wanted was to see her again and tell her how he felt, if he could put it into words.

Well, he'd seen her. Hands in his pockets, brow furrowed, Nicholas walked along the path, absentmindedly kicking at stones now and then. Seen her with Byrne, discussing an assignation. Maybe he'd spent most of his life at sea and knew little of the ways of the world, but he wasn't stupid. There had been something between Cassie and Byrne in the past; it looked like there still was.

Someone taught Cassie how to kiss. The thought made him stop, balling his hands into fists. Give him five minutes with that damned dandy, just five, and he'd wipe that superior, supercilious expression off his face. Cassie was his, blast it! She always had been, even if he was just

185

beginning to realize it. The hell of it was, she had no reason to prefer him, rough-hewn, ill-mannered, to Byrne, with his sophisticated ways. None at all.

He stopped again and looked up at the house, at the windows to the music room, his face grimly determined. Let Cassie have her assignation. He couldn't prevent it, even if he went to her and told her what he'd heard. If she truly wanted Byrne, she'd find a way to see him. But, by Neptune, he wasn't giving up without a fight! He strode down the path. He was going to do his damndest to get Cassie to see him as a man. Someday, she would be his.

The neighborhood was, without exception, excited about the arrival of the visitors to Sutcliffe Hall. Imagine, not only someone from the Admiralty, but a viscount and a duke, as well! This was what everyone had hoped would happen when the new earl came. He was a good man. Oh, he had his strange ways; there were some who still had their doubts about the parentage of the two little foreign girls, and others who looked askance at his hiring of Cassandra Aldrich. Most, however, forgave him any eccentricities. He was, after all, the earl, and his involvement in local affairs only added to their approval.

The ladies of the gentry had begun making plans to entertain the guests as soon as they heard of the house party, but it was Mrs. Lamb who was quickest, with an invitation to tea for that very afternoon. Cassandra, leaving the nursery after seeing the girls settled for their nap, was glad not to have been included in that invitation. She wondered what Penelope would make of Daphne Fairleigh, with her delicate features and clouds of dark hair, and smiled to herself. High time Penelope had some real competition.

The corridor to the music room was quiet and deserted in the early afternoon hush. In the usual way of things few people came here, except to clean, but all that would change very soon. Nicholas, blithely announcing plans for the ball, probably had no idea how much work it would entail. She hadn't been lying this morning when she'd told Basil she intended to start the preparations. She just doubted, now, that she'd get much done.

The music room was quiet and dim, light filtering dimly through the muslin draperies, while the holland covers on the furniture gave the room a ghostly air. Across the room was a spinet that must once have been magnificent, cream with delicate, extravagant decorations in pink and green and powder blue, but the gilt was badly tarnished and the paint was dull. The hinges of the lid groaned as Cassandra lifted it, and the tone that sounded when she touched a key was so sour that she winced.

"You used to play quite well, I remember," a voice said, seemingly from nowhere, and her hands came down on the keys in surprise, crashing a dischord that echoed eerily in the room. Basil came forward from a window embrasure, one eyebrow raised. "Surely much better than that."

"I didn't know you were here, my lord." Cassandra busied herself with lowering the lid. "Well! This will have to be tuned before the ball, and I do hope we can clean the tarnish from the gilt."

"Do you still chatter when you're frightened, Cassandra?"

She lifted her chin. "I'm not frightened."

"No? I remember one night when you chattered quite a bit. The night we—"

"You're no gentleman to remind me of that," she

snapped, moving away from the spinet. "But then, we established that long ago."

"Past history, Cassandra."

"Oh?" She looked at him over her shoulder. "Why did you want to see me, then?"

"To discuss our future."

Here it was, then. Cassandra braced herself for the inevitable. "What do you want?"

"You always were forthright. If you'd had more town bronze, learned to be a bit more devious, perhaps you'd have known enough—ah, but that is in the past, isn't it? Very well, then, Cassandra. I'll come to the point."

She gripped the back of a chair, enshrouded in its cover, keeping it between them like a shield. "Which is?"

"You could make a deal of trouble for me."

"I—!" She stared at him. "All you have to do is say the word and I'd be out of a position."

He clucked his teeth. "Come, Cassandra, do you think me such a cad as that?"

"Yes."

"No, no, no. You misunderstand me. Besides, I've changed. You needn't look at me like that. I have changed."

"Really."

"Oh yes. I've no intention of making trouble for you. If—"

"If?" she repeated when he paused. She had a very good idea what he wanted from her.

"If you make none for me."

"How could I do that, sir?"

"By telling what transpired between us."

That startled her into a sharp, bitter laugh. "As if I would!" Hadn't she spent the best part of the last six years trying to put that very event behind her? "Do you think I wish to destroy my own reputation?"

"No. I think you're smarter than that. However, women have been known to do strange things, in the name of revenge."

"You speak as if I have power over you."

"You do. Had I known you were here—but that is beside the point, now. The thing is, Cassandra, one wrong word from you, and my life will be ruined."

"Well." Slowly she came around the chair and sank down into it, ignoring the puffs of dust that rose from the holland cover. "This certainly isn't what I'd expected you to say."

His mouth twisted. "You thought, perhaps, I'd wish to take up where we left off?"

"Yes."

"You do think well of me, Cassandra, don't you?"

"With reason, sir."

"I'll give you that." His mouth twisted again. "I won't say but that a few months ago you'd have been right. However"—he swung to face her, his face serious—"I have changed. You perhaps know that I'm courting Miss Fairleigh?"

"Poor girl," Cassandra blurted.

"Thank you. As it happens, I think I might make her a passable husband."

In spite of herself, Cassandra was curious. "Does she know about you?"

"I'm not certain she does. Her brother is another matter. He's none too certain of me as it is. If he hears of this, he'll never consider me suitable for her."

"There must be money."

"You know me well, Cassandra. Yes, there's money, and as you know my pockets are always to let." He pulled

189

a chair closer to her and sat down, leaning forward. "Shall I tell you the truth?"

"Which truth? The real one, or the one that is convenient for you?"

"Both."

"By all means, then."

"The truth is, I love her."

Cassandra laughed. "Don't gammon me!"

"It's true." His face was serious. "I won't deny it was the money that interested me at first, but not anymore. It's Daphne. You've seen how sweet she is." His mouth quirked. "They always say it's the rakes that fall the hardest. Well, you behold before you a fallen man, Cassandra. I haven't been with a woman in over two months. I haven't even looked at another woman." He leaned back, his arms crossed. "I don't expect you to believe me, of course."

"I might, if I hadn't heard the same words from you before. Though I must say, the part about other women is new."

"You've grown bitter, Cassandra."

"Can you blame me?" She gestured sharply toward herself. "Look at me! This wasn't what I had planned for my life. And even the little I have I must fight to keep." She glanced away. "I think I believe you," she said, slowly. "There's something different about you. But I'm not certain it's altogether fair to Miss Fairleigh not to let her know what she's getting into."

"I'll make her a good husband." His gaze was clear and direct. "A faithful husband."

"Well, time will tell, won't it?" She rose. "I wish you would go. I've much to do here."

"Cassandra." He crossed to her, stopping her at the

door with a hand on her arm. "You haven't given me your word not to say anything."

"No, I haven't, have I," she said, and saw alarm flicker across his features. Good. Let him suffer as she once had. As soon as she had the thought, though, she dismissed it as unworthy. Unworthy of her, and rather startling. Here she had revenge in her hands, and she found it tawdry and unsatisfying. She could not, in all conscience, ruin another's life so casually. "Of course I won't tell. But don't think it's for you, Basil. I've learned how to take care of myself." She paused. "I've had to."

He peered down at her. "Do you know, I think I may have been a fool all those years ago, to let you go."

"I would have been a fool to accept you." She opened the door. "Please leave, now."

"Very well. But don't forget our secret," he said, and sauntered out.

Cassandra closed the door very, very quietly, and then sank down onto the nearest chair. Heavens, her legs were shaking. The encounter hadn't been quite so bad as she'd expected, yet, at the end, the threat had been unmistakable. What Basil would do, if she didn't comply with his demands, she didn't dare guess. She did, however, remember quite well her last encounter with him, six years ago, and what it had led to. She had no desire to go through that again.

She would keep quiet, then, protecting herself from exposure and Basil's wrath. Nicholas would never have to know the truth about her. That was a profound relief. The only problem was, she thought, rising at last and crossing the room, that Miss Fairleigh might be hurt by her silence. Doubtless she had no idea what kind of man Basil was. Mr. Fairleigh must know, however. He may have been at sea for years, but he was no one's fool. Yet he hadn't discouraged Basil. Perhaps Basil had changed. She doubted it, but perhaps he had. If so, she owed him, and herself, a chance at the future.

She was pulling the holland covers off chairs to check their condition when the door from the hall opened. Instantly she straightened, a cover clutched in her hands. "What are you doing?" Nicholas asked, strolling into the room.

"Why are you here?" she countered, not relaxing her grip. Thank heavens it wasn't Basil. This was almost as bad, however. What if Nicholas had chanced to come along while she and Basil were talking? "I thought you were at the Lambs'."

"Something came up." He grinned. "I made certain of it."

"Oh."

He glanced around. "By Neptune, this room's a mess. What are you doing with that shroud?"

"What? Oh, this. Checking to see if any of the furniture needs repairing."

"Plan on doing it yourself? I have servants for that kind of thing, Red."

"I have to know what needs doing before I can give the servants their orders, haven't I? Now." She draped the dust cover onto the chair. "Is there something you require, sir?"

"No, no." Hands clasped behind his back, he prowled the perimeter of the room. "Carry on."

"Very well." Cassandra continued her work, keeping him in sight from the corner of her eye. From time to time he would look at a chair, or step into a window embrasure to check the fit of the window. When he at last drifted over to the spinet, lifting the lid to hit a sour note, Cassandra had had quite enough. "There's really nothing for you to do here, sir. I'll note what should be done and tell the staff."

"I know." He struck another note, frowning. "Do you know, I think this spinet needs tuning."

"Really. Nicholas, you said something had come up to keep you from going to the Lambs'."

"Something did." He flashed her a smile. "My dislike of Mrs. and Miss Lamb."

"That's hardly polite behavior."

"They've got a viscount and a duke. Won't miss me."

"But—" She stopped. So he didn't know that Basil, too, had stayed behind. The knot of fear in her stomach eased. "Of course they'll miss you! I can't say I blame you, though. There." She replaced the holland cover on the last chair and stepped back. "They're all in good enough condition, thank heavens. I'll speak with Mrs. Feather about cleaning in here and then we can begin on the decorations. If you don't need me any longer, sir?"

"I think I made a mistake, Cassie," he said, abruptly.

She stopped at the door. "About what, sir?

"This blasted house party." He thrust his hands into his pockets and began to prowl the room again. "What do I know about being a host? Fear I'm making a cake of myself, Cassie."

Cassandra stepped back into the room. "Of course you're not. I think everyone's enjoying themselves."

"Or they're all too polite to say they're not. What do I have to offer them for entertainments? Just country pursuits."

"Stop fussing." She smiled at him. "They don't mind. After all, none of them seems terribly high in the instep. Well, except for Viscount Byrne," she said, at his look. "But he'd be too polite to show it if he was bored."

"Exactly my point. And now this blasted ball."

"Well, that is the one thing they're sure to enjoy."

"I won't." He hunched his shoulders. "Don't even know how to dance."

"Oh, you must have learned somewhere."

"Aboard a man of war? Ha. Only the hornpipe, and I don't think most people know that."

"No, I'm afraid not." She glanced about the room. "If you really don't need me, sir, I should go—"

"No, wait. I have an idea."

The enthusiasm in his voice put her on guard. "What?"

"You could teach me."

"To dance? No." She backed toward the door. "No, I couldn't."

"Of course you could. You've had a season, you'd know what to do. Yes. You'll teach me to dance."

"Actually, sir, what I could do is organize a dance party. Yes. We could have it one afternoon, and teach each other. Heaven knows I don't remember the steps to the country dances anymore. We'll invite people from the neighborhood—"

"Blast it, Cassie, I'll not make a cake of myself in front of everyone! No." He stood with his arms folded. "If you won't teach me to dance, I'll cancel the ball."

"You can't do that!"

"I can. Well, Cassie?"

"I told you. I don't remember the steps."

"Just one dance, Cassie, so I don't look too foolish." His smile deepened. "Just one, that's all."

"You are the most annoying man." Cassandra left the relative safety of the door and walked over to him. "Oh, very well. Let's see what I remember. In a country dance, we start like so—"

"I don't want to learn a country dance." He smiled down at her. "I want to learn the waltz."

194

Cassandra sucked in her breath. The waltz, that most seductive and intimate of dances. To perform it with him would be to court disaster. After all, look what had happened the last time they had been close. Which he hadn't even mentioned, the dratted man! She didn't want to find herself in his arms again. Undoubtedly it would be heaven, but being left alone again would be hell. "I'm afraid I don't know it, sir."

"What?" He appeared shocked, though his eyes twinkled. "And you had a season?"

"Yes, but to dance the waltz was considered fast. It still is, I believe."

He waved his hand at that. "They do it in London, I hear. So you didn't dance it at all those balls and assemblies you went to?"

"No." She breathed a tiny sigh of relief. "I'm sorry."

"Hm." His eyes were suddenly sharp. "I'll wager, though, that you learned it anyway, with your friends."

"Why—no, of course not! We'd never have done such a thing."

"No?" He grinned. "Never once felt like kicking over the traces, Cassie? Always did what people told you to do?"

"Always." Amazingly, she faced him directly with that. To have done otherwise was to admit to dangerous matters best forgotten.

"Blast." He ran a hand through his hair. "Very well, Cassie, if you say you didn't, you didn't. Guess I just won't dance at the ball after all."

He looked so woebegone that she instinctively put her hand out, touching his sleeve. "You're right. I do know the dance. A friend did show me."

The crestfallen look on his face disappeared, to be replaced by delight. "You do? Good." He grasped her

195

hands firmly and dragged her into the center of the room.

"Nicholas." Oh Lord, now what had she done? She didn't want to be any closer to him than she had to be, for the sake of her heart. "We have no music."

"Hum something," he commanded, and slipped his arm about her waist.

"Not so close, sir." If she were to survive this she would have to regain some semblance of control.

"More fun this way, Cassie."

"It isn't proper. Would you hold Penelope like this?"

"By Neptune, no!"

"That's better." She smiled up at him, now the requisite arm's length from her. "We clasp hands, like this."

"Your hands are small, Cassie."

"Now. The steps are like this. One, two, three, one, two, three."

"One, two, three." Nicholas counted under his breath, moving in the pattern she showed him. "Dashed odd, Cassie. Are you sure?"

"Quite sure. Do you have it? Good. Now you turn around, no, with me, Nicholas! There. Keep in step. Very good."

Nicholas grinned, tightening his hold. "Not so hard."

"Not so very, no." She pulled back, aware of his hand at her waist, warm and strong and possessive. "Are you sure you haven't done this before?"

"Never in my life," he said, and whirled her in an exuberant turn. Cassie's skirt swirled about his legs, and momentarily he was tangled in it, stubbing one foot against the other. Off balance, he stumbled against her and she fell back, throwing out her arms. Somehow he found his footing, his booted foot landing squarely on hers in its soft slipper. Cassandra let out a cry of protest and he pulled back, nearly overbalancing them in the other direction. She fell against him with a soft *oomph!* and instinct made her clutch at him. Instinct, and something else.

By some miracle, they managed to remain standing. Cassandra, clutching at Nicholas's arms, looked up at him, her eyes wide and startled. "Good heavens, Nicholas!"

"Blast it. I'm sorry, Cassie. Are you hurt?"

Cassandra flexed her injured foot. "No, I think it's all right. Good heavens, that was close!"

"Sorry," he said again. "Guess I shouldn't have tried that yet."

"No, you should not." She pulled back, and his arms about her tightened. For the first time she realized her danger, leaning against his chest in so intimate a way. "Nicholas—"

"You're dashed pretty, Cassie."

"Nicholas, let me go. I must see to the girls—"

"They can wait a moment." His eyes roved her face. "I can't stop thinking about last night."

She swallowed, hard. "Neither can I," she whispered.

"It was special, Cassie."

"It was—something that must never happen again, sir."

Caught off guard, Nicholas released her when she pushed against his chest again. "Why not?"

"Why not?" She gave a short, bitter laugh, standing there looking at him, loving him, loving him. Knowing that love was impossible, that he would never love her back. "Surely even you can see how unsuitable it is."

"Is it?"

"Yes!" Oh, why was he doing this to her? "Please, leave me alone. Just—leave me alone," she said, and fled.

"Cassie," he called, starting after her, and stopped. She was gone. Damn, damn, damn! He'd botched that good

197

and proper. Groaning, he dropped into a chair, running his hands over his face. Nothing had gone as he planned. He knew how to waltz, of course. He had thought to use this afternoon as a way to get close to Cassie again, to counter whatever it was Byrne had said to her, and perhaps to go on with what they had started last night. He wanted her. Oh, he wanted her, and that wanting had kept him awake all night. He was afraid now that tonight would be no different. Something had happened to him when he took her in his arms for the waltz. Though she wasn't close to him, he was so aware of her small hand in his that he could feel her pulse, and her trim waist under his hand made him feel warm and light-headed. Not that Cassie did anything to cause this peculiar reaction. She was small and compact in his embrace, holding herself separate. Proper as they come, his Cassie. But her hair, just brushing his chin, was soft, and she smelled of some sweet flower—lilac? Lavender? He didn't know. He knew only that her scent went to his head, that he reeled with it still. No wonder he had stumbled. He was half-seas over on eau de cologne, by Neptune!

So, he'd made a complete fool of himself, stepping on her foot like that. He groaned again. If there was anything worse than appearing the fool before the woman you admired, he couldn't think what it was. And he did admire Cassie.

Aye, he thought, rising and leaving the room. Admired her, respected her, liked her. Cared about her well-being, and wondered just what it was about Byrne that brought that bruised look to her eyes. Seriously considered challenging Byrne to some kind of conflict. Fisticuffs would be just about right; Nicholas would like to see that dandy's face when he drew his cork. A satisfying thought, which meant—what? Well, he liked Cassie, always had, and he needed her, like the air he breathed, like the sea that was still so much a part of him. No blasted dandy was going to take her away from him. Cassie was his.

Chapter 14

Nicholas had invited his guests to view his ship, the *Eagle*, now standing in the bay at Fairhaven after undergoing extensive repairs. All that remained to be done now were odd jobs, painting and the like, and the hiring of a captain and crew. Nicholas seemed, however, in no hurry to hire anyone.

All the guests seemed interested in the ship, and so plans were made to row out several mornings later. Cassandra had managed to convince Nicholas that simply rowing his guests to the ship wouldn't be enough, and that he would have to provide some kind of refreshment. He had immediately charged her with planning a picnic luncheon, something simple, he said.

Something simple, Cassandra thought, running down the list in her mind once more. What had begun as a pleasant outing for the guests had spread to include nearly everyone in the neighborhood, all of whom were curious about the earl's latest venture. Slowly and inexorably she was being drawn into this house party, in spite of Nicholas's promise that she need only make an occasional appearance. First the ball, and now this. At least he hadn't asked her to waltz with him again. She didn't think her feet, or her heart, could withstand it.

As it happened, most of the ladies declined the honor of actually going aboard the ship, preferring instead to explore the village and to stop into the shops. Cassandra, turning to walk with Sabrina and Daphne, looked longingly out onto the bay where the *Eagle* rode at anchor. It was her duty to entertain Nicholas's guests, even if she wasn't really his hostess, but, oh, how she wanted to row out to the ship. Ever since she was small she had thrilled to Nicholas's tales of the sea and his adventures. She had dreamed of foreign lands, of skies so distant that the very stars were unfamiliar, of meeting new people and hearing strange languages. She had dreamed of standing beside Nicholas at the helm.

Foolish dream, that one, she decided, hurrying to catch up with the others as they strolled down the High Street, but then, she'd only been a child. Her only consolation was that, when *Eagle* sailed, it would be with another captain. Nicholas would remain on shore, with her. And that was another foolish thought, she scolded herself. There never could be anything between her and Nicholas, as she well knew. The arrival of Viscount Byrne had only been a reminder of that fact.

By the time the men returned from the ship, the ladies had managed to visit all the shops, and had gathered by the carriages. Sabrina was too polite to show any impatience, but Daphne danced from foot to foot, peering anxiously toward the boat nearing the quay. "Oh, I do wish they would hurry!" she said. "Just the thought of Byrne on a boat gives me *mal de mer*."

Sabrina and Cassandra exchanged quick, amused glances. During the few days of the house party Daphne's shyness had melted, and one thing had become clear. She was fascinated by, if not exactly enamored with, Viscount Byrne. "Oliver loves ships," Sabrina said, smiling. "I sometimes think he wishes he'd been a pirate."

"Really?" Cassandra said in surprise. She had difficulty imagining the reserved, upright duke in such a role.

"Oh yes. We've discussed visiting America, but we can't just now, of course." Her smile faded. "I hate this war."

Cassandra glanced toward the quay, where the boat was now tying up. The end of the fighting on the Continent had been such a relief to everyone that she sometimes forgot that war was still being waged. "Is your home in danger?"

"No, I don't believe so. It's near New York, but it should be far enough upriver to protect it." She sighed. "I don't believe Oliver would tell me if there were danger. This has been a difficult year."

"It must have been hard, losing your grandmother."

"Yes, she was a dear." She paused. "And a child."

"Oh, I am so sorry!"

Sabrina nodded. Her face was serious, and her eyes had darkened, making her look older than she was. "Yes. It was hard. But"—she put her hand to her stomach—"we have hopes."

"Really? Oh, that is wonderful."

"Thank you." Sabrina smiled at her, looking young and almost carefree again. "I have a good feeling about it this time. Of course, Oliver is being overprotective. It's why he wouldn't let me go out to the ship. Ah, here they are." With another smile, Sabrina left Cassandra to go to her husband.

Cassandra smiled in return, though inside swelled a great, aching loneliness. What must it be like, to love and to know that your love was returned? And to have a child.

All the children she had cared for, and they weren't enough. They weren't hers. The knowledge that she would never be a mother was the most painful thing she had ever had to face.

Samuel Fairleigh was escorting his mother from the quay, both of them absorbed in conversation. Basil apparently hadn't enjoyed the experience; he looked ruffled and rather pale, and yet Daphne hung on his arm, smiling at him. Bainbridge and Sabrina walked together, more slowly, but their feelings were apparent in the way they looked at each other as they talked. That left only Cassandra, standing alone, and Nicholas, trudging slowly up the hill.

Something was wrong. She could see it in the set of his shoulders, in the furrows on his forehead. He had removed his hat, letting the wind tousle his hair, and apparently he had tugged at his neckcloth more than once, both sure signs of his agitation. He looked far more like a sailor than an earl. He also looked decidedly unhappy.

Without thought, Cassandra stepped toward him and took his arm. "Nicholas? Is all well?"

For a moment he stared blankly down at her, and then blinked. "Of course, Cassandra. Why wouldn't it be?"

He had called her by her full name, and he was using formal speech. Very bad signs, indeed. "You wish you were sailing on her, don't you."

Nicholas sighed and tugged at his neckcloth again. "Blast it, Cassie." He turned to look out at the ship. "I'd forgotten. I've gotten so involved with things on shore, I forgot. Then, repairing and outfitting her, 'twas almost like she wasn't real. But going aboard her." He stopped. "I could feel her, Cassie, alive, all around me. I can see her with all sails set and a following wind and—blast it, I didn't want to come back."

She tightened her hold on his arm. "I know."

"I hate this life, Cassie. Hate being tied to the shore." His gaze sharpened. "You do, too, I think."

"I've never been to sea, Nicholas."

"No. No, but it's in your blood, too, Cassie." His eyes softened. "You've the look of a sea sprite sometimes, when your hair is down and flowing wild. You weren't made for this life, Cassie, any more than I was."

"Nonsense." She withdrew her arm from his. "This is the life I've chosen, sir."

He followed behind her. "Is it, Cassie? Can you honestly say you're happy?"

Cassandra stopped, squaring her shoulders. "Yes. Now, come, Nicholas, we must go. The others are waiting and your guests will already be at the picnic."

"Damn the others," he said in a low, fierce voice, catching at her hand. "If I had my way, Cassie, I'd take you aboard *Eagle* and we'd sail away from all this."

She stared up at him, her throat going dry. Oh, how wonderful that sounded. If only—"We must go, sir," she said, and pulled away. After a moment, Nicholas, his head bent, followed.

The weather, which had been cloudy, had turned sunny and warm. As Cassandra had predicted, the guests were already gathered in the hollow behind the Hall, where they would be picnicking. It was an ideal setting, sheltered from the winds that blew in from the sea, with an old orchard, its trees gnarled and bent but bright with new leaves. From here it was a brief walk to the garden, or, for the more adventurous, the cliff. The servants had been busy, setting up tables with fine linen cloths, glistening china, and enough food to tempt even the most jaded appetite, lobster patties, succulent ham, and a special strawberry tart for the sweet. It was, Cassandra admitted, walking across the grass, a festive scene, rivaling any al fresco meal she had had in London. The gentlemen, though dressed in country attire of sturdy coats and high boots, still looked handsome, while the ladies in their pastel muslins flitted about like colorful butterflies. It was a sight such as she hadn't seen since her time in London, and her spirits rose. For this day, she would enjoy herself.

Samuel came up to take her arm. "May I walk with you, Miss Aldrich?"

She smiled up at him. He had never been less than polite to her, in spite of her curious position, and for that she was grateful. "Of course, sir. Though I would think you would prefer someone else. There are some lovely girls here."

"Lightweights," he said, succinctly. "Nicholas got the best."

"Sir, I assure you—"

"My apologies, ma'am. Didn't mean to imply anything." His eyes twinkled down at her. "Still, I've never seen Nick the way he is with you."

Cassandra's heart skipped a beat. "I understand, sir, you've known him a long time."

"Since we were boys. He's a good friend, and a good man."

"Yes, he is."

"Could have gone as far as he wanted, maybe even made admiral, except for what happened."

"Hmph. I didn't expect to see you here, Aldrich," a cool voice said, and Cassandra looked up to see Penelope. Instantly her spirits, bolstered by Samuel's attention, sagged. Like her, Penelope was wearing blue, but there any resemblance between their ensembles ended. Penelope's gown was of the very latest design, pale blue muslin cut a bit lower in the waist and fuller in the skirt, so that it floated about her. Embroidered leaves and flowers trimmed the hem, a cashmere shawl was draped with artful carelessness over her arms, and her narrow-brimmed bonnet was trimmed with a feather dyed the exact shade of her gown. Next to her, in plain blue broadcloth, Cassandra was forcibly reminded of who she was. Only the governess.

"Good day, Miss Lamb." Cassandra forced herself to smile. "You remember Mr. Fairleigh, I trust."

"Yes, of course." Penelope's smile was as cool as her voice as she held out her hand. "How do you do, sir."

"Good day, Miss Lamb." Samuel briefly took her hand, but his gaze slid to Beatrice, standing beside Penelope. "Miss Beatrice."

"Mr. Fairleigh." Beatrice's smile was wide and warm. "And, Cassie. How wonderful to see you again! We missed you at tea the other day."

"It would have been quite impossible for her to come," Penelope said. "You must have things to see to here, Aldrich."

"As it happens, I do," Cassandra said, glad to escape Penelope's presence. "If you'll excuse me."

Samuel smiled at her. "Of course," he said, and held out his arm to Beatrice. "Miss Beatrice, would you care to walk a bit?" To Cassandra's gratification, the last thing she saw as she walked away was the look of rage on Penelope's face.

"Cassandra," another voice called as she walked on, "may I walk with you?"

Cassandra stopped, squaring her shoulders, and at last turned. "Sir," she said, inclining her head to Viscount Byrne as he neared her. "Is aught amiss?"

"Nothing, of course," he said, smoothing down his hair. His appearance wasn't quite so impeccable as usual. "How do you manage living in the country?"

"I like it." Cassandra kept her pace brisk, so that Basil couldn't keep to his usual insolent saunter as he walked alongside her. "Don't you?"

"Good God, no. If I had to live here I'd go mad in a week." He looked at her from under his lashes, a glance that should have been feminine, but wasn't. He had entranced many a woman with that look. "I wouldn't think it would be what you'd prefer, either, Cassandra."

"Yes, well, things change. As I found out."

"Are you still blaming me, Cassandra?"

She stopped and stared up at him, amazed. "Who else is there to blame?"

He waved a languid hand. "Society's foolish rules. If not for them—"

"Nevertheless, sir, I made a mistake, and because of you. Must you continue to torment me with it?"

They walked in silence for a few moments. "I didn't realize I was tormenting you, Cassandra," he said, finally.

"Didn't realize! Good heavens, after the way things happened?"

"Yes, well, I'm sorry about that." He stopped and grasped her arm, his face unusually serious. "I mean that, Cassandra. I truly am sorry about what happened. I behaved like the worst cad. Can you possibly forgive me?"

"Good heavens!" She stared at him. "Have you really changed, or are you just pretending?"

"I think I've changed," he said, sounding surprised. "Amazing, isn't it?"

"Yes. Quite."

"You sound as if you don't believe me, Cassandra." He glanced away, and stiffened. "Who is that with Daphne?"

Cassandra looked past his shoulder. Daphne, looking sweetly pretty in a round gown of sprigged muslin with a pink satin sash, was smiling up at a besotted-looking George Lamb. "George Lamb. He is a neighbor."

Basil muttered something under his breath, becoming, for a moment, the hard, dangerous man who had ruined her life. "I'll soon put a stop to that. And, remember"—he rounded on Cassandra—"about your promise, or—"

"Is that a threat, Basil?"

To his credit, Basil glanced away. "No. No, I didn't mean it to be, Cassandra. My apologies. But seeing Daphne—damn it, I know I'm not the best match for her, but I'm trying. I don't want anything to ruin it."

In spite of herself Cassandra felt a tiny, very tiny, spurt of sympathy for him. It wasn't easy to watch someone you loved and never know if you would receive love in return. "The secret's safe with me, Basil," she said, touching his arm.

He turned and gave her the brilliant smile that had once charmed her, so many years ago. "You will not regret it, Cassie," he said, and caught up her hand, pressing a fervent kiss on it before she could pull away. Then he was gone, ambling across the grass to claim his beloved.

Good heavens! Cassandra stared after him, resisting the urge to scrub her hand against her skirt, removing the stain of his touch. She had seen him on the prowl before when she had been his prey, but never had he behaved quite like this. He really did care about Miss Fairleigh, and that meant that Cassandra held his future in her hands. How odd, when one thought of how he had changed her life. Yet, her life really wasn't so terrible. It had led her to Nicholas.

She turned, seeking him, and found him almost immediately. He was standing in a group of men, along with Mr. Lamb and other of his neighbors, but he paid them no heed. Instead, he was staring at her, frowning, though she couldn't imagine why. His only reaction when she smiled was to nod. Then he turned away, effectively dismissing her and leaving her feeling as if the sun had just gone in. Nicholas had cut her, and she didn't know why.

Sometime later Nicholas sat at the head of one of the tables that had been set out, surveying his guests and hiding his churning feelings behind a polite mask. He felt as if he were two separate people. One part of him enjoyed the day, and his guests. At times like this, he felt part of the neighborhood. People came to him for advice—as if he knew anything about managing an estate, by Neptune—and there was even talk about his becoming a magistrate. It didn't appeal to him, but, for a man who had seen his chances for a brilliant career in the navy slip away, for someone who still felt all at sea, it was flattering. He could almost get used to it, and he might, if the future were more certain. For he knew, as no one else did, that his contentment was largely due to one person. If she left, he would be lost.

With every appearance of listening to Mrs. Carlisle, the vicar's wife, he let his attention drift farther down the table, to Cassie, seated between Samuel, and, of all people, George Lamb. That had set tongues to wagging, he'd wager, though young Lamb appeared not to be paying her any heed. Instead, he'd hardly taken his eyes away from Daphne, seated on his other side. Cassie was safe from him. Not that Nicholas had ever considered him to be much of a threat. His real rival sat across from her, smooth, polished, urbane. Viscount Byrne.

Nicholas stiffened. Truth was, he'd taken a dislike to Byrne from the beginning, though he knew enough to

209

hide it. Byrne was everything he despised, a London dandy enjoying the best life had to offer, while other men fought and died to protect that life. Nicholas would have tolerated the man, though, were it not for his relationship with Cassie. For the last few days, it had rarely left his mind. What, he wondered, had they discussed that afternoon in the music room?

Cassie was laughing at something Samuel had said, appearing to be paying no heed to Byrne, but Nicholas knew better, for all Byrne pretended to be courting Daphne. Hadn't he seen, with his own eyes, Byrne kissing Cassie's hand in a lingering, passionate way? Cassie had looked uncomfortable, but that was to be expected. He knew how proper she could be. He also knew there'd been someone in her past, in London, maybe. The chances were that that someone was Byrne. He had returned, and when he left, he just might take Cassie with him.

Nicholas's eyes narrowed at that, and Mrs. Carlisle, talking about the forthcoming parish fête, faltered a bit. He no longer looked the polite country gentleman, but a warrior, fierce and intent, though he wasn't aware of it. Byrne would not have her, by Neptune! Not if he had any say in the matter. A man like Byrne would want to marry money, and position. Anyone could see he was toying with her. Cassie was sensible, he knew that, but even the most sensible woman could have her head turned by a handsome man. He wasn't going to let that happen to his Cassie. He'd stepped in to protect her before; he'd do so again. If he had to, he would lock her up, so that she couldn't leave. If he had to, he would marry her himself.

Nicholas went very still. Aye. He'd marry her. He hadn't thought seriously about it before, but as he considered it, the prospect became more and more pleasing. More and more right. Cassie belonged to him. He would do everything he could, anything he had to, to keep her. Anything.

Harriet, seated on his other side, touched his arm lightly, and he started, smiling at her. He could not, as his instincts clamored for him to do, leap up from the table and claim Cassie as his own. He would, though, and soon. Cassie was his.

Penelope was not enjoying herself. Oh, she knew she was easily the most beautiful girl at the earl's al fresco meal—for she refused to call it a picnic. So *dé classé*. The only people who might have given her competition weren't up to her weight at all. Miss Fairleigh was pretty enough, but her gown of white muslin was horridly unsophisticated. There was the Duchess of Bainbridge, too, whom Penelope had seen only from a distance during her season. Much as it galled her to admit it, she hadn't traveled in the highest circles in London. The duchess, however, was dressed in mourning. Really, no competition at all. Why, then, was Penelope alone?

Feeling more than a little grumpy, she sank gracefully down into a chair under a tree. One must always appear at one's best, no matter the circumstances, and certainly one should never let the sun work its damage on the skin. Her eyes narrowed thoughtfully as she scanned the hollow, scattered here and there with groups of people like bunches of flowers. There was the earl, talking with her father and some other men. At least he was safe for the time being. When she adjudged the time right, she would go to him and separate him from the group, continuing her campaign to win him. Then there was Mr. Fairleigh. Pleasant enough, she supposed, and, according to rumor, quite plump in the pocket. He was, however, paying an unconscionable amount of attention to her sister. What he saw in Beatrice, she didn't know. Beatrice was welcome to him, though. He had no title, and that made him completely ineligible in Penelope's eyes. That left only Viscount Byrne.

"May I join you?" a cultured voice said, and she looked up to see the Viscount.

"Please do," she said coolly, hiding her excitement as he took the chair next to her. Well. This was more like it. "So fatiguing, being out of doors like this, is it not?"

"Quite." Basil lounged back in the chair. Somewhere along the way he had managed to repair the damage wreaked on his appearance by the excursion to the earl's ship. Not a hair was out of place; his neckcloth was neatly and intricately tied; and his shirt points were white and crisp, in spite of the heat of the day. The earl could learn something about fashion from this man. "Are you enjoying yourself, Miss Lamb?"

"Oh, quite. Though I am persuaded, sir, that this kind of rustic entertainment is not quite to your taste."

"It will do. I never expect much in the way of entertainment in the country." His eyes slid to hers, and he smiled, unexpectedly. "Of course, I didn't expect to meet you, Miss Lamb. You appear as out of place here as I."

Penelope preened. "I did have a season in London, sir."

Something sparked in his eyes. "Did you? I am sorry I didn't meet you there."

Penelope kept her smile cool. Surely he wasn't laughing at her! "I am hoping to come to town next spring, sir. Perhaps we will see one another there."

"Perhaps." He leaned forward, suddenly frowning. "That is your brother with Miss Fairleigh?"

Penelope glanced across the hollow, and stiffened.

George was indeed standing with Daphne, gazing adoringly down into her face. With them, however, was Cassandra. "I wonder that Aldrich has the nerve to join them," she said, softly.

"Miss Aldrich has worked hard to make this a success," he said, absently. "The earl would be lost without her."

"Oh, indeed." Penelope invested her words with as much meaning as she could, and Basil, at last distracted, turned to look at her, one eyebrow raised.

"Like that, is it? I wondered."

"Oh, indeed," she said again. "Of course, no one knows for certain, they are being very discreet, but the earl is a man and Aldrich is passably attractive, I suppose."

Daphne and Cassandra were laughing at something George had said, drawing Basil's attention again. "You sound as if you know her rather well."

"I do. She was our governess, before we turned her off." He turned to look at her again. "She attempted to seduce my brother. Of course we couldn't have that."

"I see. So that is how she came to be with the earl."

"Yes. Taking care of those brats of his. Or so she says."

"I see," he said again, and Penelope smiled. There, she'd managed to avenge herself on Aldrich. Look at her, joining the guests as if she belonged. And, look at her, going to live with the earl. There was no doubt in Penelope's mind that, were it not for Aldrich, the earl would be hers today.

"In fact, sir, if I were you, I would remove Miss Fairleigh from her presence, before she corrupts her."

Basil stiffened. Daphne and Cassandra had glanced over at him and then away, and now were laughing. "I knew Cassandra in London, you know," he said, at last leaning back, presenting the very picture of a man at ease.

Penelope looked at him, alerted by something in his voice. "Did you, sir?"

"Yes." His smile broadened. "Intimately."

For once, Penelope forgot her pose of coolness. "Really?"

"Yes. Though it pains me to say so about a lady—of course, I am not certain one could call her a lady."

"I don't believe so, either." She paused. "You didn't wish to marry her, sir?"

"To the contrary. It was she who spurned me." He looked at her. "Of course, it is past. I would hope you'd say nothing of this to anyone. Far be it from me to ruin a lady's reputation, but—"

"But we do need to know what we are dealing with, do we not? Fear not, sir." She reached over and laid her hand on his. "I shall not breathe a word of this to a soul."

"Thank you. If you will excuse me, Miss Lamb, I really should rescue Miss Fairleigh."

"Yes, of course." She smiled up at him as he took her hand. "It has been quite interesting talking with you, sir."

"And with you, ma'am." For a moment their eyes met, the gazes of two people who perfectly understood each other, and then he walked away.

Penelope rose and strolled toward the group of men where the earl still stood, her spirits vastly improved. It was Aldrich who had made her life so frustrating of late. Soon, though, she would be gone. Viscount Byrne had just handed Penelope the perfect weapon. She intended to use it.

Chapter 15

The nightmare came again that night. Nicholas lay still on his back, an arm flung over his eyes, as if to shut out the grisly images. It came less and less often these days, as he gradually let go of the past, though he knew the guilt would be with him forever. When first he had arrived at the Hall he'd had it nearly every night. Now it came only if something happened to remind him. Being aboard the *Eagle* today had been a forcible reminder, making him realize anew all he had lost. Ashore he might have authority and even, it seemed, the respect and affection of his neighbors. It wasn't enough, though. It wasn't the life he had trained for, the life he'd always wanted. Only Cassie made it bearable.

Cassie. The thought of her sent an urgent need through him to see her. Flinging the covers back, he swung his legs over the side of the bed and crossed to the door, his bare feet covering the distance in a few long strides. Only when he struck his shin against the doorjamb did he realize that he was hardly dressed properly for an evening call. Blast, making such a call at all was improper. But he had to see her, talk to her, he thought, struggling into the nightshirt he so rarely wore and then covering that with his old,

215

worn dressing gown. He had to assure himself she was still with him. It wasn't only going aboard his ship that had triggered the nightmare. It was seeing her with Byrne, and knowing he might lose her. He couldn't let that happen.

The floorboard outside Cassandra's door, always a reliable signal that someone was there, squeaked. Cassandra shot up in bed, reaching for the tinder to light her candle with fingers that shook slightly. The day had been trying, the evening long, and she had hardly slept, except for an occasional light doze. Now she knew what she was so nervous about. Basil. As she had feared, he had no intention of leaving her alone. "Who is it?" she called as the door opened. "Who's there?"

Nicholas stepped into the room, his hair mussed and his expression sheepish, so that he looked like a little boy. "Evening, Cassie. Did I wake you?"

"Nicholas!" She clutched the covers to her chest. "What in the world?"

"Couldn't sleep." He glanced around her room, and then, ignoring the chair, sat on the edge of her bed. "By Neptune, I didn't realize how small this room is. You deserve better."

" 'Tis close to the children. Nicholas—"

"All the work you've done on this house, and your own room is bare." He shook his head. "Should do something about it, Cassie. Better yet, there are better rooms downstairs."

"I belong on the nursery floor. Nicholas, what are you doing here?"

"Told you. Couldn't sleep." His eyes flickered to her, and then away. "Thought I'd like to talk to someone. If you want me to leave, I will."

"Was it the nightmare again, Nicholas?"

He turned astonished eyes on her. "How the devil do you know about that?"

"Kirby mentioned it once. He didn't say anything else, though." She leaned back against the pillows, primly straightening her ruffled nightcap. "If you need to talk I've no objection, but please do keep your voice down. I don't want to waken the children, or the nursery maid."

"This is blasted improper of me, isn't it? I'm sorry, Cassie, I wasn't thinking. I'll go."

"No." To her own surprise she reached out and grasped his arm. "No, please stay."

"Do you mean that?"

"I suppose I do. But only"—she fixed her best governess look on him—"to talk."

"What else?" he said, feigning surprise, and she frowned. "Ah, Cassie. You're safe with me. Don't you know that?"

"Yes." She settled back, waiting for him to begin, but he only sat, head down, picking at a stray thread in his dressing gown. "I believe your guests are enjoying themselves."

"Yes." He looked up. "Cassie, is there anything between you and Byrne?"

"Good heavens!" She stared at him, about to protest, when a little imp, long ignored, urged her to something different. "And what if there is?"

"Blast it, Cassie!" He leaned toward her, gripping her wrist. "The man's not fit to swab the deck, let alone dangle after you."

"Nicholas."

"I won't have it, Cassie." He rose and took a turn around the room, pushing his hand into hair, which was already mussed. "Do you hear me? I won't allow it."

"Nicholas, there's nothing. I promise you. Nothing."

He eyed her from beneath lowered brows. "Then why did you try to make me believe there is?"

"I was only funning you. I told you, Nicholas, we knew each other once. That is all."

"Is it?"

She glanced away. "I won't deny I was attracted to him once, but that was a long time ago. I've changed. In any event, he's courting Miss Fairleigh."

"I don't know what Sam is about, to allow that," he growled, at last sitting beside her.

"Well, thank heavens it's none of our affair. Mr. Fairleigh seemed to like your ship."

"Aye." He paused. "Said I should skipper her myself."

"Well, why don't you? It is what you want."

"I can't, Cassie. I have responsibilities here."

"And you asked me why I was so proper," she mocked, gently.

"Aye." He reached for her hand. "Things do change, don't they, Cassie?"

"Aye." She twined her fingers through his, reveling in the contact. For just this night, these stolen moments, they were no longer the earl and his governess, but a man and a woman. The man she loved. "Tell me about the dream."

He shook his head. "Doesn't matter now, Cassie."

"It must, if it bothers you like this."

"It's nothing I want to burden you with."

"Nicholas." She briefly tightened her grip. "You've been there for me so often. Won't you let me do this for you?" When he looked at her without answering, she went on. "Something happened aboard the ship today."

"Yes." He pulled his hand away, leaving hers feeling cold and bereft. She tucked it next to her, as if for comfort. "Sam got to talking about old times. Reminded me that we always said we'd go into the merchant trade together."

"You and Mr. Fairleigh?"

"Aye. And John Northrup."

"I don't believe I've ever heard you mention him before."

"He died in battle."

"Oh, I'm so sorry, Nicholas." She reached out her hand to him, and then withdrew it. Something in the way he sat, very still, his shoulders hunched, told her he didn't want to be touched. "Did you know him long?"

"Aye. Since entering the navy. We were all midshipmen together. Don't know if we'd have got through it without each other." He rose abruptly and began pacing, his height making her tiny room seem even smaller. "Life in the navy is hell, Cassie," he said, bluntly. "Never told you that, did I?"

"No," she said, her voice faint. All Nicholas's tales had been of glory and adventure. "You never did."

"Sorry, Cassie, but it's the truth. A warship is hell. Several hundred men, all crammed together, away from home for years, with only lousy food and pretty damn poor pay. Worse, you live either in boredom, between actions, or fear. Midshipmen have it a little better. At least we started off as officers, and we had our own mess. Dirty, smelly place, and during an action it was used as the surgery, but we were away from the rest of the crew." He shoved his hands into his pockets. "A warship lives on discipline. Isn't any different in the midshipmen's mess, and a new boy coming aboard has to prove himself. Well, I was strong for my age and able to give a good account of myself, and so did Sam. Northrup, though, was small, and he had a strange sense of humor, got him into trouble any number of times. Game 'un, always ready to fight, but

219

small. So Sam and I took him over. Became good friends, too."

"Was it always so bad, Nicholas?"

"No. Sometimes. Battles were hard." His voice was clipped. "But we grew up. Learned about navigation and seamanship, and because we were officers we had some authority and a chance at better things. We all wanted to go far, the three of us. Don't get me wrong, Cassie. The life was hard, but it was the life for me."

Cassandra wrapped her arms about her knees. "Mm-hm. And you survived it."

"Aye. Sam was the first of us to get his own command. Then I did, a sixth-rate at first, only twenty-eight guns, but then a fourth-rate with fifty guns. There was talk my next command would be a third-rate, or maybe even a second-rate. I was on my way up in the world, Cassie. I was twenty-four years old."

"Where were you?"

"Mediterranean. By this time the worst at sea was over. All we basically were doing was enforcing the blockades." He paused. "Did I mention that Northrup was my lieutenant?

"No."

"Best seaman I ever saw. Should have had his own command. But he had that strange sense of humor, as I said, and he offended someone in the Admiralty. Anyway. It was the beginning of action in the Peninsula. We were part of a convoy, making sure the supplies got to the army all right. We were off Gibraltar, a foggy, dismal day, couldn't see a hundred yards ahead. Got the surprise of my life when this ship suddenly appeared, not fifty yards off. There wasn't any wind, we couldn't veer off, and I couldn't spot her colors at first. Could tell by her design she wasn't English-built, but we'd captured and taken over so many foreign ships that that didn't mean anything. Then I saw her flag. She was French."

"A warship?"

"No, that kind of action was pretty much over after Trafalgar. She was a trader. We didn't know that, then." He sank down on her bed, his hands loosely clasped between his legs. "Anyway, a merchant ship's guns are just as deadly as a ship of the line's, at that range."

"But would a trader want to do battle?"

"No, not usually, but we were too close. We beat to quarters, prepared for action. It should have been easy. Hell, Cassie, he only had a few guns. I had fifty. He didn't have a chance." He took a deep breath. "Our first broadside took his mizzenmast. Crew was scurrying on deck, trying to cut it loose and trying to get the ship into position for another barrage, and we came around, raked him from the other side. Thought he was done for then, but he still had some surprises left for us. He drove straight for us, Cassie, head to head, and his bowsprit crossed ours. We were all tangled together, like this," he said, putting his fingertips together and holding them in a V shape.

"Oh," Cassandra said. She barely understood what he was talking about, and yet she could see it, the two ships locked together at the bows, the very front, and unable to get free. "What happened?"

"I decided to board him. Barely gave the order when those Frenchies gave a god-awful yell and started boarding us. Nothing to do then but fight, hand to hand."

"Good heavens!"

"I had charge of one group of men, Northrup and the other officers had others. Not much you can do in a situation like that but fight, with everything you have. I had my sword out and was laying about with it—"

"Were you hurt?"

221

He blinked, as if startled. "Nothing to signify. Accounted for a few Frenchies. It was—"

"What?" she prompted when he didn't go on.

"Nothing. A good fight."

"Oh." She had the feeling that wasn't what he'd planned to say, not with that fierce light in his eyes. All her life she had seen Nicholas as her champion, her friend. Now she saw another side of him. He was a warrior.

"After a while we started to beat them back. The deck was pretty slippery by then, and I went down on my knee. As I got up I heard someone yell to me to look out, and sure enough, there was a Frenchy, standing over me with a belaying pin."

"Oh my Lord!"

"He caught me on the arm, here, just as I managed to get up." Nicholas indicated his left forearm. "He broke it. Didn't even feel it until later. All I cared about was getting him. I did." He paused. "Felt someone behind me, just as I finished. I was—when something like this happens, you get out of yourself, somehow. Things you'd never do otherwise, you do. Once I started fighting, I couldn't stop. There was—it wasn't pleasure, Cassie, but there's something. I never felt so alive, as I did then, ready to take on the world. Ready to fight anyone. Well, there was this person behind me, and I didn't care who it was. I spun around and struck. Cut the man nearly in half." He paused again. "It was Northrup."

"Oh no!"

"Turned out he saw me fall and he was protecting my back, and I killed him." His head lowered. "He died in my arms."

Cassandra knelt up on the bed. "Nicholas, you didn't know—"

"I should have known, damn it! It was my ship. God."

He ran a hand over his face. "His eyes were open, staring at God knows what. He looked surprised. I still see that look sometimes. In the nightmare."

"Oh, Nicholas. Oh, how awful."

"I live it over and over, but it always comes out the same. I killed my best friend."

"You didn't mean to."

"Fact remains, Cassie, I did. Well, we beat the Frenchy. Didn't matter. Northrup was dead."

"But, in the heat of battle—"

"They hauled me up before a court of inquiry. Can't have officers killing other officers, after all. And that's what the magistrates said. In the heat of battle. They let me go back to sea." He took a deep breath. "But I never got a better ship after that. Never rose higher in the ranks, never got a better command." His voice softened. "And I've never forgotten what I did."

Cassandra leaned forward and put her arms around his shoulders, laying her head against his back. Now she knew why he never discussed battles. There was no glory in them for him. There was nothing she could say, nothing she could do to comfort him except to hold him. Nicholas, however, apparently didn't want comfort. Instead, with a force he'd never before shown her, he hauled her onto his lap, into his arms.

"Nicholas," she protested, but it was a feeble protest, as his lips traveled over her face, her brows, her cheeks. Oh, how long had she dreamed of this! To be held by him, to have him see her, not as the young girl he had once rescued, not as a properly distant governess, but as a woman. His woman, and only his. It couldn't last, of course. In a moment, she would pull away. For now, though, she reveled in his touch, arching her head back

223

as his lips pressed demanding kisses on her throat. There was no one else. There never had been.

Nicholas reached up and pulled off her nightcap, her hair spilling in glorious profusion over her shoulders. "I love your hair." He buried his face in it, rubbing the strands against his fingers, and his warm breath on her neck sent shivers through her. "It smells of—lavender?"

"Lilac."

"Lilac. It suits you, Cassie." His mouth moved further on her neck and found a sensitive spot, making her head drop back again. "My beautiful Cassie. I want you."

Cassandra's eyes flew open. He did, indeed, want her. She could feel it. "Nicholas, what are you doing?"

Nicholas's voice was muffled as his lips pushed at the collar of her nightshift. "Making love to you."

"You can't!" She pushed at his shoulders. It was like trying to move a stone wall. They couldn't do this. She couldn't. She couldn't take the chance again. "Oh please."

Nicholas raised his head. His eyes were heavy, sleepy-looking. "Ah, Cassie. When you touched me—"

"I didn't mean to start anything," she babbled. "I wanted to comfort you, you were so upset—"

"It's not comfort I want, Cassie."

She pulled back, evading his lips. "Nicholas, please."

His grip tightened, and his head dropped to her shoulder. For a moment, there was silence. "Ah, Cassie. I'm sorry."

"Nicholas, please let me go."

"I didn't mean to scare you. I'd never want to hurt you. But, oh God, Cassie." He pressed his head harder against her, between the curve of her neck and shoulder. "I close my eyes, and I see it all over again. I see him."

"Hush." Cassandra pressed his head to her breast and

rocked him back and forth. The impropriety of their embrace no longer mattered. Nicholas needed her. Just as he had always been there for her, so she couldn't turn him away now. "It's past, Nicholas. It's over."

His fingers dug into her arms. "I still see his face."

"You didn't mean to do it, Nicholas. Oh please, stop torturing yourself this way." She framed his face in her hands. It was rough with stubble, lined from the sun. Her fingers ached to explore it. "You didn't mean to do it."

Nicholas gazed up at her. "You believe in me."

"Yes, Nicholas. Always."

"Oh God." Abruptly he grabbed her, pulling her closer. Cassandra barely had time to react before his lips were on hers, hard, warm, demanding.

"Nicholas." She twisted her head away, though that last kiss had sent fire through her veins. "No, please——"

"I need you, Cassie." He caught her chin in his hand. "Don't turn me away."

He needed her. Cassie gazed into his eyes, seeing their fear and vulnerability and something else, something warm that made her heart leap. He needed her. And she needed him, too, as she had never needed anyone. She needed love, his love. It couldn't be wrong.

This time when his head bent she didn't turn away, but lifted her lips eagerly to his. This time she returned his embrace, holding on to him as if for her very life. It was madness, what she was doing, but it was sweet madness. He deepened the kiss and she responded instinctively, tilting her head to give him access, opening her mouth to admit his eager tongue, using her own tongue in a way that made him groan. She allowed his weight to bear her back on the bed; allowed his hands to roam where they would, pulling at the buttons of her nightshift, stroking lovingly over her breasts, her waist, her hips. And then it was no longer a question of allowing him to do these things, but a matter of allowing herself to flow with him. She could no more have stopped him, or herself, than she could the tides. They came together in a surging current, and she felt the waves lifting her, higher, higher. Yet it was all right, because Nicholas was there with her, holding her. The waves peaked, crested. From somewhere she heard a cry, sharp and high-pitched, and only dimly recognized it as her own. Then she was floating, drifting, in a dark warm sea, held safely in Nicholas's arms.

A long time later Cassandra lay on her side in the narrow bed, curled contentedly against Nicholas's warm body, falling into a deep, dreamless sleep. Rest didn't come so easily to Nicholas, however. Too much had happened today, the emotions of the afternoon, his nightmare, and now this, the tumultuous loving. And something else, something he hadn't expected and which had knocked him on his beam ends. Cassie meant the world to him, there was no question of that, and tonight she had given herself to him without reservation. It had been special, precious. Yet, at the height of their loving he had discovered something that stunned him. Cassie was sweet, warm, loving, and his, but not his alone. Cassie was not a virgin. He was not her first lover. And how he would deal with that, he didn't know.

Chapter 16

Cassandra woke alone. Sleepily she turned over, her arm reaching for Nicholas and finding only emptiness. Blinking, she leaned up on her elbow. It hadn't been a dream. The bed was mussed in a way it never was when she slept alone, and the imprint of his head was still on her pillow. There was even a golden hair lying on the pillowslip. Cassandra picked it up delicately between forefinger and thumb and grinned at it. Nicholas's hair, precious because it was his. Oh, she was behaving foolishly, like a besotted girl, but she couldn't help it. She was in love. After last night, she had little doubt that that love was returned.

She went through the morning lighthearted and light-footed, smiling and singing snatches of silly songs. It didn't matter that her body ached in odd places, or that there were bruises on her arms from Nicholas's fierce grip. Last night had been magical, wonderful. Nothing ever would be the same again.

As had become her custom, she joined the guests at luncheon, listening to them talk of their plans for the afternoon. Some were going riding, over the rolling hills of the South Downs. Most of the ladies planned to go into the village to visit the shops and then take tea with Mrs.

Carlisle, and several expressed a desire for a walk. Nicholas said nothing to any of these plans. His head was bent and he toyed with his food, pushing a bit of beefsteak around with his fork. Cassandra wondered if his nightmare still bothered him.

"You'll come, won't you, Cassandra?" Sabrina said, breaking into her thoughts.

"Hm?" Cassandra looked up and smiled. "No, I fear I cannot. I promised Juanita and Elena I would take them to the cove today and let them wade, it's been so warm. But I do thank you for asking." She glanced again at the head of the table, to see Nicholas watching her. As her gaze met his, however, he looked away. Some of Cassandra's euphoria faded.

"Did you and mine host have a quarrel?" Basil said to her in a low voice as they rose from the table.

Cassandra stiffened, pulling away from the proprietary hand he had rested on her back. "No, of course not." Far from it. However, it was better if the guests thought that, rather than the truth. "Whatever makes you think that?"

"I noticed he didn't speak to you during luncheon. He watched you, though."

"Oh? I didn't notice."

"I don't think you were meant to. He looked elsewhere if he thought you could see. He had a strange look on his face, too." Basil bared his teeth in a smile. "Angling after him isn't doing you any good, is it, Cassandra?"

"You haven't changed," she said in a low voice, aware of the others, waiting for them in the hall. Some had glanced curiously back into the dining room. Including Nicholas. "You are as spiteful and malicious as ever."

"Ah no, Cassandra. Merely an interested observer."

"Well, I'll thank you to stop observing me." She pulled away from him, her lips pursing with annoyance. Basil had lost the right to any say in what she did long ago. However, he was right about one thing. Something was wrong with Nicholas. After last night, she couldn't imagine what it was.

She caught up with him just as he was leaving his study, preparatory to going riding with the gentlemen. Since he was usually home in the afternoons she had thought she would have the chance to speak to him while the children napped, but unfortunately this was all she could manage. "Nicholas," she called from the stairs as he crossed the hall, which was otherwise empty. "Please, wait."

Nicholas stopped, glancing about the hall, gazing toward the door. Looking, in fact, anywhere but at her. "Have to join the others, Cassandra. Don't have much time."

His use of her full name was puzzling. "Nicholas, is something wrong?" She stepped closer to him. His eyes settled for a moment on her face, and then skittered away.

"Nothing's wrong, Cassandra. I don't have time to talk."

"Is it the nightmare?" She moved closer, and he stepped back. "Is it bothering you that you told me about it?"

"No."

"Then, Nicholas—"

"There's nothing." He clapped his hat onto his head. "Have to go," he said, and fled the house, leaving Cassandra standing in the hall, alone and bewildered. How could he just leave, after last night? Oh no. Not again. It couldn't be happening again.

Matters didn't improve during the day. At dinner Nicholas appeared to be his usual self, except that, again, he wouldn't look at her. Cassandra had little appetite for the meal. All afternoon the dread had been growing inside her, and the panic. She had made another mistake, the same mistake, and she feared very much that she would have to pay, and pay dearly. Though it had seemed like tragedy the last time, she knew now that only her pride had been bruised. This, though, was far more serious. This time her heart was involved.

Pleading a headache, she went directly upstairs after dinner. She couldn't rest, though, couldn't settle to reading or mending or planning the girls' lessons for the next day. At odd moments she would catch herself staring into nothingness, a pen poised in her hand, the ink long dried on the tip, and she would apply herself to her work again with greater diligence, to no avail. Finally she gave up, and began pacing her narrow room, until the headache she had pretended to became all too real. It was too much, this waiting and wondering and worrying. Nicholas would not come to her tonight, that she knew. Yet she couldn't stand another day of this uncertainty. She would have to go to him.

The great house was quiet and dim as she slipped down the stairs. Somehow, without her noticing it, the time had passed and everyone was abed. There was, however, light showing under Nicholas's door. She paused, hand raised to knock, and then lifted her chin. No. She wasn't going to give him a chance to turn her away. Lips set in a firm line, she turned the handle and went in.

"Who is it—good God!" Nicholas jumped up from his chair by the fireplace. Cassie, of all people. Cassie, so beautiful, and so faithless. "Cassandra, what in Neptune's name do you think you are doing?"

Cassandra came into the room, eyeing him warily. "I need to talk to you, Nicholas," she said, closing the door.

"Well, you can't do it here. Good God, Cassie, if anyone saw you come in—"

"That didn't seem to matter to you last night."

"Last night was different."

"Yes, so I gathered." She drew the chair out from his writing table and sat facing him, hands folded in her lap. His room suited her, she saw in one quick glance. In contrast to the countess's room's former shabby opulence, it had the clean, stripped-down appearance of a ship at sea. The furniture was simple, light pine, and the coverlet was midnight blue. The walls were pale cream, and were decorated with little beyond a brass chronometer, a barometer, and a painting of a ship under full sail. No carpets covered the wide board floors, which had been polished to a high gloss. Nicholas had evidently tried to recreate as much of his former environment as he could. Had she not been so upset, she might have felt some compassion for him at that. "We do need to talk."

"Yes, but not here."

"Where, then? And when? You avoided me all day."

"That's not true," he mumbled, rising and turning away, though he hadn't wanted to face her, or the truth about her. "Nothing's wrong, Cassandra. Go back to bed."

"You're sorry about last night," she said, her voice and eyes steady. "You didn't mean it to happen, certainly not with me, and now you regret it. But you don't know how to tell me—"

"Good God, Cassie!" He wheeled to face her, gripping the back of his chair. "How could I regret last night? I was alone, and I'd had that damned nightmare. You made me feel alive, Cassie." He paused. "Never felt that way before."

"Neither have I."

"Hm."

"Then what is it, Nicholas?" she asked, leaning forward, her face creased. "Tell me. I need to know."

"God." He dropped into his chair, rubbing his hand over his face. He had hoped to escape this. What he had learned about Cassandra last night had changed all his perceptions of her. Clearly she was a woman of experience, and, to his knowledge, women of experience didn't make such a fuss. Unless she expected him to marry her. Funny. He'd almost asked her, last night. "There's something I need to know, Cassie."

"Yes, what?"

He raised his head and looked directly at her. "Who was he?"

"Who was who?"

"Who was the man that came before me?"

She sucked in her breath. "I don't think that's any of your affair!"

"It damned well is my affair!" he roared, slamming his hand down on the arm of his chair. "I thought you were pure, Cassie. I thought I was taking your virginity, and, by Neptune, what a gift that was! And then to find out—" His face was set. "Who was he?"

"It doesn't matter." She rubbed her forehead with her fingertips. "It was a very long time ago."

"Was it Byrne?"

She shook her head. "No."

"Who, then?"

"No one you know." Her hands dropped. "And you don't have the right to know, no matter what you may think. It's in the past."

"Not as far as I'm concerned."

"Are you trying to tell me you were never with another woman before last night?" she demanded.

"No, of course not, but—"

232

"Then don't condemn me, Nicholas St. John! You're no better than I am."

"It's different, Cassie. It's all right for a man—"

"Oh, of course," she said, bitterly. "All very well for a man, but not for a woman."

"I can't help it, Cassie." He held his hands up, then let them drop in his lap. "It's the way I feel."

"That I'm soiled goods?"

"No," he said, but he looked away, unable to meet her steady gaze. "Of course not."

"I see." She sat back, arms limp in her lap, as if she had lost all strength. She looked much older than she had a few moments ago, and the familiar urge to comfort her, protect her, rose in him. This time he didn't give in to it. "What do we do now, then?"

"I don't know, Cassie. I—don't know."

"I see," she said again, and rose. "Well. This was never intended to be more than a temporary position. I'll leave."

He looked up, stricken. "Cassie—"

"I'll wait until you find a new governess, of course. But then I'll go."

"Cassie," he called. She stopped at the door, her back to him, her head slightly turned. "Why did you do it?"

Cassandra closed her eyes for just a moment. Then, without a word, she stepped out the door and was gone, leaving him far more alone than he had ever been in his life.

There were entertainments yet to plan, menus to oversee, a ball to organize. Much as she might want to, Cassandra could not give in to the dark depression that had settled upon her. Instead, she smiled at the guests, talked

233

with the servants, hugged the children. If there was a certain mechanical quality to her actions, if her eyes had taken on a lost, empty look, no one remarked upon it. Nicholas certainly didn't, but then, he rarely looked directly at her these days.

"This is how it used to be," Beatrice said, leaning back in her chair at the day nursery table and setting down her teacup. "When we used to visit you to escape from Mama."

Over the rim of her own cup Cassandra smiled politely at Beatrice and Amanda, her two visitors. It was foggy and misty, much like her mood, and Nicholas's guests had been forced to find entertainment within doors. The two Lamb girls, however, had been adamant. It was Cassandra they wished to see. "What does your mother think of this?" she asked.

"Oh, she doesn't know." Amanda brushed back a strand of hair that had come loose. "She believes we're visiting with Miss Fairleigh. It's not quite a bouncer. We will see her before we leave." She smirked at her sister. "Beatrice wants to see Mr. Fairleigh, anyway."

"I do not!" Beatrice exclaimed. "Mandy, such a thing to say!"

"I'm afraid he's not here," Cassandra said, and saw disappointment flicker in Beatrice's eyes. "I understand he went to the village."

"Oh." Beatrice raised her cup with studied nonchalance. "It doesn't signify."

"You'll have to wait until the ball tomorrow night, Bea."

"Amanda." Beatrice glared at her. "You'll have Cassandra thinking I've set my cap for the man."

"Well, you have."

"He's a very nice man," Cassandra said, rising, before

the sisterly squabbling could get out of hand. "Would you care to see the music room? 'Tis where the ball will be held."

"Oh yes!" Amanda jumped up. "We're ever so excited about it, Cassandra, aren't you? Imagine, a real ball, here in Fairhaven!"

"Yes." Cassandra quietly opened the door of the night nursery and looked in. Juanita and Elena were curled on their beds, taking their afternoon naps, while Mary Ann, the nursery maid, sat nearby, a pile of mending on her lap. Cassandra nodded to her and closed the door. She could leave them for now, though for the last few days she had left the safety of this room as little as possible. Thank heavens she had Beatrice and Amanda with her, in case they did encounter Nicholas. "It has been a great deal of work, though," she added, leading them out into the hallway.

"I thought you looked burnt to the socket."

"Mandy." This time Beatrice sounded more exasperated than angry. "I'm sorry, Cassandra. I don't know what's making her say such outrageous things today."

" 'Tis all right." Cassandra opened the door to the music room and stepped in. "What do you think?"

"Oh." Both girls spoke at once, staring about the room with wide eyes. For a moment Cassandra emerged from her fog, seeing the room through their eyes. It did look nice. Even though the day was gray, everything sparkled, from the tall windows, to the long mirrors on the walls, to the chandeliers. The parquet floor had been polished to a high gloss, and the holland covers had been removed to reveal chairs of white and gilt with red velvet seats. Even the spinet had been restored to its former glory. It was a magnificent room, rivaling any ballroom she had seen in London, and a fitting setting for Nicholas's ball.

She wished she wouldn't have to attend it tomorrow night.

"Tomorrow we'll bring in the flowers," she said, in an effort to distract herself. "The neighbors have been wonderful, letting us raid their gardens. There was so much, I didn't know what to choose, but the duchess and Mrs. Fairleigh have both been very helpful. Heaven knows I've never had to plan a ball before."

"Yes, Mama had something to say about that," Amanda said, and waltzed onto the floor, her arms raised as if she were in the embrace of an imaginary partner.

"I am sorry, Cassandra," Beatrice said in a low voice, though Amanda, humming to herself, paid them no heed. "I don't know why she's saying such things."

Cassandra smiled. "It doesn't bother me, Beatrice. She always has been outspoken."

"I know, but she really should know enough to mind her tongue. Especially when you—"

"When I what?" Cassandra asked when Beatrice stopped.

"I'm sorry, Cassandra, I didn't mean to say anything. But you do look tired." She pulled back to study Cassandra's face. "And unhappy. Is anything wrong?"

"No, of course not. What could be wrong?"

"Have you and the earl quarreled?"

"Beatrice." Cassandra stared at her. "What a thing to say."

"You did, didn't you?" Beatrice said. "Oh, Cassie."

The sympathy was very nearly Cassandra's undoing. The tears that she had held back, burning at her eyes, for days, now surged forward. She composed herself only by a great effort. "It—nothing happened. It doesn't mean anything."

"Oh, Cassie," Beatrice said again. "And I had so hoped—"

"What?"

"Well, anyone could see how you felt about him, the day he first came to the manor. And you deserve it, Cassie."

"No. I'm getting what I deserve now." Because she had deceived Nicholas, no matter how unwittingly. It was true that she had never expected to be intimate with him. It was only natural she had expected to keep her secret, and yet now it felt wrong. Loving him as she did, knowing how he had always been there for her in the past, perhaps she should have trusted him. Or, perhaps not. It was altogether possible he would have reacted in the same way. The man she had always thought of as her hero had failed her, and it hurt.

"Why? Because he's an earl and you're a governess? Surely you don't believe that, Cassie."

Cassandra shrugged. "It's the way of the world." Somewhere in the house a clock chimed, and she paused to count the strokes. "The children will be waking soon. I must go."

"Yes, of course. Mandy," Beatrice called, and Amanda, who had danced to the far end of the room, began twirling toward them. "Won't you let me help you?"

Cassandra managed a smile, putting her hand on Beatrice's arm. "There's no help for this, Bea." She could just imagine Beatrice's reaction if she did tell her what had happened. "I do appreciate the thought."

"Well?" Amanda spun to a stop before them, her hair tousled and her cheeks charmingly flushed. "Did you find out what's wrong, Bea?"

Beatrice glared at her. "Amanda," she said, drawing

out each syllable, and Cassandra laughed. It was the first time she'd felt like laughing in days.

"I love you both." She threw her arms around them in a quick, fierce hug, and then pulled back. How she would miss them when she had to leave. "Now. Let us go have a comfortable coze," she said, and led the way out of the room.

The sea was dead calm and glassy, with wisps of fog hovering only a few feet above the surface. It deadened all sound, muffling the scrape of the oars in their locks as Nicholas rowed out to the *Eagle*. Not a day to be out on the water, not in the ordinary way of things, but matters were far from ordinary. The sea was the world he knew, the only place he felt he truly belonged. For too long he had denied himself its solace, concentrating instead on becoming a country gentleman, living up to his responsibilities. All that had gained him was loneliness, and pain. He had lost something precious, and he didn't know how to get it back.

Kirby, who had decided he was much more comfortable aboard a ship, even one at anchor, than on land, saluted him when he climbed aboard. Nicholas nodded, going directly to the captain's cabin in the stern. As with everything else on the ship, the Americans had made this functional room attractive in a spare, simple way. Tiny paned windows stretched across the stern, and under them was a padded settee. In the center of the room, under the skylight, was a table, bolted down, while the bunk was built up against a bulkhead. Nicholas had felt at home here immediately, except for one thing. He would never command this ship.

Paper crackled in his coat pocket as he sank down onto

the settee. Frowning, he reached in and pulled out the letter that had arrived just this morning. His man of affairs had found a captain to skipper the *Eagle*, someone with experience and a good reputation. Nicholas would interview him, of course, and decide whether the man was suitable, and in the meantime the new skipper would begin to assemble a crew. Events were underway. Soon the *Eagle* would set sail, without him.

Maybe he wouldn't have felt so low about that had things not turned out as they had ashore. Until recently he hadn't realized how he was settling into his new life; how much the friendship of his neighbors meant to him, and how good it felt to stay in one place for a time. Cassie was an important part of that life. Cassie, who he had watched grow, who had always behaved with utmost propriety, a lady to her fingertips. His sweet Cassie, who had betrayed him.

The sound of water splashing outside made him turn to peer out the window. Just visible under the hull was another small boat, with Samuel pulling at the oars. Frowning, Nicholas stuffed the letter into his pocket and went up on deck. Blast, he didn't want this. He'd come out to the *Eagle* to try to find peace. That he hadn't was another matter.

"Ahoy." Samuel climbed over the rail, smiling. "Permission to come aboard, Cap'n."

"Of course." Nicholas's smile felt tight. "Dirty day to be out for a sail, Sam."

"They're playing cards back at the Hall. I got bored." Hands in pocket, Samuel surveyed the ship, from topmast to deck. "I envy you this, Nick."

"Come below. Got some good brandy and cheroots." Nicholas led the way back to the cabin, regretting his lost solitude. He liked Sam. No question, though, that he was a reminder of something else Nicholas would prefer to forget.

"The Yankees know how to build 'em," Samuel said, studying the cabin with the same thoroughness, before accepting a glass of brandy. "Too bad you're not skippering her."

"Cassie said the same thing," Nicholas said, and instantly regretted it.

Samuel looked at him over the rim of the glass. "Miss Aldrich seems to know you, Nick." Nicholas shrugged and turned away. "You two have a quarrel?"

"Blast it, of course not." Nicholas sat on the settee again, making much of trimming the end of his cheroot and lighting it. "Cassie's a friend."

"Mm-hm." Samuel sat beside him, and they blew clouds of smoke in silence. "Remember when this was all we wanted?"

"Aye. A ship of our own, to sail wherever we desired. I remember. And then things changed." He sipped from his glass. Cassie had changed. Or, more likely, she never had been what he thought. He was the first to admit that women were a mystery to him.

"The way life is, I guess."

"Aye. But what do you do, Sam, when you find out someone's not what you thought?"

Samuel's glance was sharp. "You still thinking about Northrup?"

"What!" Nicholas stared at him. Northrup was the farthest thing from his mind. "What do you mean?"

"You changed after what happened. Only natural. But you didn't mean to do it, Nick."

Nicholas rose, uneasy with this line of talk, and began pacing the cabin. "Blast it, I know it, but—"

"Something like that changes a man. War changes a

man." Samuel took a long swallow. "Makes you look at yourself a different way, and sometimes you don't like what you see. But I know one thing, Nick." He set his glass down on the table, hard. "You would never have done it deliberately."

"No." Nicholas stared back at him. Odd, but what had happened with Northrup seemed curiously distant, as if it had happened to someone else. "Sam, I don't like talking about this."

"Don't blame you." Samuel rose and poured himself more brandy. "Just one thing I want to know, Nick. When are you going to put it behind you and get on with your life?"

"I have put it behind me."

"Have you? Well, I know you, Nick. You're pretty damned hard on people when they make a mistake, including yourself. Don't you think it's about time you forgave yourself?"

"I have." As he spoke, he realized it was true. It was in the past. It hadn't been, though, until he had told Cassie about it.

"Good." He clapped Nicholas on the shoulder. "Whatever you're quarreling with Miss Aldrich about, let that go, too."

"That's different," he blurted.

"Is it? Not to put too fine a point on it, you both look like hell, Nick. Whatever happened, she's suffering for it."

Nicholas paced the cabin again. "I don't understand women, Sam."

"Who does? I'll tell you one thing, though. You could do a lot worse." He grinned. "So, for that matter, could I."

"Blast it, what do you want with Cassie?"

"Hold off, there!" Samuel held up his hands as Nicholas advanced upon him. "It's not Miss Aldrich I'm interested in. It's Miss Lamb. Miss Beatrice Lamb." His grin widened. "You sound jealous as the devil."

"I'm not." Nicholas stowed the brandy decanter back in the cabinet with enough force to make the liquid slosh back and forth. "Let's go back to the Hall, find something else to do besides whist, or cutting up at each other."

"Fine. But take my advice, Nick." Samuel hit him on the shoulder again. "Let the past go."

Let the past go. The words stayed with Nicholas through the remainder of the day, as he rowed back to shore, as he mingled with his guests. It's past, Nicholas, Cassie had said. The trouble was, it wasn't past, not for him. Some other man had held her, kissed her. Some other man had been the first. Blast it, that hurt. Cassie had always looked at him in a certain way, even when she was a child. God knows he'd liked that, needed it. Even now, when she tried to keep her distance, she still looked at him in that way sometimes. It had been balm to a soul sickened by war, wearied by life. It had made him feel alive again. Learning it was all a lie, that once some other man had meant more to her, was painful. The hell of it was that, in spite of everything, he still wanted her. He thought he always would.

The guests gathered in the drawing room after dinner for cards and conversation. Everyone was anticipating the ball tomorrow night, and that gave some animation to the talk. After nearly two weeks, the house party had run its course. Enjoyable it had been, but people had their own lives and were eager to return to them. Nicholas wasn't sure if he would be glad, or sorry, to see them go.

"My lord"—Hargreaves appeared in the doorway—"there are visitors, sir."

Nicholas turned from the table, where he held an indifferent hand of whist. "Well, then, show them in. Who is, anyway? The Lambs? Or—"

"No, my lord. They aren't local. The Marquess and Marchioness of Shand."

"Who?" Nicholas looked quickly at his guests, but they appeared as mystified as he.

"We've met them in town," Sabrina said, "but usually they stay in Yorkshire, where they live. They're not young."

Yorkshire. That rang a bell in his memory. "Why are they here?" Nicholas appealed to her.

"I have no idea."

"You can't keep them standing, sir," Cassandra put in quietly. His eyes flicked to hers, and then away. Her face was white. "There's room for them. I'll have Mrs. Feather see to it. But, my lord, I think I should say—"

"Yes, yes, have a room prepared. Very well, Hargreaves, show them in, and let's find out what this is all about."

"Yes, my lord." Hargreaves went out and returned a few moments later, followed by a couple in traveling dress. Sabrina's comment that they were old was an understatement; their hair was white, their faces lined. Yet both held themselves proudly erect. "The Marquess and Marchioness of Shand."

Nicholas crossed the room to them, his hand outstretched. "Welcome to Sutcliffe Hall. I am the Earl of Lynton."

Unexpectedly, the marquess's eyes gleamed. "Nicholas St. John, eh? Well, we've heard about you." His gnarled, wrinkled hand grasped Nicholas's firmly. "Sorry to show up without warning, but we came as soon as we heard."

"Oh?" Nicholas gestured them toward chairs, staring at them in fascination. The marchioness was a plump

243

little dumpling of a woman, smiling at everyone; the marquess was tall and spare, with strong bones. He reminded Nicholas of someone. "You have the advantage of me, I fear."

"Didn't David tell you about us?" Lady Shand said.

"David? Good God. David Maidstone?" Good God. His eyes sought Cassandra, standing poised in the doorway to the hall.

"Of course he didn't," Lord Shand said, exchanging an exasperated look with his wife. "That boy will never grow up."

"Now, Jason," Lady Shand reproved gently. "Yes, David Maidstone. We are his parents."

"Worse luck," the marquess muttered, and his wife sent him another look.

"We do apologize for arriving like this, but once we had David's letter, we couldn't wait." She beamed at him. "We've come for our grandchildren."

Chapter 17

"They're lovely little girls," Cassandra said, leading Lady Shand down the corridor to the night nursery. She was very much the governess again, very proper and self-contained. "Of course they're asleep now, but when they're awake, they're a joy to be with. Active, of course, and very sweet."

"It will be good to have little ones in the house again," Lady Shand said. "There are days when the Grange is so quiet. We had seven sons, you know."

"Good heavens! No, I didn't."

"David is our youngest. We never did know quite what to do with him. Oh, look at them."

Cassandra had opened the door of the night nursery, and the two women tiptoed in. Elena was sprawled atop the covers, her thumb securely in place in her mouth, while Juanita, quieter even in sleep, lay still on her back, her outflung arm the only sign of childish abandon. *Mis angeles*, Cassandra thought. "Juanita, and Elena," she whispered, pointing them out. "I shall have to tell them about you in the morning. I wish I knew how to say 'grandmother' in Spanish."

"*Abuela*," Lady Shand said, surprising her. "Jason and

I have been learning the language. After all, it would be a shame if we couldn't talk to our own grandchildren."

"Most commendable of you, my lady." Cassandra smiled at the nursery maid and then walked out, going into the day nursery. Her back to the marchioness, she lighted the lamp there with remarkably steady hands. "You'll want to know more about them, of course."

"Yes. What a pleasant room." Lady Shand smiled as she looked around. "Not at all like the schoolrooms I remember."

"I've tried to make their surroundings as pleasant as possible, so they could learn." Cassandra sat across the table from her. "Are you certain you wouldn't rather rest, ma'am? You've had a long journey."

"They're my babies. I want to know everything about them." She smiled. "You look surprised, Miss Aldrich."

"Oh no. It's just that I thought—"

"David led you to believe we would never accept them. Oh, that boy." She shook her head. "He said as much in his letter to us. Rather as if he's still trying to defy us. I don't understand him, Miss Aldrich, I'll tell you that frankly. I love him, but I never did understand him. Well. That is neither here nor there. The important thing is that those babies have a home."

"This will likely upset them," Cassandra said, choosing her words carefully. "Elena is young enough that she adapts quickly, but Juanita's had more trouble. She still remembers her mother, you see."

"Poor child. Well, we'll just have to love them and make them feel as if they belong. My daughter-in-law is so excited." She smiled. "My oldest son's wife. She's barren, poor thing. Well, we certainly have enough sons and grandsons to carry on the title, so that isn't a problem.

But she would like children. She's looking forward to mothering these two."

"I'm glad." Cassandra forced a smile. Captain Maidstone had indeed misled them, making them think that his family would repudiate the girls. Instead, they apparently stood ready, not only to give them a home, but to love them. For that, Cassandra thought, she should be glad. She wasn't.

"Well." Lady Shand rose. "I am tired, and now that I've seen my babies I can rest. Will you help me find my room, dear?"

"Of course." Cassandra took the woman's arm and helped her down the stairs, smiling and talking as if nothing in the world were amiss. It was only later, when she returned to the nursery floor, that she let her mask slip. Opening the door of the night nursery, she looked in. *Mis angeles,* she thought again, and turned sharply away. She would not cry.

Cassandra was just beginning to get undressed for the night when there was a light tap on the door, making her freeze. *Nicholas.* How she knew she couldn't say, but she did. Pulling her dress back up over her shoulders, she went to the door and opened it a crack. Nicholas stood there, clad only in breeches and shirt. The muscled shoulders that sometimes made him look bulky in a fashionable coat now showed to advantage, making her mouth grow dry. "What is it?" she whispered.

"Came to see if you're all right," he whispered back.

"Yes." He looked tired, she noted. There were lines around his eyes that hadn't been there before, and his hair was mussed. "Is that all?"

"Aye. Well—could I come in, Cassie?"

"I don't think it's a good idea, sir."

He made a sharp gesture with his hand. "Nothing's going to happen."

"Oh yes. On that you're right, my lord."

"Blast." He thrust his hand into his hair. "I want to talk to you about the children.

Cassandra hesitated. "Very well. Just a moment." Closing the door, she did up her dress with fingers made clumsy by haste. Nicholas was stubborn. The sooner she let him say what he wished, the sooner he would leave.

Eventually she opened the door again, and he stepped in. Immediately the memories flooded back, sharp and clear, of the last time he had been in this room. His eyes met hers, and in them she saw the same remembrance, making her look away. Dangerous thoughts. "Well, sir?"

He thrust his hands into his pockets and prowled the room. "Something of a surprise, wasn't it? The Shands arriving like that."

"Yes." Cassandra stood still and calm, her hands folded before her. "They're not quite what I expected."

"No. The next time I see Maidstone I'll—"

"What?" she prompted, when he didn't go on.

"I was going to say I'd kill him." He gave her a smile that looked more like a grimace. "Not very funny, is it."

"No. But he did lead you to believe his parents would have nothing to do with the children, and when they didn't come, I assumed he was right."

"They never had my letter, apparently. If they had, they would have come sooner."

In that case, he would never have hired her, Cassandra thought. How differently things would have turned out, if not for that one mishap. "They belong with their family."

"Aye. I'll miss the little devils, though." He stopped, looking directly at her. "I'll miss you."

"We both know I cannot stay."

"Aye." He turned away. "Samuel told me today I should let the past go. He was talking about Northrup, but . . ."

Cassandra closed her eyes, fighting for composure. "You can't let it go, can you."

"No. I can't." His eyes met hers. "I'm sorry, Cassie. I can't."

"Neither can I," she said, though she was talking of more recent events. His rejection of her was something that would hurt for a long, long time. " 'Tis late, sir, and this isn't doing any good. You must go."

He nodded. "You're right. I won't bother you any longer." At the door, though, he paused. "I'm sorry, Cassie," he said, and went out.

The flowers decorating the music room were all in place, the chandeliers had been lighted with wax tapers, and the orchestra hired from Dover was tuning up in the gallery. In the kitchen Cook and the kitchen maids scurried about, preparing the supper that would be served at midnight; in their rooms, the guests donned their finest clothes. Even the weather had cooperated, producing a night that was cool, but clear. Everything was at last ready for the first grand ball to be held at Sutcliffe Hall in many a year.

Cassandra took one last look around the music room and then hurried out. She had just enough time to change and then be back when the guests began to arrive. Thank heavens she wouldn't have to stand in the receiving line with Nicholas, but she would be needed, all the same. Organizing the ball was her responsibility. There were certain to be details to be seen to, problems to be solved tonight. For her the ball was not something to anticipate with pleasure. It was, instead, something to be endured.

A black-uniformed maid curtsied as Cassandra whirled into her room, making her stop short. "Della," she said. "What in the world are you doing here?"

Della curtsied again. "Mrs. Feather sent me to help you dress, ma'am. Earl's orders," she added.

"Oh, really. No, please don't curtsy to me, Della, I'm certainly not a grand lady. And I don't need help dressing."

"If you please, ma'am, Mrs. Feather will give me a tongue-lashing if I don't do as she says."

Cassandra sighed. "Oh, very well. Though why she should think—what in the world is that?"

Della, taking a gown from the wardrobe, turned. "Your gown, ma'am."

"It most certainly is not. I don't own anything in that particular shade of green."

"But Mrs. Feather said to bring it to you, ma'am." Della stood with the gown draped carefully over her outstretched arms. "She said it was new, for tonight."

"Well, I didn't order anything new. Oh, very well, let me see it."

"Yes, ma'am," Della said, and held the gown up.

Cassandra gasped. "Good heavens," she said, stepping toward Della, her hand outstretched to softly touch the shining fabric of what was undoubtedly the most magnificent gown she had ever seen. Emerald green satin, low in the bodice and banded about the high waist, with short puffed sleeves. Luxurious satin, with traceries of gold thread embroidered in flowers and leaves and vines about the hem and bodice; emerald green, to set off her complexion and turn her hair to flame. Mrs. Feather had never ordered this gown. She did, however, have a very good idea who had.

How dare he! Almost instantly, her awe turned to rage, and she spun away, crossing to her dresser and pulling her brush through her hair with short, sharp strokes. There was no question that this had come from Nicholas. How dare he do such a thing, purchasing so extravagant and seductive a gown that even now the servants must be whispering about it? How dare he think she could be bought!

"Ma'am?" Della said, her voice tentative. Cassandra looked at the maid's reflection in the mirror, and sighed. This wasn't Della's fault. And oh, it was a beautiful gown. She'd wear it, she decided, setting down the brush. She would also have something to say to Nicholas about it, later.

A little while later, gazing at her reflection in her mirror, she almost forgot her anger. Della proved to be talented with fashioning coiffures, pulling Cassandra's hair back and pinning it up, so that curls cascaded down to her shoulders, left bare by the gown. And oh, such a gown as it was. It fit her like a dream, tight across the bodice, flowing softly to the floor. If there was anything wrong with it, it was that it was cut lower than anything she'd ever worn, displaying an expanse of skin she usually kept hidden. Even that, though, was part of its charm. She had no jewelry, but Nicholas had apparently thought of everything else; long gloves of white kid rested in tissue paper on her dressing table, while white satin evening slippers awaited her in her wardrobe. Feeling a bit as if she were in a dream, Cassandra pulled on the gloves, stepped into the slippers, and turned to the pier glass, to confront someone she had nearly forgotten existed. Tonight she was not Miss Aldrich, plain, quiet governess. Tonight she was Cassie, and almost anything seemed possible.

Because it had taken her longer to dress than she had

expected, most of the guests were already in the music room when Cassandra came in. The sight of the crowded room made her check in dismay at her lateness, and that very action made people turn to look at her. She could feel herself going red. Oh dear, she hadn't meant to make a grand entrance, but people were staring at her with expressions she was too rattled to read, and it seemed oddly silent. Feeling like Cinderella at the ball, she stepped into the music room, and people turned away, chatting. Everything was normal.

Except for Nicholas. He was standing across the room, near the spinet, with Mrs. Lamb and Penelope, and his eyes were riveted on her. Trapped by that sea blue gaze, Cassandra could only return the look. In that moment there was no one else present, no guests, no orchestra, no servants discreetly circulating with glasses of champagne. They were, again, not earl and governess, but simply a man and a woman, linked together by a bond as strong as steel, and as fragile as trust. In that moment, everything she had ever felt for Nicholas welled up within her. She loved him. It didn't matter that he had failed her. He was not a hero, not a god. He was only a man, and she loved him. She always would.

"I say, Miss Aldrich, you look fine as fivepence," a voice said nearby. It jarred her, brought her back to the world, reminded her that the differences between her and Nicholas were still there, still real, and as unbridgeable as ever.

Blinking, she turned to see George Lamb. At another time she might have derived considerable amusement from his ensemble, a coat of mulberry velvet worn over a puce waistcoat figured in gold, and breeches of white satin, but tonight she hardly noticed it. "Thank you, Mr. Lamb. Are you enjoying yourself?"

"Just got here, what? I say, Miss Aldrich, there's the earl, opening the ball. Would you like to dance?"

Across the room, Nicholas was leading Lady Shand onto the floor for the first dance of the evening, a cotillion. Cassandra forced herself to smile. Dancing with George was the last thing in the world she wanted. It had, however, been a long time since anyone had looked at her so admiringly. "Thank you, sir, but I do not plan to dance tonight."

"Not dance! But Miss Aldrich, you must."

"I cannot, sir. I am only the governess, after all." Keeping her smile firmly in place, she stepped away. "Pray excuse me. I must make certain everything is going smoothly."

Cassandra could feel people's eyes on her again as she crossed the room, fully intending to find a chair in a secluded corner and stay there all evening. She could just imagine what people were saying about her, a servant, wearing such a fine gown. If there had been gossip about her before, it would surely intensify now. Oddly enough, that thought didn't bother her so much as it once had. She could live through gossip and scandal. She'd proven that. What she wasn't certain she could survive was the pain of Nicholas's rejection.

"Well." Basil loomed up before her, his quizzing glass raised. "Well. What have we here?"

"Good evening, sir." She was in no mood for an encounter with him, but to cut him openly would only cause more problems. Never far from her mind was the thought of the very real trouble he could cause her. Though, again, that didn't seem to matter as it once had. "You are enjoying the ball?"

"I am, now." Leisurely his gaze traveled over her.

"That is a fine gown, Cassandra. What did you have to do to earn it?"

She stepped back, her face flaming with color. "You are insulting, sir!"

"Am I? My apologies. I didn't mean to be." Surprisingly a look that might have been regret passed over his face. "I forgot where I am."

"Even in town such a question would be an affront."

"Your show of indignation bores me, Cassandra," he drawled. "I have already apologized, have I not? You should take it as a compliment."

"A compliment!"

"You look very well, Cassandra. Very well." He raised the glass again. "Makes me think I was quite foolish six years ago."

"Good evening, Byrne. Cassandra."

Cassandra turned, startled. Nicholas had come up behind them so quietly she hadn't heard him. She wasn't certain whether to be relieved, or chagrined, at his presence. "Good evening, sir," she said, her voice subdued and her eyes downcast. "Is all proceeding well?"

"The ball is fine." Nicholas's voice was clipped. "Is everything all right here?"

"Yes." But what, she wondered, had he heard?

"Do you feel you need to rescue Miss Aldrich, Lynton?" Basil sounded amused. "But I assure you, she'll come to no harm with me."

"She had better not, Byrne. Because, if she does—"

"Oh, please!" Cassandra protested. Caught between the two men, she felt frustratingly helpless. Other women might appreciate being fought over, but she didn't. Not in this way. In his own way, each man was devastatingly attractive, and equally as dangerous. Basil was the epit-

254

ome of the London dandy, with his exquisitely tailored coat of black superfine and his expertly styled hair. His danger lay in words and innuendo. Nicholas, too, was dressed in faultless black and white, but there any resemblance ended. His shoulders, as always, were too broad for London tailoring, and his hair had not been mussed by his valet's careful hands, but by his own actions. Most importantly, he radiated an air of vitality that the other man, with his fashionable languor, could never hope to achieve. In a fight Nicholas would use far more direct weapons than words. Innuendo was a woman's weapon, Cassandra thought, and for the first time she felt nothing but contempt for the exquisite Viscount Byrne.

"If he is bothering you, Cassie," Nicholas said.

"He is not." Cassandra's voice was crisp. "You are both acting like schoolboys. Juanita and Elena have better manners than you do."

Both men eyed her with astonishment. "Cassie—"

"Cassandra—"

"You, sir, have guests to see to. And you, Viscount, should pay attention to Miss Fairleigh. Now if you'll excuse me, I have things to do." With that, she stalked off, knowing both men were staring at her, and not caring. She'd had quite enough of them both for one night.

The first guests she encountered were the Marquess and Marchioness of Shand. Lady Shand, in a gown of shimmering lilac silk that exactly suited her, was seated, watching the others, while Lord Shand stood behind her, tall and spare, a hand on her shoulder. After just one day Cassandra liked them both quite a bit, even if they had come to take her angels away. How could they know how much she had come to care for the girls? She was, after all, only the governess.

"Good evening, my lord. My lady," she said in return to their greetings. "How do you, tonight?"

"Oh, very well, dear." Lady Shand's eyes sparkled. "We rarely go to town anymore, you know, and so something like this is a treat for us." She patted the chair next to her. "Please, sit with me for a moment."

Cassandra hesitated and then sat; she could find no graceful way to refuse. "For a moment only, ma'am. If anything goes wrong, I'll need to see to it."

"Oh, but surely you're allowed to enjoy yourself this evening, too? That is a lovely gown, by the way."

"Thank you." Was that all she was to hear tonight, comments on the blasted gown? One would think no one else here was dressed in their finery.

"I must say, you handled that situation well."

"Ma'am?"

"Lynton and Viscount Byrne." She laughed softly. "I have never seen two men look so flustered."

Cassandra flushed again. Chances were everyone had seen the encounter and was discussing it. Well, let them! She hadn't asked for what had happened. "They were being disagreeable. But I find that being a governess works just as well with grown men as with children."

Lady Shand laughed again, with genuine delight. "You are a prize, Miss Aldrich. Lynton was lucky to find you."

"Thank you," Cassandra murmured, plucking at her skirt. She didn't want to like Lady Shand, but she did. She liked her sense of humor, her forthright manner of speaking, and her kindness. Seeing her with Juanita and Elena this morning had been a revelation. Both girls had been wary at first, clinging to Cassandra for reassurance, but by the end of the morning they had been happy to go to their *abuela,* who showed no hesitation at all in joining in their games. Any worry Cassandra may have had, about their being properly cared-for, was gone. Lady Shand would make certain they would receive, not only a proper upbringing, but love, as well. What more could she ask, Cassandra wondered, and was startled to feel tears pressing behind her eyes.

"We shall have to find someone for the babies," Lady Shand went on. "Our own Nurse is much too old."

"I'm sure you'll find someone, ma'am. There must be any number of people who would be glad for such a position."

"Will you be staying on here, Miss Aldrich?"

"Heavens no! Oh, I see. You think because I've helped plan the house party and the ball—"

"No, my dear." Lady Shand laid her hand on Cassandra's arm. "We think no such thing of you."

Cassandra smiled, shaking her head. "Thank you for that. Though, to be honest, I didn't think you did. You've been much too nice to me."

"Well, my dear, you've taken such good care of our grandchildren. I do appreciate that."

"I'll miss them." Cassandra gazed off across the room, not seeing a thing for the mist in her eyes. "At first the earl needed me, to help him settle in. I've also helped with the house and the entertaining, because, quite frankly, he didn't know what to do." She turned back, forcing a smile. "He's much better at it now."

"I suspect he'd hate to lose you, though."

"Oh no, my work here is done. I'm sure I'll have no trouble securing another position."

From behind them Lord Shand, who had stood quiet all this time, cleared his throat with a deep rumble that made them both start. "Ahem. Maria. About what we discussed—"

"Yes, Jason." Lady Shand smiled up at her husband.

"I'm getting to it. Miss Aldrich." She took Cassandra's hand between her cool, wrinkled ones. "Since you are in need of a position, why not come with us?"

"What? But, ma'am—"

"I'm sure we'll never find anyone so qualified as you. It is clear you are a lady, even if you must work for a living. And we'll offer quite generous wages, won't we, Jason?" She rushed on before Cassandra could object. "I know Yorkshire isn't what you are used to, but it can be beautiful, and the Grange is comfortable. You would have your own suite of rooms, and your own staff, and, of course, a holiday every year."

"It's a very generous offer, ma'am, but—"

"And you love the children." Lady Shand's eyes held hers. "I can't think of anyone else who could offer that. Please, my dear"—she gripped Cassandra's hand harder—"please say you'll at least consider it."

Cassandra glanced across the room again. A country dance had begun during their discussion, and Nicholas, partnering Harriet, looked content and sure of himself. She wasn't needed here anymore. "Yes," Cassandra said, turning back. "I'll take the position."

It was a very long night. Under other circumstances Nicholas thought he'd probably be enjoying himself. Being a host was surprisingly easy, once the planning was done. All he really had to do was greet his guests, make conversation, and dance, if he so desired. Everything else was being taken care of for him. Cassie's doing. Without her nothing would run smoothly at all. He had to be grateful to her for that. Yet, it was because of her that his mood was so low.

Along with several other couples, he was engaged in a

country dance, forming a line with the gentlemen on one side, the ladies on the others, while each couple took turns dancing the length of the line. The steps were intricate and baffling, and he should have been watching to see how they were done. Instead, all his concentration was focused on Cassandra. By Neptune, when she had entered the music room wearing that gown, he had felt his heart race and his breathing grow short. He'd known she was pretty, but, blast it, tonight she was beautiful, breathtaking. He hadn't been able to take his eyes off her. Trouble was, every man in the room had noticed her, too. First George, the cause of her downfall, and then that blasted Byrne had approached her. It was too much. Blast it, Cassie was his!

She was safe enough for the moment, sitting with the Shands. Nice people, if you forgot they were going to take Juanita and Elena away. To his own surprise, he'd miss the little girls. There was, however, a more serious problem for him to face. He'd hired Cassie as a governess. What would happen when there were no longer children at the Hall?

Harriet reached out her hands to him, and he realized with a start that they were at the head of the line. It was their turn to dance. Blast, he should have paid attention to the steps. Feeling like a fool, he took Harriet's hands and began the steps, hoping he wouldn't tread on her feet. Hoping that, when the dance was done, he would be able to do what he had wanted all evening, and seek Cassie out.

It was not to be. Constantly, as he made his way across the room toward the windows and fresh air, he was hailed by friends and acquaintances, and his opinions were solicited. What did he think about local politics, about the American war now that Napoleon had been defeated, about different farming methods? It was far more agreeable than dancing, and so he joined the group of men, but, when the orchestra struck up a waltz, he stiffened, looking about the room. Cassie. Where was Cassie? He couldn't see her anywhere, but he did see Penelope, advancing upon him with a purposeful gleam in her eye. Good God. Hastily he excused himself and fled, to the sanctuary of a window embrasure.

"What—who is it?" a startled voice demanded as he parted the drapes and stepped into the embrasure. Good, it was cool here, and a man could breathe. Even better, the one person he wanted to see was sitting here in a chair, alone.

"Hello, Cassie." He leaned against the wall, grinning at her. "You hiding, too?"

"Certainly not." Cassandra turned her head away, using her dance card to fan herself. "I merely wanted some air."

"You're not dancing."

"It wouldn't be proper."

"Bother proper, Cassie! Don't you ever get tired of it?"

"Easy for you to say! I've been accosted by every man here tonight, and the women are talking about me."

"Well, I've just escaped from Penelope, so we're even."

Cassandra laughed, a choked little sound. "Poor earl, being pursued by the ladies."

"Not that funny, Cassie," he said, but he smiled. "Seriously, though. If anyone's bothering you, come to me. I'll handle him for you."

Cassandra looked up at him, all laughter gone from her face. "Nicholas, why in the world did you buy me this gown?"

"Thought you'd like it. Looks good on you, Cassie."

"Never mind that! Think of what people are saying."

"To hell with them," he said, suddenly angry with her, with society, with the need to be proper at all costs. He didn't care about any of it. He knew only that, in spite of everything, he was happiest when Cassie was nearby. "Let's dance," he said, catching her hand and hauling her to her feet.

"Nicholas!" she protested as he pulled her from the window, onto the floor. " 'Tis a waltz."

"I don't care what people think, Cassie."

"But you don't know how to waltz."

"I lied."

She stared up at him. "You—why in the world would you do such a thing?"

His hand tightened at her waist, and he whirled her around, making her clutch at him to keep her balance. He liked it. Cassie, in his arms again. "Why do you think?"

"I—oh. You scoundrel!"

"Aye." He grinned at her. "Forgive me, Cassie?"

"I am tired of you men, and the tricks you play."

"What tricks have I ever played on you, Cassie, besides this?" He paused. "Or are you talking about Byrne?"

"I don't wish to discuss him."

"No, not here," he agreed, and spun her back toward the window.

"Nicholas—"

"We have to talk, Cassie," he said firmly. Once inside the embrasure he released her, catching hold of her hand and pulling her outside. "We'll be private here."

"If you had to drag me outside, you could at least have brought me to the terrace."

"There are other people there."

"Yes, well, it's muddy here."

"Cassie." Lightly, quickly, his hands moved up her arms, and he felt her go still. Cassie, his Cassie. God, he'd missed her these past days. Missed talking to her, missed seeing her smile, missed holding her. And all because of his silly pride. Well, no, it was more than that, but pride was part of it. Samuel was right. He did have to let the past go. "About what happened between us——"

"I don't want to talk about it, Nicholas."

"I think we have to. Anyway, think you'll like what I have to say."

"Oh?"

"Aye. See, I've been thinking about it, Cassie. Thinking about, well, you know." He fumbled for the words, and found the ones he knew would work. "And what I thought is this, see? I've decided to forgive you."

Cassandra stared up at him, her face very still. Then, to his utter astonishment, she raised her hand and slapped him full across his face.

Chapter 18

Penelope smiled politely up at Mr. Gregory as they waltzed. After all, one must behave as a lady, even when one was seething with anger. The earl was a dolt. Why else had he not realized that she wished to waltz with him? She certainly had given him enough signs. In fact, she had never been so obvious with a man in her life. She had never needed to be. He was a dolt. There was just no other explanation.

It didn't change her plans. If anything, it only made her more determined. She was going to marry the earl, and she would do whatever she had to, to catch him. First, however, she had to dispose of Aldrich. *That* was what made her so angry, the sight of Aldrich, in that incredible gown, waltzing with the earl. Penelope knew she looked as lovely as usual, in a gown of blue silk banded about the hem with silver cord, but somehow tonight Aldrich made her feel like a *jeune fille*. The nerve of her! Everyone knew, of course, that she'd set her cap for him, but before tonight she'd been discreet about it. Now she didn't seem to care who knew. But she wouldn't win. Oh no. Penelope had a weapon that Aldrich could never counter, and she was about to use it. Before the evening was over, Aldrich would be in disgrace, and she, Penelope, would be that much closer to attaining her goal.

Penelope smiled again, a genuinely ravishing smile that made Mr. Gregory blink, though she didn't notice. Soon, she would have her wish. She would be the Countess of Lynton, and Aldrich would be gone.

"Ow!" Nicholas drew back in surprise, his hand flying to his cheek. "Blast it, Cassie, what did you do that for?"

"You'll forgive me. Forgive me!" Cassandra's voice trembled with anger. "Of all the unmitigated nerve—"

"Now, just wait, Cassie." He caught her arm as she turned to go in. "Yes, I forgive you. What's so bad about that?"

"If you can't see it, then I don't know why I should explain."

"Blast it, if that's not just like a woman." He shook his head. "Explain it to me, Cassie. Help me understand."

"You wish to understand, my lord? Very well, then. It is this. I will not be made to feel a pariah for something that happened long ago, and that doesn't even concern you."

"It damned well does concern me, Cassie. I had every right to think I was the first—"

"You blasted, arrogant son of a—sea dog!"

"Cassie!"

"Who do you think you are? The great Nicholas St. John, who comes waltzing into my life whenever he wishes and decides to tell me how to live? That won't wash any longer, my lord. I'm not a little girl anymore. I see you for what you are. You're not a hero. You're a man."

"That's all I ever claimed to be, Cassie," he said quietly. "A man, and men make mistakes." He paused. "It's hard, being a hero. If that's what you need, you'd better look for someone besides me."

"I don't need a hero. I need someone who'll see me as I am." Helplessly, she stared at him. "I thought that was you."

"I never meant to hurt you, Cassie."

"I know." She glanced away. "There's no future here for me, for us. I thought—well, never mind."

"You'll always have a home here," he said, stopping her as she reached the window.

"No, Nicholas." She turned and gave him a sad smile. "Lord and Lady Shand have offered me a position as governess. When they leave, I'll leave with them."

He blinked. "When did this happen?"

"Tonight." She paused by the window, her hand on the frame. "It's for the best," she said, and went in, leaving him as lost and alone as he had ever been in his life.

"Excuse me, my lord." The footman held out a folded piece of paper. "The lady asked me to give this to you."

Basil, leaning against the wall and wondering what had happened to make Cassandra storm out of the music room, looked up. "The lady? What lady?" he asked, making no move to take the paper.

"She asked me not to say. I believe the note explains everything," the footman said with a wink.

"Ah. Very well then." Basil took the note. "Thank you, my good man."

The footman waited for a moment, while Basil studied him with cool nonchalance. Finally, realizing he wasn't going to receive a vail for delivering the note, he walked off, his shoulders stiff. Basil's lip twisted to one side in a sardonic smile. He'd never see the man again. Why waste precious coin on him?

He scanned the room quickly before unfolding the note. No one seemed to pay him any particular heed, not even any of the ladies. Anticipation quickened his pulse. It had been a very long time since he'd received a note in such a way. Which lady, he wondered, desired an assignation with him?

A moment later he refolded the note with quick, precise gestures. He was a fast reader and he rarely forgot anything he read, but this particular note would always be emblazoned on his memory. She wished to meet with him, because she could no longer bear the distance between them. They had the past in common, and could have it again, if he would come to the Persian Room in precisely one half hour. It was signed, simply, "C." Cassandra, of course, and what a delightfully appropriate place she had chosen for a liaison. He knew it, had known it all along. Under that proper exterior she affected she still desired him. Far be it from him to disoblige a lady.

Smiling, he secreted the note in his pocket. The Persian Room, in one half hour. He would be there.

Everything was ready, Penelope thought, not quite half an hour later. Her notes had been dispatched, given to footmen with a sizable enough vail to ensure their forgetfulness. Viscount Byrne was still present in the music room, talking to Lord Shand and appearing the soul of discretion, but Aldrich was nowhere to be seen. Apparently she had already received her note, and left. Good. As the crowning touch, the crucial element of her plot, she had asked the earl, in her prettiest manner, to conduct a tour of the house, beginning with the bookroom. The secret door fascinated her, she said, and she was certain those who had never seen it would be interested, as well. The earl's reaction to that had been puzzled, but polite. Of course he would show people around if they wished. He would just find out if anyone else wished to come along, and then he would be with her. They should, by Penelope's calculation, reach the bookroom in time to hear Aldrich and the viscount discussing their past, their intimate past, through the door that opened into the Persian Room—

Penelope stilled, panic suddenly welling inside her. The secret door. Had she opened it? Yes, of course she had, when she'd gone into the bookroom earlier. Hadn't she? She was certain she had, and yet the doubt remained, growing and growing until it consumed her. She had to check. It would take just a moment.

Without a word of excuse to Reverend Carlisle, who was expounding on the immorality of the waltz, she turned and fled, nearly running down the hall to the bookroom. She dared not look into the Persian Room, lest Aldrich see her, and yet if Aldrich were already there she'd be certain to hear the noise from the bookroom. There was no help for it, though. That door had to be open when the guests entered the bookroom.

Moonlight streamed into the bookroom when she at last entered it, filling the room with shadows and odd shapes. Making her way to the far corner of the room, she stumbled over a stool and exclaimed at the pain. A corner of the library table was the next object she encountered, and a chair seemed to appear from nowhere right in her path. She dared not light a candle, lest the glow spill into the next room. Fortunately, she was almost to her destination. She trailed her fingers along the rows of books until she came to the corner and froze. The secret door was closed.

But she had opened it! She remembered that clearly now. Some overzealous servant must have come in and closed it. There was no time to lose. She had to open it again, and quietly. Willing herself to calmness, Penelope counted in from the wall. Ten, eleven, twelve—there! She lifted the book, and was met with silence and a wall that refused to move.

She stared at the wall in horror. It had been the twelfth book, she was certain of it! Frantically she pulled at the next book, and the next, but still, nothing happened. Perhaps she had the wrong shelf? But no, the twelfth book on the shelf below did nothing, nor did its counterpart on the shelf above. Nearly weeping with frustration she slammed the book back, not caring about the noise she might make. Her plan, her beautiful plan, was ruined, and all because of some stupid book. Oh, nothing was going right tonight. It was Aldrich's fault, all of it. If she had her here, she'd—well, she'd do this! With all her strength, Penelope struck at the books.

The twelfth book on the third shelf lifted, just a bit, from the force of the blow. There was a click, followed by a grinding sound, and the shelf unexpectedly swung inward. Leaning on the shelf, Penelope lost her balance, and tumbled into the Persian Room.

The room was dimly lighted by the candles in a three-branched candelabra. Viscount Byrne, studying a particularly florid nude through his quizzing glass, turned at Penelope's precipitate entrance, one eyebrow raised. "Well," he said, letting the quizzing glass drop and ambling toward her, smiling. "So you're my mysterious correspondent."

A footman handed Cassandra a note as soon as she returned to the music room. Murmuring a distracted thanks, she glanced about the room, seeking Nicholas. Not because she wished to see him, but, rather, the opposite. If she knew where he was, then she would also know how to avoid him. There. He was across the room, talking to a group of people. Her heart contracted. Nicholas. So dear, and so lost to her.

The paper crackled in her hand and she looked down, realizing with vague surprise that she had crumpled it. Now who would be sending her a note? she wondered, unfolding it. She scanned its contents, frowning. It made no sense. The handwriting was crabbed and nearly illegible, but even in a clear hand the message would have been meaningless. Juanita and Elena, unable to sleep because of the excitement of the ball, had, according to the note, crept down to see the guests, and then had broken free. They had last been seen running into the Persian Room. Or so the note said. The signature was a scrawl that Cassandra couldn't make out, no matter how hard she tried.

Odd. Frowning, she turned the note over, looking for more information, but there was nothing. She would have been alarmed, had she thought there was any truth to it, but she knew quite well there wasn't. After the incident with Nicholas she had fled to the nursery and stayed there, composing herself. When she had at last left, the children were tucked in their beds, fast asleep, and even the nursery maid's head was nodding. Since she'd returned directly to the music room, there had been no time for the girls to get into the kind of mischief this note alleged. Odd, she thought again. Someone was obviously playing some kind of a prank on her. But who?

Looking up, she saw Nicholas coming toward her, a group of laughing, chatting people in his wake. She stepped aside in time to avoid another encounter with him, though she was very aware of the look he slanted her. "Where is everyone going?" she asked, as the group approached.

"Oh, Miss Aldrich, 'tis so exciting!" Daphne, looking remarkably pretty in blue silk that brought out the color of her eyes, smiled at her. She was, Cassandra noted, holding onto George's arm, which made her wonder where Basil was. "The earl is going to show us again how the secret door in the bookroom works."

"Oh. How interesting."

"It was my sister's idea," George said. "Penelope, don't you know. Don't see her now, though, do you?"

Cassandra glanced about the room. "No, I don't."

"Come with us, Miss Aldrich," Daphne said impulsively. "We have the most marvelous news."

"Really?" Cassandra let herself be swept along. "What is it?"

"My brother is going to marry Beatrice Lamb. He spoke to Mr. Lamb just tonight."

"Why, that is good news. I must wish them happy."

"Penelope wasn't half mad about it." George grinned. "Should have seen her face, Miss Aldrich, when she heard. She's mad because Beatrice is getting married before her." His smile softened as he looked down at Daphne. "Don't tell anyone, but that might not be the only engagement tonight. Daphne and I—that is, as soon as I speak to Mr. Fairleigh."

"Good heavens! That is wonderful," Cassandra said,

after a moment's startled silence. What did that mean for Basil, and her own future? She glanced about again, but he, like Penelope, was nowhere to be seen.

"Do come with us, Miss Aldrich," Daphne said again. The group, having been supplied with candles, was now going out into the hall. "I think a secret door is so exciting."

"So long as we don't go into the Persian Room," George said, and Daphne, turning pink, giggled.

His words jolted Cassandra's memory, and she touched the note again. Odd. What could possibly have been the purpose of sending it to her? Almost without thinking about it, she joined the group, wondering just what was going on in the Persian Room.

Penelope, breathless from her frantic search for the catch to the secret door, and stunned by her fall, grasped the edge of a table for support. "What are you doing here?" she demanded, having long ago learned to attack first.

"I might ask you the same thing." Basil, smiling, urbane, leaned on the table near her, and she backed away. "Or didn't you send me this note?"

Penelope looked with horror at the paper he dangled between thumb and forefinger, and then recovered. "Whyever would I do that?"

"To meet me here."

"I wouldn't do something like that! I am a lady. It sounds more like something Aldrich would do."

"Ah. Then you know how it's signed."

"I—is it? Did she really send it to you?"

He grinned. "You play the innocent well, Penelope."

"I don't know what you mean, sir."

"Come, come, no pretense with me. We're two of a kind, you and me. We use people. And I think I can guess why you sent this."

"I never did!"

"Do you know, you're really rather pretty," he mused, studying her.

"Pretty!" She drew herself up. "I'll have you know I'm the beauty of the neighborhood."

"Mm. Really? But I like you like this, you know." He reached out to touch her hair, and she drew back, sharply. "With your hair just a little mussed, and your gown just a little askew. Mm. Much more approachable. But I wonder, Penny."

"Miss Lamb to you, sir!"

"Why did you want me to think Cassandra was here?"

The question jolted Penelope back to herself, and a sense of her own danger. If she didn't leave, now, she would be caught in the room, and her scheme exposed. "I must go," she gasped.

"No, wait."

"I can't—"

"Your gown is caught. Or do you wish to go back to the ball with a tear in a very interesting place?"

"Ooh!" Tears of frustration filled her eyes. Her gown was indeed caught, near her hip, on a filigreed edge of the table, and getting it free would take more patience than she had at the moment. "Oh, the dratted thing."

"Let me."

"No!"

"If you want to get free, Penny, hold still." Basil's manicured fingers carefully worked at the material, the back of his hand just brushing her hip. "There."

Instantly Penelope pulled away, and then was caught

up short. Basil still held a fold of her gown in his hand. "Unhand me, sir!"

"You really are very pretty, when you forget to act icy. Is there warmth underneath, I wonder?"

"Oh, please—"

Basil's hand slid around her, grasping the edge of the table, trapping her. "Let's just see how cool you really are," he said, and brought his mouth down on hers.

"Mmph!" Penelope struggled, but he knew quite well what he was doing. Though he didn't touch her, he continued to grasp the table on either side, keeping her prisoner. He wooed her with his lips, his tongue, never once resorting to force, and of a sudden the ice princess melted. She had never been treated like this! No man had ever dared to kiss her in such a way, so long and deep and yet persuasive; the most she had ever allowed was a chaste kiss on her cheek. Never had her senses been assaulted in such a way, so that she could think of no one but him. Fire sizzled through her veins, spreading even to her toes, so that she knew she would never be cold again.

Basil at last released her and smiled down at her. She leaned against the table, as if for support, her eyes half closed, her hair now more than a little mussed, and a sweet, fatuous smile on her face. "Well. Not so cold, after all," he said, softly, and at that moment there was a noise at the secret door from the bookroom. He turned, and Penelope looked over his shoulder, to see Nicholas and his entourage.

"Oh no!" Penelope wailed, pushing against Basil and finally gaining her freedom. "It wasn't supposed to be like this! It was supposed to be you."

Cassandra, who had just stepped into the room, drew back in surprise. "Me!"

"Yes, you! You're the one the viscount wants, not me. You're the one who had an affair with him!"

273

Chapter 19

Silence reigned in the room in the wake of Penelope's declaration. The group turned startled eyes on Cassandra. Only in Nicholas's did she read more: sadness, knowledge, and betrayal. "I don't know what she's talking about—"

"Nonsense." Basil's voice, unexpectedly crisp, cut across Cassandra's feeble protest. "Miss Aldrich and I have never been more than acquaintances. I don't know what gave you such an idea."

"But you told me," Penelope began.

"You must have misunderstood," he said, coldly.

"What is going on here?" Nicholas demanded, at last taking charge, and, as quickly as that, Basil's face changed. Lounging back against the table, he smiled, and his arm snaked out to catch Penelope about the waist, though she struggled.

"Forgive us, Lynton. Now, my love, don't struggle so. We are well and fairly caught."

"This wasn't how it was supposed to be!" Penelope cried.

"No, my love, but they know all about us, now. We've been caught in a compromising position." Penelope's

274

mouth dropped open at that. "So, you see, my love, there is nothing we can do. I apologize, Lynton, for abusing your hospitality in this way."

Nicholas nodded. "Fair enough. Though there's someone else you should speak to, I think."

"Of course." His gaze flicked past Nicholas to Daphne, who, looking horrified and fascinated at once, was clinging to George. A bleak expression crossed his face, and passed. "I'll speak to your father, shall I, darling?"

"No!" Penelope protested. He silenced her with a swift kiss, and the dazed, fatuous look returned to her face. "Yes."

"Good." He smiled down at her, and only Cassandra noticed that the smile was just a little bit forced. "Come, my dear. Let us go find your father." He inclined his head toward Nicholas, took Penelope's arm, and walked away.

"Well!" Lady Shand exclaimed. "I must say that that was interesting." As if that had been a signal of sorts, the group began chattering about the last few moments. Only Nicholas remained silent, and Cassandra. He leaned against the bookcase that made up the secret door, gazing steadily at her. Her own head was bent, against the hurt and accusation in his eyes. "And whatever is this room, sir?" someone from the group called out.

"Nothing," Nicholas said hastily, and turned, blocking the entrance to the Persian Room. "Come, let us return to the ball. There's been enough excitement for one night."

"Supper will be served soon," Cassandra chimed in. "We wouldn't want to miss that, and I should just make sure everything's all right."

"Everything will be fine, dear." Lady Shand's eyes were knowing as she patted Cassandra on the arm. "Poor Miss Lamb, she must have been quite overset, to say what she did," she said in a lower voice, leaning her head toward Cassandra. "But I don't think anyone will believe it for a second, especially after what Lord Byrne said."

"Thank you, ma'am." Cassandra's voice was stiff. Perhaps no one would quite believe it, but they would always wonder, in spite of Basil's denial. Why had he done it? It had been unexpected, an act of gallantry from a man she had never thought capable of being gallant. She wondered just how much it had cost him.

"Come, ma'am. Let us return to the ball," she said, and, giving the older lady her arm, led her out of the room. So much had happened in the last few minutes, so much had changed, that she couldn't quite take it in. The farce was over. Her reputation was safe, but at what cost? For she still had to face Nicholas. Never had she dreaded anything quite so much.

The grand ball at Sutcliffe Hall was held to be a great success, one that would be talked about for days to come. Not only had the dancing been superb and the refreshments excellent, but it had produced no fewer than three betrothals. No one was very much surprised that Mr. Fairleigh had proposed to Miss Beatrice Lamb. George Lamb's engagement to Daphne Fairleigh was more startling, however, so young they both were, and the match between Penelope and Viscount Byrne was the most shocking of all. Why, no one had even known they were courting. There was talk of some incident in the bookroom at the Hall, but no one quite knew what it was. It was no matter. The viscount, who had removed from the Hall to the Crown and Anchor, was as polished and polite as ever, while Penelope visibly preened at having made such a catch. And, best of all, the young ladies in the neighborhood thought, the earl was still unattached.

At the Hall, the guests who had attended the house party were packing to return to their normal lives. The Fairleighs were returning to London, where they planned to host the Lambs for a visit; the Duke and Duchess of Bainbridge were traveling on to Bainbridge Abbey. Lord and Lady Shand also were preparing to leave, this time with their two young granddaughters. Soon the Hall would be empty, and life would return to its usual routine.

Cassandra planned to leave with the Shands, but the day before their departure Nicholas asked that she stay for a few days, to make sure his household was organized properly. Because the request was phrased so formally, Cassandra accepted, though it went against her better judgment. Since the night of the ball they had managed to avoid each other quite successfully, and she hoped to continue doing so. Facing Nicholas and seeing again that look in his eyes could only bring her pain. She knew he wondered about the truth of Penelope's accusation, knew he had always suspected it, but, after the way he had reacted in the past, she had no desire to tell him anything. Too much, and not enough, had already been said.

It was a clear, sunny morning when the large traveling carriage with the Shand crest drew up before Sutcliffe Hall. A baggage coach had already been loaded with various trunks and boxes, including all the belongings of two tiny girls. Cassandra stood with Elena and Juanita on the drive, watching as the carriage came to a stop. Elena, excited, pointed to the horses, but Juanita held back, clinging to her hand. Cassandra had been careful to explain to them, as best she could, what was going to happen, that they now would have a family of their very own to love them and that soon she would be there to take care of them. She made the entire journey sound like a grand adventure. Juanita, however, seemed only to know that, once again in her young life, she was being uprooted.

"I do wish you were coming with us, Miss Aldrich," Lady Shand said, walking down the steps of the Hall toward them. "I fear the girls will miss you terribly."

Cassandra forced a smile. "The earl really does need me, ma'am. When it comes to household matters, he hasn't the slightest idea what to do."

Lady Shand's eyes twinkled. "Perhaps he'll soon have a wife to see to such things for him."

"I wouldn't know, ma'am." Cassandra went down on one knee, straightening Juanita's collar, tugging Elena's skirt down about her chubby legs. "Mary Ann will take good care of the girls," she went on, speaking of the nursery maid, whom the Shands had hired, "and I shall be there in a few days."

"I cannot change your mind?"

"No, ma'am."

"Oh, very well. But do please remember to hire a post chaise rather than taking the stage. It will be so much more comfortable for you. You have enough for the chaise?"

"Yes, Lord Shand spoke to me about it last night. Now, Juanita, Elena, listen to me," she said, and two pairs of big, solemn eyes gazed up at her. "You're going to be going on a long journey. Isn't that exciting? But, remember, you must mind Mary Ann, and you must do whatever your *abuela* says."

"Roja come, too?" Elena said.

"No, *angel*, not yet. In a few days."

Elena let out a howl. "I want Roja!" she cried, and threw herself into Cassandra's arms.

"Me tambien!" Juanita's lower lip trembled. "Roja, me too!"

"Oh." Squeezing her eyes shut, Cassandra gathered both children close, shaking with the force of their sobs. "Oh, *mis bebes, mis angeles. Se amo.* I love you. I love you both." She kissed them each soundly and then rose, though they still clung to her. "Go with *Abuelita,* now. Go on." Gently disengaging their fingers from her skirt, she turned them toward the carriage. "I'll see you soon. I promise."

Mary Ann came and took their hands, bending to smile at them, and though both children looked back, they went with her, dragging their feet. Cassandra bit the inside of her lips. Farther and farther away, across the drive, into the carriage. The door closed; the coachman took up the reins. The carriage turned and drove away, heading down the drive until it was no longer in sight, and only clouds of dust showed its passage.

Gravel crunched beside Cassandra. "Are you all right?" Nicholas asked, and her face crumpled.

"Mis angeles," she gasped. "Oh, *mis angeles!"*

"Cassie." Nicholas put a firm arm around her shoulders and turned her toward the house. "Come."

"I'm s-s-sorry, I never break down like this."

"Hush." Nicholas led her inside, to his study. "I know."

"I never cry."

"I know. Sit here, Cassie." He pressed her gently into a chair. "Is there anything I can get for you? Brandy, or maybe tea?"

"No." She pulled out her handkerchief and mopped at her face. "I'm sorry to be such a watering pot, Nicholas."

"It's all right, Cassie."

"I don't know why I'm acting this way. I was only their governess."

Nicholas perched on the edge of his desk. "You've been more than that, Cassie, much more. Time you admitted it."

Cassandra looked up at him, and stuffed her handkerchief into her pocket. "I must go. There's much for me to see to before I leave—"

"Sit down." His voice, carrying the command of the quarterdeck, cut across hers. "We have things to talk about."

"I don't know what."

"Don't you? You've been avoiding me, Cassie."

"I could say the same to you."

"Yes, well." He glanced away. "I suppose I have. But, blast it, Cassie, can you blame me, after the other night?"

"Yes!" she shouted, suddenly angry. She was tired of his acting like the one who had been hurt, tired of feeling guilty for something that was long over. Oh, it felt good to be angry, really angry, instead of holding in her emotions, as a proper governess should. "I am not your property, Nicholas, and I never have been. What did you expect, that I wouldn't live my life, just because you weren't around?"

"I didn't expect you to have an *affaire, d*amn it!"

"I didn't have an *affaire.*" She paused. "More like an encounter."

He dropped into a chair facing her. "So you admit it."

"How can I deny it? You knew immediately."

"With Byrne?"

"Yes."

"Damn it. Damn it." He got up, and began to pace the room. "Why didn't you tell me? I asked you, I gave you every chance—why didn't you tell me?"

"It was past—"

"Oh no, it wasn't. Not for me."

280

She swallowed. "I know. I was afraid of what you'd do if you knew, with Basil in the house——"

"Blast it, Cassie, I wouldn't have done anything to embarrass you."

"Oh, wouldn't you! You were angry enough."

"I was hurt! Damn it, Cassie, why didn't you tell me? Why didn't you?"

"I was ashamed!" she cried, and threw her hands up in front of her face. "I was ashamed," she repeated, her voice lower, duller.

"Ah, Cassie." He crouched before her. "I didn't mean to make you feel that way."

"But you did." She wiped again at her eyes. " 'Tis nothing new. I've lived with the shame of it for six years."

"He seduced you?"

"Yes." She looked up at him, and sighed. "You may as well sit down, Nicholas. It's a long story."

He rose and crossed to a chair. "Blast it, if I had him here——"

"He's not completely to blame."

"The hell he's not."

"He's not." Her eyes met his. "I knew what I was doing. At least, I thought I did."

"How could you have? A man like that, and how old were you? Eighteen? You didn't stand a chance, Cassie."

Cassandra looked down at her hands, and shrugged. "Regardless. No one forced me into anything. I was old enough, and I knew of his reputation."

"And you thought maybe you could reform him."

For the first time, her gaze faltered. "Well, yes."

"Then, Cassie——"

"Are you going to let me tell this, or not?" she demanded.

He thrust his hand into his hair. "Oh, very well. Go on. You were eighteen?"

"Yes. It was my first season." She gave a laugh that lacked humor. "My only season, as it turned out. I lied to you, Nicholas, when I told you I didn't take. I did. I was a success." Her fingers pleated her skirt. "My parents were gone by this time, and so my aunt offered to sponsor me for the season."

"And your sisters?"

"They were married already. I'd never been out of Gloucestershire before, and I'd never met anyone other than the local boys." *And you.* Nicholas had been as lost to her, then, though, as he was now. "Society is strange. My aunt despaired of me. My figure wasn't slender enough, my height was only average, and my hair! Someone, though, decided to proclaim me an Original, and so I became popular. Soon I had many suitors. The only problem I seemed to have was choosing among them. Then I fell in love."

Nicholas's hands gripped the arms of his chair. "With Byrne?"

"Yes. Oh, this is hard." She searched the ceiling, as if for guidance. "Do you remember what it is like, to be so young and to feel that way? So happy and excited and yet scared, too? I know now it wasn't love." *Because it's nothing like what I feel for you.* "It was, oh, the dancing and the music and all the attention, all going to my head. You can't imagine what that felt like. In Norton, I was the plain Aldrich girl, the bluestocking. In London I was a success. It was wonderful. And then he asked me to marry him."

"Byrne did?"

"Yes."

"The same Byrne who was here at the Hall?"

"Yes. But there was a problem."

"Ah. Somehow, I'm not surprised."

"I don't think he's quite so bad as you do," she retorted.

"Ha."

"Well, I don't anymore. Of course, then—well, I had no dowry, you see. He said he wasn't concerned, but he thought his parents would be. He said he would talk to his father, and then speak to my uncle the next day."

"And?"

"And—oh, this is hard," she said again. "I believed him, of course. So, when he said he wanted us to seal our love, I—well, we did."

Nicholas rose abruptly, his hands clenched, his knuckles showing white. "The bastard. If I had him here—"

"Sit down, Nicholas." Cassandra's voice held a governess's authority. "He'll be punished."

"He deserves to be," Nicholas growled, but he sat down again. "What happened then?"

"Nothing. At least, not right away. The next day I refused to go out. My aunt and uncle knew what was happening, and they were in alt. We waited all day for Basil to come to talk to my uncle. He never did." Her hands bunched in her lap, the only sign of her agitation. After all these years, the memories still hurt. "We had several engagements that evening, and my aunt insisted we go. I was convinced there'd been some mishap and that I'd see him and he'd explain everything. Instead." She swallowed, hard. "Instead, when we attended the first rout, people whispered behind their hands when they saw me, and then turned away. They cut me, Nicholas." The pain and bewilderment of that moment were in her voice. "I didn't know why, but a few moments later my aunt made me leave."

"Cassie." Nicholas's voice was filled with concern. "Are you all right?"

"Yes. I—I—do you know what he did?"

"No, sweetheart. What?"

"He and his friends had made a wager about me. It was on the books at his club. He made a wager, and he won—"

Nicholas erupted, bounding up from his chair. "The bastard! He'll pay for that. No, don't try to stop me, Cassie." He strode across the room. "I'll make him pay if it's the last thing I do—"

"He's marrying Penelope. That's punishment enough."

He stared at her from the door. "You take this damned lightly, Cassie."

"I've had six years to get used to it. I'm not quite done, Nicholas. Don't you wish to hear the rest of it before you go off to draw his cork?"

"I don't need to. I already know. He abandoned you."

"Yes. He never had any intention of marrying me. Oh, I know why, now. I had no dowry, no lineage, and he said that since the betrothal had never been announced, it had never really happened."

"Damn him."

"It was a very long time ago, Nicholas. It's over and done and I survived it."

"Survived it!" Nicholas paced the room. "Blast it, Cassie, look at the way you've lived all these years! Always at the beck and call of people who could dismiss you like that!" He snapped his fingers. "What kind of life is that?"

"It hasn't been so bad." Now that she'd told him her story, she felt a curious kind of peace. Her secret was out. She no longer had to worry about it. "It was hard at the time, I won't deny that. To see people I thought were my friends turn against me—well, it hurt. But I learned from it." She studied her fingernails. "I've done some thinking about it, Nicholas, and I've come to the conclusion that, in some way, this was meant to happen." *Because it led me back to you.* "I was a silly girl then. All the things that used to matter to me I put away, because they weren't fashionable. I wasn't myself. If I'd married one of my suitors, I don't know what I would have turned into. Probably just another bored society matron trapped in an unhappy marriage and wondering where it had all gone wrong. Heaven knows, I saw enough of that. Instead, I learned from what happened." She gazed up at him. "I learned to avoid scandal, and I learned to be very proper. But I've kept myself intact, even if only in here," she indicated her heart, "and I like to think I'm stronger for it."

"But alone."

"By my choice."

"Not really. Or did your family stand by you?"

"Well—no, not completely. My poor aunt was devastated. My uncle reacted much as you did, but there was nothing he could do. I left London. I stayed with one of my sisters for a time, until I realized how difficult it was for her. Because I was another mouth to feed, not because of the scandal," she said, at sight of his face. "That was when I decided to go out as a governess. It hasn't been a bad life, Nicholas."

"You were cut by friends, went through scandal, and have been living alone, and you call that not a bad life?" He shook his head. "I shall never understand women. Why aren't you angry with him?"

She stared at him steadily. "Is what he did any worse than what you did?"

"What I did—blast it, Cassie, you can't compare us!"

"You rejected me, too, Nicholas," she pointed out.

285

"That was different."

"No, it wasn't! It hurt me, Nicholas, ten times worse than anything Basil could ever do to me. I trusted you."

He stared at her from across the room. "I trusted you, too, Cassie. It's why I reacted as I did."

"It had nothing to do with you—oh, never mind, you'll never understand."

"No, Cassie, I won't. Blast it, do you have any idea what you've meant to me all these years?"

"What I've meant to you?"

"Yes. You were only a little girl, but you became everything I fought for. When life at sea got too boring or rough, when we were in battle—it didn't matter where I was. All the noise and heat, the guns firing and making the ship shake as if she were coming apart, men screaming, blood everywhere—all through it I'd think of you and I'd hold on. I hated what I was doing. Hated it. But it was all right, because I was doing it for you. As long as you were safe, it was all right." His face twisted. "And then to learn that you—never mind."

"You and I have never quite seen each other as we really are, have we?"

"What do you mean?"

"I am not a paragon, Nicholas. Just as you are not a hero."

"I never claimed to be, Cassie."

"I know you didn't." She rose. Her legs felt shaky, as if she were recovering from a long illness. "I told Mrs. Feather I'd speak with her this morning, so she would know exactly what you want her to do."

"Cassie. I'm trying to let the past go. What I said, the other night, I meant it. I do forgive you."

Cassandra turned from the door. "I know you think that's what you should do, Nicholas."

He made a gesture with his hand. "It's all I can do."

"I see. But can you forget, as well?" Silence greeted her. "I see."

"Cassie—"

"I'll be leaving tomorrow, Nicholas."

"Cassie." His voice was urgent. "Don't go. Don't leave me."

Cassandra's hand slipped from the door handle. "Why should I stay?"

"Because I want you to. Blast it, I need you, Cassie."

"Need?"

"Yes. I need you."

Cassandra closed her eyes. Need, not love. It wasn't enough. "Good-bye, Nicholas," she said, and went out.

Chapter 20

A post chaise, hired for the long drive to Yorkshire, stood waiting in the drive, the job horses hitched to it blowing and stamping with impatience. The postilion, seated on the last horse, from where he would control his team, turned, watching while a footman packed bandboxes and a battered trunk into the boot. Amid all this bustle the only center of stillness was Cassandra, wearing her gray traveling dress and bonnet and standing on the bottom stair of the Hall, hands clasped before her. Only when everything was packed and ready did she step down onto the drive, allowing herself to be helped into the post chaise by the footman. With an impatient flick of the rein the postilion started his team, and the chaise rolled down the drive, away from Sutcliffe Hall.

Nicholas turned away from the study window before the chaise was quite out of sight. They were gone, all gone. Samuel, his friend; the two little girls who had so unexpectedly endeared themselves to him; and Cassie, his Cassie. The house rang with the silence, the emptiness, echoing inside him. He felt hollow, numb. They were gone, and never in his life had he been quite so alone.

Kirby, back at the Hall now that it was just him and

Nicholas again, put his head in through the door. "Be you wantin' anything, Cap'n? Coffee or something?"

"Nothing, Kirby." Nicholas was vaguely surprised to notice that his voice sounded normal. Strange, when he felt so distant and empty. "I've work to do. Leave me."

Kirby hesitated. "House feels different, don't it? Without the little girls running around."

Nicholas sat behind his desk and reached for the morning's post. "Leave me, Kirby," he repeated.

"Aye, Cap'n. Never thought that having a woman aboard would make such a difference, but—"

"Kirby."

"Aye, Cap'n." Kirby withdrew his head, and then looked in again. "You ask me, we should go back to sea," he said, and pulled the door shut behind him.

"No one asked you!" Nicholas roared, at last angered at the interruptions, when all he wanted was to be left alone. Go back to sea. As if that would solve his problems. Aye, it would have, once. Go to sea, and escape everything on land, the uncaring father, the schoolmaster who thought he'd amount to nothing, the baffling ways of landlubbers. Somehow, though, none of those things seemed very important when compared with this awful, aching emptiness. This he would carry with him to the end of his days, no matter where he was.

Best not to think about it. Picking up a penknife, he slit open each envelope methodically and began to read his correspondence. A note from the Duchess of Bainbridge, thanking him for his hospitality. A letter from an old, barely remembered shipboard acquaintance, asking for work. And a report from Captain Gilman, skipper of the *Eagle*.

Nicholas pushed all other correspondence aside to concentrate on this last. In just a few days, Gilman wrote, he had managed to put together a crew he was certain the earl would approve. A remarkable feat, Nicholas thought, scanning the remainder of the letter, considering the vast amounts of men needed to run the Royal Navy. Most seamen, however, would rather ship out on a merchant ship than with the navy, given that pay and conditions were usually better. Probably that explained Gilman's success. All that was needed now was to find a cargo, and to settle on a destination. Nicholas had an idea about that. Canton, in China. Aye, Canton, for tea and porcelain and delicate silks. It was a place he'd always wanted to visit. He'd never get there now, though. He was the Earl of Lynton, and was tied to the land.

Crumpling Captain Gilman's neatly detailed report into a ball, he flung it across the room. Blast the man! Blast the land, and blast being an earl! He didn't want it. He'd never wanted it. The only thing that had made his life bearable these last months was Cassie.

Cassie. Oh God, Cassie. Groaning, he put his face in his hands. Cassie was gone, and this time he never would see her again. It had been different, all those years ago, when she had been a child and he a young man set on a glorious career. Then the future had lain before him. Now, though, he was stuck, and she was gone. In one day he had lost the two things he loved most in this world, Cassie, and the sea.

It took a few moments for the word he had used to penetrate. When it did, he raised his head, staring unseeingly across the room. Love? Did he love Cassie? Nonsense, a man like him, knowing only the sea and a man's life—how could he love a woman? But he did. The knowledge of it resonated inside him, filling the empty void. He loved Cassie. He always had. Why the hell hadn't he realized it before it was too late?

But it wasn't too late. If he rode hard and fast, he could catch the post chaise. Nicholas jumped up and was halfway across the room when the flaw in that plan struck him. He loved Cassie, aye, and needed her, far more than he had ever needed the sea. But, God! She didn't feel the same. How could she, when she had allowed another man to kiss her, touch her, make her his? The circumstances didn't matter. She had gone with another man, and that wasn't something he thought he could ever forget.

Let the past go. Samuel's words echoed in his mind as he sank into a chair, drawing his hands over his face. Aye, good advice, but how could he? When he closed his eyes he saw them together, Cassie and her lover—Cassie and him. The image superimposed itself on the earlier, hurtful one. Cassie, in his arms, in his bed, kissing him, touching him. Cassie, responding to him as no other woman ever had. In his memory he saw her, heard her; saw the delight and wonder on her face, heard the surprise in her gasps, reactions that had told him, had he only realized it, that what she felt during their loving was totally new to her.

The thought jolted him from the chair. By Neptune, he *had* been the first. Maybe not physically, but what did that matter? Cassie was right. Her past was past, just as his was. What mattered was the present, and the future. No one, no one, had taught her how to kiss, how to make love. No one but him. By Neptune, he had been every sort of a fool.

"Kirby!" he bellowed as he ran into the hall. "Blast it, man, where are you?"

Kirby scuttled into the hall. "Aye, Cap'n? What is it?"

"Pack my sea chest, Kirby, for a long voyage. And pack something for yourself while we're at it."

"Cap'n, are we—"

"Aye. We're taking command of the *Eagle.*"

"Aye, Cap'n!" Kirby grinned. "Knew you couldn't let her go."

"No, I can't," he said, grinning, but it wasn't the ship he was thinking of. "Get everything ready and bring it to the ship. I'll meet you there."

"Aye, Cap'n." Kirby saluted smartly and ran up the stairs. Nicholas, already out the door, yelling to have his horse brought round, didn't notice. He was going after Cassie, and this time he wasn't going to let her get away, by Neptune! This time, he thought, swinging up into the saddle, he was going to take what he wanted, and be damned to the consequences.

In several months of living on land Nicholas had yet to become comfortable on the back of a horse, but he didn't care. Head bent low over his mount's neck, he galloped hell for leather down the road, knowing only that he had to catch Cassie. He couldn't let her leave him. *Don't go, don't go, don't go*. The horse's hooves pounded out the rhythm, and he found himself repeating the words end-lessly. *Don't go, don't go, don't go!*

He galloped past the Crown and Anchor and tore through the village, causing people on the High Street to turn and exclaim in surprise. So caught up was he in his goal that it wasn't until he had gone a good quarter mile beyond the village that he realized what he had seen at the inn. There was a post chaise there, standing empty, its team unhitched, with several men bending over the wheel. Abruptly he tugged on the reins, and the horse, struggling, stopped. It couldn't be, could it? Coincidence if it were the same chaise, but if so, Cassie was at the Crown and Anchor. Nicholas looked down the road ahead, where the chaise may already have traveled, and then back. He had to know. Cursing himself for a fool for the time he would lose, he turned his horse and galloped back, through the village again, to the inn. "Hold him," he commanded, tossing the reins to the groom who ran up at his approach, before he had barely dismounted. "Whose carriage is that?"

"It's a job carriage, my lord," the ostler stammered. "Had some trouble with the axle, so they stopped to repair it."

"Who was in it? Come, man, I haven't got all day."

"A lady, sir. She's inside—"

"Thank you." Nicholas wheeled off toward the inn, threw the door open, and stomped inside.

"My lord!" The innkeeper, wiping his hands on an apron, came out of a room to the right. "Is something wrong?"

"Miss Aldrich. Is she here?"

"In the private parlor, my lord. My lord, will you want anything—"

"Thank you," Nicholas said, and pushed past him. A man had just descended from the stairs and stood in the hall, and Nicholas, uncaring, jostled him as well.

"I say! Watch where you're going, Lynton!" a cultured voice said, the only voice that could penetrate Nicholas's determination. Viscount Byrne, grinning at him. "Come for Cassandra, have you? Then you've come to your senses at last."

Hardly pausing in his stride, Nicholas drew back his fist and planted it firmly in Basil's midsection. Basil bent double with an *oomph!* as the air went out of him, and Nicholas followed that blow with a solid left to Basil's eye. He strode on, leaving Basil hunched on the floor, and the innkeeper staring after him.

Cassandra was just sipping from her second cup of tea when the door to the private parlor crashed open. "Nicholas!" she gasped, half-rising. Never had she seen him looking like this, his hair in disarray, his eyes intent and determined, power and authority radiating from him. He looked thoroughly dangerous, and thoroughly male. "What in the world?"

"I've come for you, Cassie," he stated, standing with his feet planted apart and his hands on his hips.

"Oh, have you." Cassandra poured herself more tea, though it was the last thing in the world she wanted. "Do please close the door, or do you want everyone in the village to know our business?"

Nicholas stared at her and then, thrusting his hand into his hair, turned to close the door. "Cassie—"

"What is it you want, Nicholas?" she asked in her coolest voice. Not again. She wasn't going to go through this again.

"I've come to take you home."

"Home? I have no home, Nicholas. You should know that."

He slammed his hands down on the table, leaning over her. "Your home is with me."

"Please sit down, Nicholas, or do you really expect me to carry on a conversation with you looming over me?"

"Blast it, Cassie," he said, but he fell into a chair, facing her. "Why won't you listen to me?"

Inwardly Cassie smiled. She'd taken some of the wind out of his sails. "If you'd talk reasonably instead of issuing commands, perhaps I would listen. Now. "She stirred sugar into her tea. "What were you saying?"

Nicholas leaned forward. "I want you to come with me, Cassie."

"Why?"

He stared at her. "Why?"

"Yes. Why?"

"Why? Because I—because I need you, blast it."

"Oh. I see. You have a butler, a housekeeper, a cook, and a whole houseful of servants, but you need me."

"Blast it, not that kind of need, Cassie!"

"What kind of need, then?"

"I need. "He glanced away. "I need you to make me feel whole, to make me feel as if I belong. I'm lost without you, Cassie. All my life I've been searching for something, and I never knew what it was, until you left me." He looked at her then, his eyes defenseless, vulnerable. "I need you by my side, in my life, in my bed. Come with me, Cassie. Marry me."

Cassandra's breath caught in her throat. To marry him! To be with him, never to have to leave, to have a home and family of her own. To have Nicholas. She almost flung herself at him, crying out her acceptance. Almost. Because need wasn't enough, not nearly enough. "What about the past?"

"Hang the blasted past! Forget the past. It means nothing to me."

"It did."

"I was a fool. Blast it, Cassie, what more do I have to say? I was wrong, I was blind, forgive me! Come with me, Cassie. The house is empty without you. I'm empty without you."

"Nicholas—"

"Blast it, Cassie, I love you!"

Cassandra launched herself at him, landing so hard in his arms that his chair rocked back. "Oh, Nicholas!"

"Cassie!" Nicholas threw out his arm to regain his balance, while his other arm instinctively went around her waist, holding her to him. "Does this mean—"

Cassandra dotted his face with kisses. "Oh, Nicholas, I love you, too."

He reared back. "You do?"

"Yes." She beamed up at him. "I always have."

"Always?"

"Since I was a little girl."

"I'm no hero, Cassie."

"And I'm no paragon. I think we've established that already."

"I don't need a paragon," he growled, and brought his mouth down on hers. It was a long, hard, and thoroughly satisfactory kiss, and when it was over Cassandra rested in his arms, her head on his shoulder, hearing the thumping of his heart. "Will you come with me, Cassie?"

She nestled her head against him. "Where?"

"Anywhere. Home."

"Home is where you are, Nicholas."

"Is it, by Neptune." A slow grin spread across his face, and he rose, setting her on her feet. "Where are your things?"

"Still in the chaise, I believe."

"Then we'll have to get them," he said, and swung her up into his arms.

"Nicholas!" she cried, clutching him about the neck. "Oh, do please let me down."

"I'm never letting you go again." Kicking open the door, he stepped into the hall.

"But what will people say?"

"I don't give a damn what people will say."

Cassandra considered that. "Well, neither do I," she said, and kissed him on the cheek.

"My lord!" the innkeeper exclaimed as Nicholas continued down the hall.

"Out of my way, man," Nicholas said, elbowing his way past him.

"But my lord, Viscount Byrne—"

"Hang the Viscount Byrne!"

Over Nicholas's shoulder Cassandra saw Basil, sitting on a chair, staring at them and sporting what looked like the beginning of a fine black eye. Nicholas's smile was grimly satisfied. "Did you do that?" she asked as he stepped into the innyard.

"Yes."

"Oh, Nicholas!" She kissed him soundly on the cheek. "I do love you."

Nicholas's face had gone red, but he was grinning. "My horse," he called to the groom, who, wide-eyed, brought it over. With surprising gentleness Nicholas deposited Cassandra on the saddle, and then mounted behind her, his arms going around her for the reins. "Are Miss Aldrich's belongings still in the chaise?"

"Yes, my lord."

"Good. I want them sent to the *Eagle*. My ship, in the harbor."

Cassandra turned to stare at him. "The *Eagle?* But what about Sutcliffe Hall?"

"The Hall took care of itself before, it'll do so again."

"You're going back to sea?"

"We're going to sea," he corrected her, and his face softened. "I want to show you the beauty of the world, Cassie. I want you with me, wherever we go. You see"— he swallowed—"home is where you are, too."

"Oh, Nicholas!" And as the vicar drove by in his pony cart, as the grooms and the innkeeper and even Basil crowded into the innyard to watch, Cassandra threw her arms around Nicholas's neck and kissed him full on the mouth. To the scandalized delight of the onlookers, they were still locked in an embrace as they rode away. The news would soon spread through the neighborhood. The earl and the scandalous Miss Aldrich were together at last.

Epilogue

Lambton Manor
Fairhaven, Sussex
August, 1814.

To the Honorable Countess of Lynton,

My dear Cassandra, how strange it feels to address you in such a way! We had the news of your wedding to the earl just this morning. Penelope is in a rare taking over it, but the rest of us are so happy for you. How romantic it was, for the earl to carry you away from the inn and onto his ship. No one has talked of anything else, since. Please don't think we've been gossiping, but you must admit this is the most exciting thing that has happened around here in ever so long. I wish you happy, Cassandra, and I hope you will return here soon.

Yours in friendship, etc, etc,
Beatrice Lamb

On the quarterdeck of the *Eagle*, Cassandra folded the letter and smiled. It had taken some time to reach her, as the *Eagle* had been anchored off Liverpool for some weeks, so that she could visit the Shands and see Juanita and Elena one more time. Now, though, the day had come to leave.

Nicholas, standing beside her, overseeing the working of his ship as the crew prepared to hoist anchor, turned, smiling. "Well? Are we outcasts?"

"Hardly. You're still the earl, and we are married, after all. That excuses a lot." She returned the smile. "You never did quite understand about land ways."

"No, by Neptune. A lot of fuss about nothing."

"Well, I'm not so certain I'd call it nothing." She leaned against his shoulder, holding out her hand to admire the plain gold band she now wore. "Think of the scandal."

He looked down at her. "Are you sorry, Cassie?"

"No, of course not." She beamed up at him. "You were right, when you told me what people think doesn't matter. Think of what I'd be missing."

"Aye. You'd be in Yorkshire now. And I'd be alone." He dropped a kiss on her forehead, and then straightened. "All set, Mr. Archer?"

"Aye, Captain." Mr. Archer, the *Eagle*'s first mate, saluted sharply from the main deck. "All set."

"Hoist the anchor," Nicholas said, and began issuing the complicated series of commands that would loose the sails and send the *Eagle* on her way. He was at sea again, and he had Cassie with him. He was content.

As the *Eagle*'s sails caught the wind and filled, as the ship began to come alive, Nicholas slipped his arm about his wife's waist and drew her close. The past was left behind. The earl and his lady had set sail, toward their new life together.

FEEL THE FIRE IN CAROL FINCH'S ROMANCES!

BELOVED BETRAYAL (2346, $3.95)

Sabrina Spencer donned a gray wig and veiled hat before blackmailing rugged Ridge Tanner into guiding her to Fort Canby. But the costume soon became her prison—the beauty had fallen head over heels in love!

LOVE'S HIDDEN TREASURE (2980, $4.50)

Shandra d'Evereux felt her heart throb beneath the stolen map she'd hidden in her bodice when Nolan Elliot swept her out onto the veranda. It was hard to concentrate on her mission with that wily rogue around!

MONTANA MOONFIRE (3263, $4.95)

Just as debutante Victoria Flemming-Cassidy was about to marry an oh-so-suitable mate, the towering preacher, Dru Sullivan flung her over his shoulder and headed West! Suddenly, Tori realized she had been given the best present for a bride: a night of passion with a real man!

THUNDER'S TENDER TOUCH (2809, $4.50)

Refined Piper Malone needed bounty-hunter, Vince Logan to recover her swindled inheritance. She thought she could coolly dismiss him after he did the job, but she never counted on the hot flood of desire she felt whenever he was near!

PENELOPE NERI'S STORIES WILL WARM YOU THROUGH THE LONGEST, COLDEST NIGHT!

BELOVED SCOUNDREL	(1799, $3.95/$4.95)
CHERISH THE NIGHT	(3654, $5.99/$6.99)
CRIMSON ANGEL	(3359, $4.50/$5.50)
DESERT CAPTIVE	(2447, $3.95/$4.95)
FOREVER AND BEYOND	(3115, $4.95/$5.95)
FOREVER IN HIS ARMS	(3385, $4.95/$5.95)
JASMINE PARADISE	(3062, $4.50/$5.50)
MIDNIGHT CAPTIVE	(2593, $3.95/$4.95)
NO SWEETER PARADISE	(4024, $5.99/$6.99)
PASSION'S BETRAYAL	(3291, $4.50/$5.50)
SEA JEWEL	(3013, $4.50/$5.50)

Available wherever paperbacks are sold, or order direct from the Publisher. Send cover price plus 50¢ per copy for mailing and handling to Penguin USA, P.O. Box 999, c/o Dept. 17109, Bergenfield, NJ 07621.Residents of New York and Tennessee must include sales tax. DO NOT SEND CASH.